Vapor Trail

Also by Chuck Logan

Absolute Zero
Hunter's Moon
The Price of Blood
The Big Law

Chuck Logan

Vapor Trail

HarperCollins*Publishers*

This is a work of fiction. The characters, incidents, and dialogues are products of the author's imagination and are not to be construed as real. Any resemblance to actual persons, living or dead, is entirely coincidental.

FIRST EDITION

Designed by
Joseph Rutt

Printed on acid-free paper

Library of Congress Cataloging-in-Publication Data

Logan, Chuck.
Vapor trail / Chuck Logan.—1st ed.
p. cm.
ISBN 0-06-018573-2
1. Ex-police officers—Fiction. 2. Clergy—Crimes against—Fiction. 3. Vigilantes—Fiction. 4. Minnesota—Fiction. I. Title.
PS3562.O4453 V37 2003
813'.54—dc21   2002031779

03 04 05 06 07 ❖/RRD 10 9 8 7 6 5 4 3 2 1

FOR DAN CONAWAY

Vapor Trail

Chapter One

Angel stepped carefully over a crack in the sidewalk. Like in the kid's game, she chanted under her breath, but changed the words, *Step on a crack, you get your body back.* Then, reminded of her serious work this evening, she picked up the pace and simplified the chant to an occasional refrain, *I'm not here. Not here. Not here . . .*

She had learned to make herself invisible when she was eleven. To leave her body entirely.

She knew it was a mind trick. She knew that here and now, physically, her body was walking, down the main street, in Stillwater, Minnesota, under a sweltering 104-degree July sky. The 84 percent humidity draped her face like a dishrag. Sweat trickled down her back and her stomach and collected in the crotch of the tights she wore underneath her sweatpants. She knew she was sweating because she was way overdressed for the weather.

She wasn't dumb. She knew she had a problem.

The people out there looking in, with all the big words in their mouths, had names for it. When she heard the term *dissociative fugue,* she imagined a cannonade of piano keys. She thought of Bach. She had read that other cultures understood the necessity to occasionally escape your life. Eskimos called it *pibloktoq.* To the Miskito Indians of Honduras and Nicaragua, it was *gris siknis.* The Navaho had their "frenzy" witchcraft, and the one she really liked the sound of—*amok*—came from Western Pacific cultures.

Personally, she preferred to keep it simple and was fond of the glass analogy. *Of course they never took it far enough; the question was not whether the glass was half full or half empty, but rather what happened when the goddamn glass boiled over and started steaming away.*

And all that stuff about identity disorders and multiple personalities reminded her of the old movie *The Three Faces of Eve.*

But this wasn't about Eve, was it?

No. This was about fuckin' Adam.

But even invisible she had dressed with great care for this night's work.

The thick, wraparound praying mantis sunglasses distorted her face, and she intentionally overapplied the lipstick and the makeup. She wore her cheap woolly wig, not her good wig. The cheap wig was the color of dust and complemented her baggy oatmeal-colored sweatsuit and her scuffed tennies.

But the genius touch was under the sweatsuit. A custom-made padding suit called a body pod by the costume designers who'd sewn it together at the Guthrie Theater in Minneapolis, who then had rented it to the Phipps Center for the Arts in Hudson, Wisconsin.

Which was where Angel had stolen it from a prop wardrobe, along with a pair of black tennis shoes with two-inch-lifts.

The tight-fitting body stocking was made of Lycra with generous foam pads expertly sculpted to add the appearance of thirty pounds to her hips, rear end, and stomach.

The rig was light but bulky and made walking feel like being swaddled in inflated balloons.

She'd topped off her outfit with a flimsy navy blue nylon jacket stamped on the left chest and across the back with the scripted name of St. Paul's minor league baseball team: Saints.

So Angel rolled when she walked with the round-shouldered gait of a person who'd accepted the extra pounds of cottage cheese slung on her butt and hips and thighs. A full green cloth shopping bag dangled from one hand and bumped behind her on the concrete.

Layered in cheap cloth like a bag lady, she appeared odd moving along main street on the blazing late afternoon. The pedestrian traffic was smartly turned out sleeveless, in shorts, showing bare arms, expensive orthodontics, and tanned legs. Shoppers cruising the boutiques and antique stores did not look twice at Angel. She suggested the animated contents of an overstuffed trash closet that had burst out onto the street. People saw throwaway clothes on a throwaway person whose bottom-heavy body had veered out of control.

They averted their eyes.

Behind her sunglasses Angel studied the fleeting stares. *Hi there. So look right through me.*

Good.

See. Invisible.

So she tramped unnoticed down the main drag, left the shops behind, on past the historical society, past the patchy whitewashed walls of the old territorial prison and continued on, past Battle Hollow where a Sioux war party annihilated a Chippewa band in 1837.

Up the bluff the real estate took a nosedive where the city sewer stopped, and she arrived at the North End.

Angel took a left and climbed up a steep broken-asphalt street and into a gritty maze of ravines and gravel dead-end lanes. Her Goodwill camouflage blended right in with this little corner of Minnesota Appalachia. The yards had gone to seed, and weeds grew past the hubcaps of rusted cars hoisted on blocks. Paint peeled on the sagging trim and doorjambs of old frame houses. She paused in front of a house that tilted on its sinking foundations.

The broad-shouldered man in the sleeveless Harley T-shirt sat on his slumping porch. Just like he had the last two evenings at this time. An overgrown vacant lot separated his house from the yard of St. Martin's church.

She bent and adjusted the contents of her shopping bag so he could get a good look at her.

He wore tattoos, a red bandanna, and sweat. He was drinking a can of Pig's Eye Ale. He watched Angel straighten up and plod through the listing wrought-iron gate and into the church grounds.

"Big ass," he said as he mashed the empty can in his fist, dropped it, and went inside to avoid the sun.

Pleased, Angel turned her attention to the church. She knew that the North End was also known as Dutch Town and that St. Martins had once served a faithful enclave of German Catholics. The date *1864* was chiseled in the cornerstone. But the congregation had drifted off, and now the small stone Gothic building persisted virtually empty of parishioners. Neglect showed in the overgrown vines that clambered on the limestone walls. Coming up the flagstone walk, she noticed the lawn. Several slabs of new sod glistenened under a sprinkler; the rest of the lawn was a tightly woven mat of crabgrass, creeping charley, burdock, and dandelions. The new priest was trying to fix the place up. But it was a gesture. He was more custodian than clergyman.

She trailed her hand over the arched stone entry as she walked through the door. Her hand came away cool.

She did not touch the fount of holy water. She did not bless herself.

Our father.

Yeah, right.

Angel had stopped praying to God when she was eleven.

She went inside and looked around while she pulled on a pair of latex gloves. It was dark in here. Cooler. She could almost hear the drip of the dead Latin Mass sweat out from the damp stone.

That's when the sadness hit her. The awful double-edged stab of love and hate.

Help me, You.

Just don't touch me.

The church newsletter lying on a table just inside the door was a mimeographed sheet. Ticking down the items, Angel found the announcement: *Basic Drawing; an art class for all ages taught by Father Victor A. Moros.*

So the priest was up to his old tricks. Angel confirmed the time set aside for penance: 6:00-6:30 P.M. Tuesday.

It was 6:02 on a Tuesday. Supper time. No one around, except the priest in the confessional in a hallway off to the right of the altar. Angel stood in the empty church with two old-world statues for company. The Roman goddess on the left and the corpse with the outstretched nailed hands in an alcove on the right. Candles guttered in the ornate gloom.

Is this really the way You want us to think of You?

She looked down the nave at a brooding wedge of stained glass and the clumsy images imprisoned in it: a knife-wielding Abraham was getting ready to stab his son Isaac. Just like God was willing to sacrifice Jesus. What a bloody-minded bunch of Aztecs they were.

Angel stared down the aisle of pews to the vaulted chancel, the organ, the choir stalls, and the altar. She could not imagine a place more removed from trees and clouds and fresh air. Her skin crawled. The old cramped stone and tired wood closed in on her. Cold rigid angles. Tortured figures imprisoned in the fractured windows. In all this heat, goose bumps prickled on her arms. Being here was like standing inside the replica of a man's mind.

Father Moros heard the scuff of rubber soles. The bell on the door to the private confessional booth jingled as the door opened. The confessional was one room with two doors and was divided by a wooden partition. He placed a bookmark in the Liturgy of Hours. He had been reading Psalm 144.

Lord, what is man, that thou takest knowledge of him! Or the son of man, that thou makest account of him!

Man is like to vanity: his days are as a shadow that passeth away.

He adjusted the purple stole around his neck and faced the grille. Cheap perfume, Ponds facial cream, and hairspray seeped through the partition.

The dime-store essence reminded him of the trailer-park Anglo girls he'd grown up with in El Paso. In Albuquerque the confessional had reeked of Estée Lauder. He allowed himself a smile. He had come full circle.

Nothing happened. Some squirming from the other side; perhaps the penitent was having difficulty with the kneeling rest.

So Father Moros offered a prompt in his habitual avuncular tone. "May the Lord be in your heart and help you confess your sins with true sorrow."

"It's been years since my last confession, but I do feel sorrow," said the penitent. A low voice, strained and hard to place.

"Yes, my child."

"I'm not your child, and you sure as hell aren't my father."

Victor Armondo Moros sat up at the sharp tone. Here was something different to break up the hot afternoon. The intensity in the tightly controlled voice intrigued him. The passion of it.

"How can I help you?" he asked sincerely, in a less officious tone.

"I'm not real sure. See, I'm not what you'd call a good Catholic; I mean I've never done something like this before."

"This?"

"You know, *explain* something like this."

"I'm here to listen," Moros said.

"First I need to go back over the rules. I mean if I tell you something, you keep it to yourself, right?"

"Of course."

"Even if it could get somebody in trouble?" The tight voice rose, strained.

"I'm here as a minister of the church to hear your sins if you are sorry for what you've done," Moros said.

"Yes, but you won't tell anybody?" The voice rose again.

"I'm bound by the seal of confession to keep what we talk about in confidence. The seal of the confession is absolute."

"Okay, the thing is, I feel real bad, but I don't think I offended God. I think I pleased God. But there are parts to it that I don't understand."

"What parts?"

"Well, the basic part, like why does God permit evil? Why do children have to suffer? This stuff that's been in the news—those priests and that cardinal in Boston—that really bothers me a lot."

Moros took a deep contemplative breath as he scanned the agony of the Church. "It's the mystery of evil."

"You have to do better than that," the voice parried sharply.

"Like, I know this woman who has six kids, and she went to confessional and told the priest she's gotta go on the birth control because her family was killing her, and the priest tells her birth control is a sin that will send her to hell. So you guys have quick answers for some stuff, don't you?"

Moros hunched forward, closer to the grille. "One can assume that God created the best possible world, but he gave us free will. So evil comes into the world through the choices some individuals make . . ."

"But why?"

Moros inclined his head. "Perhaps because the human heart is vulnerable to the whole parade of venal and mortal sins. We must never forget that God has a rival who wants to collect our souls."

Then the penitent's words tumbled out in a rush. "There was this man. It was real big in the news. But this was before you came here, so you probably didn't hear about it."

"What?" Father Moros was taken aback by the personal reference, but before he could say another word the penitent raced on.

"He violated this child, and they let him get away with it. They said some of the people on the jury would not believe a kid over an adult, and that's why they acquitted him. I mean, that's not right. This guy was a teacher, and he got this six-year-old to play with his thing, you know, he told him it was a popsicle and got him to . . ."

"Please, calm down," Father Moros said, not prepared for the lurch of velocity building in the language coming through the grille.

"I'm sorry, but I have to get this off my chest; it bothers me so much I can't sleep. Okay?"

Father Moros nodded his head. *Yes. Yes.* This was the work he was called to do. The thing every priest knew could walk through the door at any time. And now here it was. "Go on." Moros fingered the rosary in his hand for reassurance and found the black beads shiny with sweat.

"All right," the penitent said. "I always thought God was, you know, like a real fierce micromanager, that he was involved in everything. But maybe it turns out he's more laid back, and sometimes he uses ordinary people to make things come out right. Is that possible?"

Father Moros wondered if she was on medication. This was swerving on the line that separated the spiritual and civil spheres.

"Well, is it?" the voice said, quavering. When Father Moros didn't answer, the penitent began to cry.

The anguish in her voice brought him back on task. "Are you ready to confess your sins?" he asked.

"Yes." The penitent's voice caught in a sob. "You see, they wouldn't stop him. Somebody had to stop him, or he'd hurt more children. I mean, they were going to let him go back to work in the same school where he did that to the boy. So I went to his house when he was all alone. I took a gun and I shot him and he died, and nobody knows who did it except you, me, and God."

It was silent in the confessional for ten seconds. Angel kneeled awkwardly on the prie-dieu. She could smell the Tic Tacs on the priest's breath not more than a foot away through the grille. And Old Spice aftershave. With her left hand she picked up the printed form on the top of the kneeling rest. It was titled: "Summary of the Rite of Reconciliation of Individual Penitents." Her right hand reached into the shopping bag.

"Wait a minute, I get it," Angel said. She cleared her throat, composed herself, and recited from the form: "Oh, my God, I am heartily sorry for having offended Thee, and I detest all my sins because I dread the loss of heaven and the pains of hell, but most of all because they offend Thee, my God."

There was more on the form, but Angel was now preoccupied

with the Ruger Mark II .22-caliber pistol she had removed from the shopping bag. The plastic Mountain Dew bottle duct-taped over the barrel made it cumbersome.

On the other side of the screen Father Moros hung his head. *What a horrible thing. Could it be true?* But Angel's act of contrition put him back on familiar ground. Automatically, he began to recite the prayer of absolution.

"God, Father of mercies, through the death and resurrection of His Son has reconciled the world to himself and sent the Holy Spirit among us for the forgiveness of sins; through the ministry of the Church may God give you pardon and peace, and I absolve you from your sins in the name of the Father, and the Son, and of the Holy Spirit."

Angel read along silently from the form as the priest droned the prayer, and then she said "Amen," as it directed the penitent to respond. She raised the pistol slowly, bringing the bulbous makeshift silencer in line with the small rectangular screen over the kneeling rest.

"There's one more thing," Angel said.

"What?" Father Moros asked.

"This is your lucky day," Angel said. "I think you're going to see God."

"I don't quite understand . . . ," Father Moros said.

The texture of light in the screen shifted slightly, and Angel placed the end of the green bottle dead center in the grille and extended her arm. "Tell me, Father Moros, why did you have to leave the parish in Albuquerque in such a hurry?"

"Wait a minute . . ." Moros tensed, combative.

"I thought you guys went in for little boys. But your thing is teenage girls, huh?" Angel said.

For a moment Moros was stunned. Where did this come from? How? Then he gritted his teeth to contain the welling anger, raised his fists, and shouted at the screen. "Lies, all lies. Not even lies; more like stupid gossip . . ."

Angel jerked the trigger twice in rapid succession, the sound of the hammer falling on the chamber louder than the muted *clap-clap* of the muzzle. *Relax, stop shaking, see, it works—the bottle soaked up most of the blast.* Furniture crashed on the other side of the partition followed by a meaty thump on the carpet. Then nothing.

Angel picked up the two ejected shell casings off the carpet, then exited the private confession door and entered the face-to-face confession door. The priest had pitched back off his chair, knocked over a lamp, and lay on his side on the floor. Angel was not even breathing heavily. She did notice that the priest had sleek black hair that was combed back with great care. Perhaps he was vain. Whatever. Hit in the right cheek and throat, he was still breathing. She was a little disappointed that his eyes were clamped shut. One of the things she relished in the memory of Ronald Dolman's last seconds was the fear in his eyes. Angel quickly shot him again in the temple, and he shuddered and the breathing stopped. The small entry wounds leaked threads of blood. The small .22-caliber bullet did not exit the skull. Tidy. Self-contained.

Efficiently, Angel retrieved the tiny spent cartridge casing and stripped off the wig, shoes, gloves, jacket, sweatsuit, and the bulky body stocking.

Her disguise hid skimpy shorts, a sports top, lean runner's legs, and a flat tummy. Angel set the awkward stage shoes aside and pulled a pair of Nikes from the shopping bag, pulled them on, and laced them tight.

The shopping bag contained a backpack. Promptly, she stuffed the pack with the sunglasses, the shopping bag, the clothes, padding, the wig, the paper bag containing the pistol and the plastic bottle silencer, which was now ragged with three holes. She removed a damp washcloth from a Ziploc bag and wiped off the cosmetics and lipstick, carefully replaced the cloth, closed the plastic bag, and dropped it in the pack.

Then, ritually, she left the signature.

Okay. Take one last quick look around. Angel cocked her head. There was this narrow stained-glass window over the askew confessor's chair. Except it wasn't real stained glass. It was Contact paper, like from Menard's.

"Fake," Angel said as she slipped on the pack.

Then she ducked from the confession booth and paused in the hallway to make sure she was alone in the church. No one in sight. Not a sound. Just a faint blur of gunpowder smeared in the air.

Like incense.

She walked under the blind plaster eyes of Jesus and Mary, went down the hallway on the left side of the altar, and exited through the back door. The walls of the church and the rectory shielded her from the street. She crossed the backyard patio and disappeared down a brushy knob and came out on a gravel road. It only took a few minutes to trot through the dusty North End streets. Soon the Nikes thudded on city pavement.

Angel opened up her stride.

A jogger gliding in Patagonia shorts and top, she slipped anonymously past the whispering sprinklers on the chemically enhanced emerald lawns with their little signs: Warning—Unsafe for Children and Pets. She ran past the gleaming SUVs parked in the broad driveways and the meticulously painted gingerbread trim of the old North Hill homes.

Another one down. Four to go.

Chapter Two

Now who the hell was calling before five in the morning?

Groggy, Broker grabbed the ringing phone beside the bed, brought it to his ear, and mumbled, "What?"

"Broker." The brusque male voice in the phone receiver sounded like a cop's voice. A cop who'd been up all night. A cop Broker knew.

"John? That you?" Broker said.

"Yeah. C'mon, wake up."

Broker blinked, looked around, and tried to focus his eyes. All he saw was black, as if he were suspended in warm ink. He shook himself and sat up. When you got a call in the dark at his age, it meant:

"Somebody's dead," he said as the careful knitting around his heart drew tight. *Dad?*

"Yeah, somebody's dead," John Eisenhower said. "Relax, it's nobody we know."

Broker sat up straighter. "So what . . . ?"

John talked over him. "Remember all those times I saved your life?"

"Bullshit, you never saved my life," Broker protested.

"Okay, what about those times I saved your job when we were in St. Paul together?"

John had a point there; they'd come up together in the St. Paul department, and more than once he'd run interference when Broker had tangled with the bureaucrats. "Okay, okay. What's up?" Broker yawned.

"Is your license current?"

"Yeah."

"Then I need a big favor," John said.

"When?"

"Starting at about daylight," John said.

"Great." Broker knuckled the sleep from his eyes. "You know where I'm at?"

"Guy like you comes into my county, I make it my business to know where you're at. That's why I'm the sheriff."

Phil Broker was keeping to the back roads this summer. He had to figure a few things out. That said, Milton Dane's river house was still a nice place to start the day, even after an early wake-up call from the Washington County sheriff.

Even when you're estranged from your wife.

Even—count 'em and weep—on your forty-eighth birthday.

Broker sat up on Milt's king-size bed, so his sweat dribbled down his bare chest and pooled in his belly button. Real smart. He had not turned on the air-conditioning, preferring to sleep with the windows open. He'd been hoping for a breeze off the river. There was no breeze. Just the ceiling fans stirring the humidity in slow circles.

Now it wasn't even dawn yet, and the relative humidity had to be way over seventy. Yesterday the humidity had topped eighty, which was tropical.

Broker sat for a while and stared out banks of tall, east-facing windows as the darkness ebbed away, and, slowly, the St. Croix River came into focus, motionless as a painted floor. Gray mist draped the bluffs on the Wisconsin side. Still no breeze.

It would be another green furnace of a day.

It was mid-July, and Broker was in between relationships and houses. His own home was up in Devil's Rock on Lake Superior, a twenty-minute drive from the Canadian border. But the house was haunted with too many memories of his marriage and especially of his five-year-old daughter, Kit. Her stuffed animals lay undisturbed where they'd dropped from her fingers when she'd visited him in May. At first he'd left the toys where they'd fallen because they were random reminders. Days passed and then weeks, and they started to look like tiny bodies at a crime scene. So he locked the house, traveled south to the Cities, and agreed to look after Milt's place on the river north of Stillwater. He'd guided Milt on what had turned out to be an extreme canoe trip a year ago October. Now Milt, an attorney, had taken Jolene Sommer, a former client of his, to Italy to see Florence.

Broker had never been to Tuscany, but his estranged wife had received her mail there. Major Nina Pryce and their daughter had taken up residence in Lucca, a walled medieval town on the road less traveled between Pisa and Florence.

He didn't know why Nina was there. She didn't wear a uniform anymore. The nature of her work was classified. And then she and Kit had just disappeared.

Broker got up from the king-size bed and passed beneath a throng of African masks and Asian dragons that peered down from the walls and the post-and-beam ceiling. Milt had transformed the upper level of the river house into a bachelor heaven; the walls were decorated with his vacation booty. The master bedroom opened on the kitchen. The kitchen patio doors led to the broad deck.

So now, as on every recent morning, he padded into the kitchen and confronted the rectangular cyclops eye of the laptop on the table. The screen saver fluttered gently in the thin light; a winter scene to mock the current heat wave, snowflakes trickling down against a hillside of snow-frosted pine trees. He clicked onto the Internet icon, went into the message center, and selected GET MESSAGES.

He typed in his password: LUDDITEONE.

And got the prompt at the bottom of the screen: NO NEW MESSAGES ON SERVER.

Broker exhaled and disconnected from the Net. No communication from Nina since Kit returned to Italy in May. Not one call, e-mail, or letter. She and Kit had vanished down into a secure government rabbit hole. Broker suspected it was the culmination of a process that had started right after 9/11.

Initially, after the attack, and despite their personal issues, Nina had called regularly explaining that her duties might, and then would, make it impossible to keep Kit with her in Europe.

Fine. Broker was more than ready to take over his end of their shared child care. Then, right after Kit's visit in May, the messages became ambiguous. Kit's transfer to her father's care was put off. Then communication had abruptly stopped.

Broker didn't exactly have a lot of recourse to penetrate the silence. There was no one he could talk to about his wife's situation. The unit that Nina had triumphantly gender-crashed herself into did not officially exist.

"Fucking Delta." Broker swore softly.

So he drew the only conclusion he could from the silence: whatever Nina was doing at the moment, his daughter was somehow included in it.

Not knowing was worse than knowing. It has been bad enough when he admitted to Nina he had strayed with Jolene Sommer.

Nina was quick to thrust back with a confession of her own weak moment with a Ranger officer.

Make that a *young* Ranger officer. Squeaky young. Smooth young. The kind of young that didn't have to compensate for the torn rotator cuff, the stressed knees, the back injury, and various shrapnel deposits. Carefully, Broker lined up forty-eight years of knotted scar tissue, stood up, and walked to the bathroom. Some things still worked. A kidneyful of pee crashed into the bowl. He flushed, washed his hands, and threw some water on his face. Then he turned and studied himself in the mirror on the door.

So this was forty-eight.

One hundred eighty pounds shrunk tight on a six-foot frame looked back at him. He was still holding his own against the sags of gravity; still hollow-cheeked, tucked in here, a dangle there. He had his love handles down to an inch of pinch. No second help-ings. No dessert. His usually thick dark hair was cut high and tight, more than summer short; a monk's vow of discipline. His eyebrows remained his defining feature, joining in a bushy line over his gray eyes. A pale white, raised centipede of stitched scar tissue crawled out of his hairline, angled down his forehead, and curled around his left temple. Two more puncture scars were less obvious on his left arm: one high on the biceps, the other just above the elbow. He wiggled his fingers and his toes to test the numbness. He'd been stabbed in the arm and had almost frozen to death, and he carried frostbitten nerve endings as a reminder. That was last year's adventure; that's when he met Milt and Jolene. Her husband, Hank, had saved his life, and Broker had not been able to return the favor.

Continue onward.

Broker squinted out the windows at the false dawn and figured he could work a run in before John showed up. He pulled on shorts, socks, and shoes. He went into the kitchen, filled the teakettle, set it on the stove, switched the burner to the lowest setting, and filled an electric grinder with coffee beans. Then he drank a glass of water and tied a red bandanna around his forehead for a sweat rag.

Five miles and forty minutes would bring him back to coffee water nearly at a boil. As he laced his shoes, he glanced at the Gary Larson Far Side birthday card lying on the kitchen table. It had appeared inserted inside the screen door yesterday morning. On the front there was a circus scene of a dog riding a unicycle on the high wire with a cat in its mouth and a vase balanced on its head. The dog was trying to keep a hula hoop and three juggling balls in motion.

He reread the caption:

High above the hushed crowd, Rex tried to remain focused. Still, he couldn't shake one nagging thought: he was an old dog and this was a new trick.

The card was signed: Janey.

In a burlesque of his wife's disappearance, he had bumped into an old girlfriend at the Cub grocery in town last week. Lean and tanned, Janey Hensen had dropped two dress sizes since the last time he'd seen her.

Working ten years deep undercover for the Minnesota Bureau of Criminal Apprehension, Broker had acquired reflexes, like sensing when he was being watched. And that's what had happened in the dairy aisle at the grocery store. Reaching for the nonfat vanilla yogurt he'd felt the short hairs on the back of his neck tickle up, and he turned around and locked into Janey's green eyes.

Fancy meeting you, she'd said.

Janey always was good. She could make a cliché chime with laughter and irony and secrets.

And she had inclined her head forward so her tawny blond hair fell across her eyes in a sort of visual echo just in case he needed reminding how she used to look at him across a bedroom.

Sixteen years ago.

So this and that.

And fancy running into Phil Broker, who was separated from his wife and getting skinny as he closed in on fifty. And she saw that he saw she was getting skinny with a vengeance as she braced for forty.

It was typical of Janey to remember his birthday, and she would have followed him from the store to see where he was staying. He could almost visualize her waltzing up the stairs to Milt's deck.

He told himself to get serious. Better that John had called than Janey.

So he walked down the stairs and out onto the driveway and into a humid morning the color and consistency of simmering tapioca. The toe of his running shoe caught in the trap rock, and he stumbled. *Getting clumsy.*

Getting old.

Vaguely, he wondered what John Eisenhower had for him.

But then he rallied. As he launched into his run, he lost the clumsiness and experienced a floaty moment of weightlessness and sheer bewilderment.

You never planned on living this long, did you? So what do you do now?

Chapter Three

Milt's steep gravel driveway was a clammy maze twisting up the bluff through an oak woods. Broker lost the faint light in the trees, pushed through the soggy shadows, and jogged to the top. Lathered and panting, he turned north on Highway 95.

He blinked sweat and looked around. Across the river, Wisconsin hid in a veil of mist. On the Minnesota side, fields of dew-soaked corn and hay hugged the earth like wet green fur. The air gurgling in his lungs was seven parts water, three parts alfalfa haze.

His Nikes thudded on pavement. His knees began to ache. So run through the ache. He concentrated on the first fat yellow stick of sunlight that melted into his back. On the cicadas that buzzed in the fields . . .

A horn blared. *Yikes.*

Broker felt the mass of the vehicle loom behind him, heard the motor, and then the burned-rubber screech of tires skidding on hot asphalt. He jumped sideways, across the gravel shoulder into the damp weeds as the white Bronco swerved to a stop in front of him.

Panting, blinking sweat, Broker watched John Eisenhower get out. Usually John, with his tidy blond mustache, came on like a well-groomed German butcher: thick with muscle, starched, a suggestion of freshly scrubbed dots of blood. This, however, was a rumpled John Eisenhower wearing a sweated-through blue T-shirt out over baggy jeans and his pager and service pistol. Eisenhower drew himself up and inspected Broker, looked up at the sky, then back at Broker. After several beats he shook his head and said, "Running in the fucking sun. No hat."

"How you doing, John?" Broker said.

They stared at each other for a few more beats.

"You look like you've been up all night," Broker said as he studied Eisenhower's face. This morning the sheriff's usually ruddy complexion was gray as wrinkled newsprint. His eyelids quivered.

"I been up all night," John said. His management style was to always find one thing to appreciate about a person. He pointed at Broker's cropped head. "I like the hair."

"Thanks," Broker said. "So you still wearing white socks, with your wingtips?" John was this clean freak, anal, squared away— a real straight copper. Except when he got into his dark side. Then he was into being real tricky. When he was into his real tricky mode, he always seemed to come looking for Broker.

Like now.

"How'd you find me?" Broker squinted in the sun.

"Jeff," John said.

"Jeff gave his word not to blow my getaway," Broker said. Tom Jeffords was Broker's neighbor up on the north shore of Lake Superior. He was also the Cook County sheriff.

"Gave his civilian word, not his brother sheriff word. Especially after I told him I intended to put you to work," John said. "But he didn't appreciate getting called at midnight."

"Midnight, huh?"

"Yeah. Get in the truck," John said.

Broker got in the passenger side. John reached in back, searched around, and tossed Broker a wrinkled sweatshirt. "Wipe yourself off; all the sweat is going to shrink my leather seats."

As Broker swabbed off a surface layer of sweat, John whipped the Bronco in a tight U-turn and headed back toward Milt's driveway.

"So who's dead?" Broker said.

John grimaced and took a long stare into a passing cornfield. Then he jerked his thumb at a rural mailbox that zipped by. "Biggest complaint this summer is mailbox bashings. Kids get drunk and go down the road at one in the morning with baseball bats and wail on mailboxes." John ground his teeth. "Second-biggest complaint is property line disputes."

Broker bided his time, letting his friend unwind.

John reached under his seat, pulled up a manila envelope, and tossed it in Broker's lap. Broker undid the tie fastener and took out a plastic evidence bag. It contained a silver medallion on a chain. The medal was three-quarters of an inch long, appeared to be silver, and was engraved with a crude icon of a man in robes with a halo. A premonition started to tickle the bottom of his mind.

"St. Nicholas the Wonder-worker. Seven fifty on the Internet," John said.

Broker sat quietly while an icy shiver wiggled through his chest. As they turned into Milt's driveway, Broker peered into the dark stand of oaks on either side of the road. Shadows still ruled the dawn, but they were already hot, exhausted shadows. The shadow that flickered through his heart went way past cold into layers of doubt, remorse, and something Broker didn't readily admit to feeling.

An old fear, long dormant, had raised its head.

"I got a dead priest. A dead fucking priest in Stillwater with *that* stuffed in his mouth, with all the hooha that's going on in the Church," John said, jabbing his finger at the evidence bag.

"The Saint," Broker said. But what he thought was what cops in the St. Croix River valley usually thought when the subject of the Saint came up: *This was about Harry Cantrell.*

John parked next to Broker's black Ford Ranger in back of Milt's house and settled in to gave Broker a few moments to digest the information. Broker got out of the Bronco, walked down to the shore, kicked off his shoes and socks, went out on the dock, and dived into the St. Croix to quench his sweat.

He had learned to carefully keep his worst memories confined in compartments so they didn't bleed into his life. Now, surfacing in the tepid river water, he suspected that John wanted him to visit one of them.

John was waiting on the stairs leading up to the deck when Broker walked back to the house. As they climbed the steps, Broker pointed to the evidence bag in John's hand and asked the obvious question: "You think Harry is involved?"

John pursed his lips and shrugged. "I always thought Harry knew who the Saint was. Now it's time he came clean."

Broker motioned John into the kitchen. Quickly he put a filter into the Chemex beaker, ground the mocha java beans, dumped them in the brown inverted paper cone, and poured in boiling water from the kettle on the stove. While the coffee dripped, he ducked into the bathroom, stripped off his wet shorts, and rubbed down with a towel. He pulled on dry shorts and a T-shirt and returned to the kitchen.

John had taken over adding water to the coffeemaker. Broker

poured two cups, and they went back out on the deck and sat facing each other on wooden chairs. John placed the evidence bag containing the medallion on the patio table between them.

"So lay it out," Broker said,

"You know St. Martin's, the little church on the North End in Stillwater?" John said.

"Sure. I thought it was closed up."

"Pretty much, but they stuck a new priest in there part-time just to keep it open. What they call a mission church. Father Moros was like a caretaker. Besides the janitor, the only other person there is a volunteer secretary. She's the one who went back to the church last night looking for her misplaced checkbook. She found him a little after seven," John said.

"Yeah?"

"He'd been shot sitting in the confessional. Twice through the screen in the booth. Then the shooter came around for a coup de grâce. Total of three rounds in the head and throat, something on the small side: .32 or .22, close range. The ME thinks just after six P.M."

"How'd you nail down the time?" Broker said.

"Okay—a guy who lives next door to the church is sitting on his porch. He sees a woman go into the church at six. Or—check this—he says, *It could have been a guy dressed like a woman.* But he didn't see her come out."

"He hear anything?"

"The Crime Lab guys found this green residue in the wounds, like the plastic in pop bottles. Remember *The Anarchist Cookbook*?" John said.

"Homemade silencer. Great. And they put the medallion in the mouth just like the Saint did in the Dolman case?" Broker said.

"There it is. The implication being another child molester gets his just deserts. And not just any pervert; this guy's a priest."

Broker inclined his head. "There's kinda a lot of that going around this season."

"Yeah. It's getting to be—say five Hail Mary's and give kindly old father Murphy a hand job. The media . . ." John raised his hands and pawed at something distasteful in the air. He pronounced "the media" as if he were raising Satan.

"I get the picture. What do you want?" Broker said.

"I want you to check around to see what's in Moros's background. See if the shoe fits."

"C'mon, you got people who can do that," Broker said directly.

John met Broker's squint with tired but very steady blue eyes. "I need a certain touch on this, just for a few days," he said.

"Uh-huh. Where's Harry fit in?"

John nodded. "Okay, I'm getting to that. This priest transferred into St. Martin's two months ago from Albuquerque. So last week the secretary—the one who found him—gets this anonymous call from his old parish. The caller insists Moros got chased out of Albuquerque for molesting little girls. One of those hush-hush geographic cures the Church is not supposed to be doing anymore.

"So the secretary's no dummy; she watches the news about the current priest hysteria. So she called it in. Since the Dolman case, Harry has this proprietary interest in anything that sounds like child abuse, so the call was routed to him. He made some inquiries and cleared it. We checked his computer last night, and his notes said, basically: this priest just transferred into a defunct church where the average age of the dozen remaining parishioners is seventy-two, with no kids. In his opinion, just another bullshit anonymous tip," John said.

"Sounds pretty straightforward," Broker said. "So what's the deal?"

"I just want you to check out where Harry was last night. To eliminate him from the git-go."

Suddenly on edge, Broker came forward in his chair. "He's *your* sergeant. Goddammit, John; Harry and I barely say hello to each other anymore."

John's eyes did not waver. "Harry fell off the wagon just about the time he took the complaint call last week. Looks like he drank all weekend. He came in shit-faced Monday morning and pulled a horror show in the unit. I took his badge and gun and suspended him for fifteen days. And I got it in writing from the union, he has to go into chemical dependency treatment, in-patient. We've reserved a bed for him at St. Joe's in St. Paul."

Broker rubbed his forehead, amazed. "Jesus," he said.

"He isn't answering his phone. So I want you to find him and put him in that bed. In the process, you push him hard about this case and the Saint's case. He's on the ropes, he just may come apart and tell us something," John said.

"I dunno, John, sounds like he's a sick man," Broker said.

"Fuck sick, I want you to lean on him." John put special emphasis on the *you*.

Broker exhaled and looked past John at the solid wall of heat rising over Wisconsin. "Harry always has trouble with the first half of July," he said.

Chapter Four

John got up to use the bathroom. Alone, Broker reviewed the Saint's case that had created a sensation in the St. Croix River valley and throughout the state last summer.

"The Saint" was the nickname the media attached to a vigilante killer who, in the popular mind, stepped up to dispense punishment to Ronald Dolman. Dolman had taught first grade at Timberry Trails Elementary School. Timberry was a sprawl of housing, malls, and cul-de-sacs that had popped up like pricey toadstools on the farmland south of Stillwater.

After a thorough investigation, Dolman had been charged with molesting six-year-old Tommy Horrigan. Washington County assistant prosecutor Gloria Russell had gone after Dolman with great energy. Her method of eliciting testimony from Tommy was earnest but carefully orchestrated to avoid the appearance of leading or coaching.

But the defense attorney had skillfully questioned the veracity of Tommy the child's testimony compared to Dolman the adult's. The jury handed down a troubled verdict; although believing that

Dolman was probably guilty, they could not unanimously dispel reasonable doubt.

Dolman was acquitted.

Two days after the acquittal, somebody did a Mickey Spillane on Dolman. He was found shot to death in his living room with twelve pistol rounds at close range.

Like *I the Jury*, people said.

Rumors raced through the county that Washington County detective sergeant Harry Cantrell, the original lead investigator on the case, had taken upon himself to step in and correct some basic system failure. Then there was a debate about the six spent .38-caliber cartridges that had been found next to Dolman's body. The Saint had reloaded to make his twelve-shot point. Some argued that Harry would never be so thoughtless as to leave brass lying around a crime scene. Others said that it would be just like Harry to leave the brass on purpose, to make it look like some asshole civilian.

The investigation went cold. And no one really mourned the passing of Ronald Dolman.

After Dolman's murder, thousands of people in the Twin Cities began wearing St. Paul Saints baseball jackets to show support for the vigilante. The Saint became a mythic unsolved case and a cautionary tale in metropolitan Minnesota.

In addition to being a top cop, Harry Cantrell cut a colorful figure as a drinker, womanizer, and gambler. He loved cultivating rumors about himself; the more provocative the better. And not least among the baggage he carried was an acute reputation for meting out street justice.

When John returned, Broker was studying the St. Nicholas medallion in the evidence bag. The Saint's calling card.

"Dolman was a thirty-eight, right? The famous mystery cartridges left on the scene," Broker said.

John nodded. "And the priest is a smaller caliber. It's preliminary, could be fragments. But, like I said, probably a twenty-two."

"Is this the same medallion?" Broker said.

"Looks the same to me. I'm not about to call the state Crime Lab and get the original for a comparison. I don't want that getting out. Not yet. It'll be an instant made-for-TV movie when the press gets ahold of this. We need a little breathing room." John chewed the inside of his lip. "St. Nicholas is the patron saint of children. I looked it all up again last night. *Butler's Lives of the Saints.*"

"Quaint touch," Broker said.

John nodded. "Nicholas was a bishop in Asia Minor in the fourth century. He was rich, and he donated his wealth to charity. He's associated with the legend of the three children. He knew this guy who went broke and was on the verge of selling his three daughters into prostitution. Nicholas would sneak over to the poor man's house when it was dark and toss in bags of gold to provide dowries for the daughters. So the children were saved."

"What about the Santa Claus angle?"

"That came later, after his legend got mixed up with our German ancestors who wouldn't let go of their damned evergreen."

"Well, this guy isn't tossing bags of gold."

"We'd always assumed the Saint was a guy. Now we got this witness throwing in a twist: was it a woman, or a guy in drag? And in case we're slow with the medallion—the suspect was wearing a Saints jacket."

Broker came forward in his chair again, but slower this time. He leaned his elbows on the table and gave John his full attention. "John, did you drive out here to suggest that Harry Cantrell got drunk and dressed up like a woman to go shoot a priest?"

John raised his arms and scratched at his sweaty hair with both hands in an exasperated gesture. "When Dolman got off, a lot of people in the county said, 'I ought to shoot the sonofabitch'— including me. Then somebody did. Some people think Harry was the Saint. Like I said, I'm not one of them. But he *knows* something. I always figured the Saint was a soccer mom who reached her bullshit limit, and she'd be damned if Dolman was going to come back to school and teach *her* kid. I always thought we should have looked closer at all the parents at that school. But we didn't have the resources." John shook his head. "Now I'm not so sure. I'm worried it could be someone in the county."

"Slow down. What if your witness talks to a reporter, the neighbors? There goes your breathing room," Broker said.

John smiled quickly. "Not likely. He's sweating a possession charge. He's an aging biker who sold a bag of grass to one of my undercover guys. Which put him over the line on points. He's looking at going inside. We can deal him up. He'll stay quiet."

"So who knows about the medallion?"

"The Stillwater cop who answered the call. And the Stillwater mayor and his police chief. My investigator, Lymon Greene; his sergeant, Maury Seacrest." John paused. "You know Maury."

Broker winced. "So every cop in the metro east of the Mississippi knows. What about the secretary who found the body?"

"She's cool; she didn't see the medallion. We took her statement, and she and her husband agreed to go on vacation up to Mille Lacs a few days early."

"What about the Ramsey County ME and the BCA Crime Lab guys? They processed the scene."

"They don't know. It stays quiet until I get back," John said.

"Back?" Broker sat up in his chair, skeptical. "The Saint just blew into town, and you're leaving?"

"My wife's dad just died. So the funeral's in Seattle."

"That's not immediate family, John."

"Sorry, gotta go."

Broker gave his old friend the barest smile. "What the hell are you doing?"

John's expression was clearly conflicted. "I'm understaffed. My top investigator is drunk on his ass and a total embarrassment; my other sergeants are tied up in court. *I'm* going to a funeral. My deputy chief is doing the course at the Southern Police Institute."

"Bullshit. You got Art Katzer in charge of Investigations," Broker said.

"He took off for SWAT training."

"When? At midnight when he heard about the priest and the medallion and Harry falling off the wagon?"

"Okay—I'm throwing the dice on this one. If I'm right and Harry knows who the Saint is, I'm betting you can get him to cough it up. If I'm wrong . . ." John shook his head.

"Yeah, right or wrong you bring in somebody expendable, who isn't part of your department, so it can't blow back on you," Broker said.

John grinned tightly. "I wouldn't put it that way, but, ah, yeah. So is that a yes or a no?"

"You're asking a lot," Broker said.

"I know, but I figure you can handle it. Look, there's a national scandal about the Church, and I got a dead priest with a radioactive clue stuck in his mouth that identifies him in the popular mind as a child molester. I gotta know if this priest was dirty." John paused. "We're not set up to handle a high-profile murder investigation. I don't want the state guys moving in on this before we know what we've got. And I don't want a media high carnival—the archdiocese in St. Paul doesn't need that kind of grief on top of everything else. I need someone to check out Moros's background without making any waves. I mean like invisible. I got Maury, but he doesn't exactly have the contacts you do."

Broker shrugged. "I never was a straight-ahead investigator, John. You know that."

John let a cynical smile play across his face. "C'mon, Broker. You tell people you retired because you invested wisely in real estate on the north shore years ago. And you own a resort up there. But I know that five years ago you and Nina smuggled several tons of buried gold bullion right under the noses of the Hanoi politburo, on through Laos and Thailand and into Hong Kong." John paused, got no denial, then began again.

"You live off credit cards. Banks in Bangkok and Hong Kong pay the bills. Last year your credit card totals were twice your declared income. The FBI keeps the IRS off your back because you helped the bureau penetrate the Russian Mafia three years ago."

"You're being dramatic, John," Broker said. "But I'll admit I'm just a little curious about where you got the stuff about the credit cards."

John rolled his eyes. "I sit on task-force planning sessions with all this alphabet soup: FBI, ATF, DEA, IRS. People have a few drinks, and they talk. C'mon, you pirate. Do me this favor, okay?"

They went silent, and then the silence became awkward as John started to speak and wound up chewing back false starts until finally he said, "There's a card inside on the table. It's your birthday, right?"

"Fuck you, John."

John chewed some more silence, then spoke. "Nina and Kit, you . . ."

"Don't," Broker said sharply.

John sat back and folded his heavy arms across his chest and waited. Twenty seconds. Thirty.

"Who would I report to?" Broker said.

John grinned. "Nobody. Your kind of play, totally on your own. I hire you as a Special Projects consultant."

"No paperwork, no office, no desk," Broker said.

John held up reassuring hands. "No paperwork, no desk. We can stay in touch by phone. You said your license was current?"

"Yeah, no problem there."

"So I'll get you an ID and a badge. You need a gun?"

"I still have the old forty-five. That'll do, if it comes to that."

John gave Broker a direct fatal look and said, "You know me, I don't go in for dramatics, right? But we're talking you and Harry here. If he's drinking, you wear the gun. Okay?"

Broker nodded. "Gotcha."

John nodded. "Okay then. We're on. Just keep it mostly legal."

Broker smiled thinly. "I won't alienate any voters, John. I understand you have to get reelected."

"Good. But we have to put it together fast. Like this morning. I have to go home and pack."

Broker shrugged. "Let me grab a shower and get dressed. I'll meet you at the Law Enforcement Center in half an hour." He pointed at the medallion. "What about this?"

John put it back in the envelope. "It's going in my safe until I get back." They walked down the steps toward John's truck. John shifted from foot to foot and pursed his lips. "Another thing . . ."

"What?"

"Keep an eye on this young cop who's working the case, Lymon Greene. Give me a gut read on him."

"Why's that?"

"Sometimes the sheriff is the last to hear what the troops are saying down in the trenches. I want to know why Lymon and Harry are always about an inch from fist city."

John Eisenhower got in his Bronco, fastened his seat belt, put both hands on the steering wheel. "You know what the troops call rumors about Harry being the Saint—they call it 'the elephant in the living room.'" He started the truck, then leaned forward feeling with his hand for the cold air to start coming through the A/C vent.

Broker shook his head. "Too hot to go elephant hunting."

"Broker, the guy needs help. Somebody has to have a Come-to-Jesus with him. I wish it wasn't you. But he's got most everybody else either dazzled or buffaloed." John shook his head. "I never liked Harry, going all the way back to the rookie school in St. Paul. He's got the best instincts of any cop I ever knew and the worst methods of acting on them." John paused a few beats and then stared directly at Broker. "And you know that better than anyone."

Chapter Five

Broker watched John Eisenhower's Bronco disappear up Milt's driveway and then stood soaking in the heat as he calculated Harry Cantrell's influence on his life.

Which had been in the nature of huge.

Broker knew that Harry Cantrell had trouble with the first half of July because his wife, Diane, had been murdered on a July 7 at seven o'clock.

Seventh month, seventh day, seventh hour: 777.

Harry had the numbers tattooed on his right forearm.

The story passed by word of mouth. It was never written down. It did not appear in the reports. It had become a quiet police legend that followed Broker through his career.

Harry and Broker were baby cops together. They'd sat next to each other at the academy. They'd partnered in patrol. Neither of them seriously thought of being coppers for the long haul. They'd both seen action in the latter days of the Vietnam War and looked on police work as a way of extending the tour of duty and the adrenaline rush.

They'd both liked the clash and sting of the street, but Harry was always the more willing to mix it up. He'd slap the cuffs on extra tight; he'd choke to subdue; he'd break wrists and dislocate arms. On his third month on the job he shot a drug dealer who'd had the bad sense to pull a gun. An investigation ruled it a righteous shoot.

Then came that perfect night for a domestic. Hot, no moon; cruising the streets, you could feel people's blood starting to steam up the lighted windows.

At least this time it was in a nice neighborhood, on Summit Avenue, which was just about as nice as you could get in St. Paul, Minnesota, in 1985.

They went together, two sergeants advancing fast in rank. Comers. They were filling in for patrolmen who were taking vacation time.

And that's the night Harry met Diane.

She was, like her house, very well maintained except for the swelling under her eye and the trickle of blood coming from her nose.

Hubby was a dentist who was a meticulous success at everything except, apparently, living. He was given to rages over cobwebs and dust balls. He'd found lint in his underwear drawer, and so he beat his wife.

That night she'd decided not to take it anymore and had picked up the phone. Broker and Harry took one look, then came in fast and split them up. Broker shoved the husband in one room, while Harry sat with Diane in another and persuaded her to file charges.

Harry continued to advise her through injunctions, restraining orders, and the divorce. A storybook courtship followed.

But there were some, with an eye toward Harry's dossier of brutality complaints, who said discreetly that Diane had traded one batterer for another.

Others in those racially more dubious days scoffed at the notion. Harry, they pointed out, only thumped on young black males.

Broker stood up in a Lutheran chapel as best man on the day Harry and Diane were married.

Now he thought back to being young and moist-eyed sentimental on the cathedral light pouring through stained-glass windows, getting dizzy on the fragrance of fresh flowers.

Here and now he remembered the birthday card inside on the kitchen table. He'd just broken up with his first wife, Caren, and he'd brought a new girl to the wedding. A girl he'd met taking evidence over to the BCA.

Janey.

But the dentist husband turned out to have deeper issues than anyone suspected. He held old-fashioned ideas about his marriage vows. He interpreted the death-do-us-part clause literally, and he began to harass Diane. He studied Harry's shift schedule, and he caught Diane alone in the backyard on a hot July afternoon. He went after her with his fists.

Diane was lucky; she got away with just her eyes blackened. She'd fought him off with a barbecue fork until her screams brought the neighbors. Word got out over the radios, and Broker met up with Harry in the Ramsey County emergency room.

He'd watched as she told Harry how crazy the ex had been.

Crazy, she'd said. Really crazy.

In a cold fury, Harry left the ER, got in his squad, and drove away.

Broker followed in a separate car. He knew that the ex-husband was still in his old house which was up for sale as part of the divorce settlement. So he headed for Summit Avenue and found Harry's squad parked in the driveway. He gave the address over the radio and called for backup. The front door was locked, so he went around the back and kicked through the kitchen door and found

Harry in the living room beating the dentist's head against the marble fireplace.

They talked it over:

Harry said, Go away and come back in five minutes.

Broker said, I can't let you do this.

Harry said, He's going to resist arrest. He's going to attack me with that fireplace poker right there. He didn't leave me any choice.

Broker said, I'm going to cuff him and put him in the car. Step away.

Harry said, Make me.

So they faced each other across six feet of space, with a semiconscious man between them, dripping blood on the Persian carpet. They both carried .38-caliber revolvers; their right hands were poised at hip level above their pistol butts.

Harry's eyes were too bright, eager for it. He said, I always wondered what this would be like.

Broker said, Maybe you could have got away with doing him, but you'll never be able to explain both of us.

The opposite of Harry, Broker had centered in a deadly calm, working the problem. He knew that he had to keep Harry talking.

Harry said, I know what this guy's like. He'll keep coming back on her until somebody stops him permanently.

Broker said, We'll lock him up.

Harry said, What do you mean? She has a black eye; he'll be out in a week. I'm telling you, he's going to kill her.

Broker said, No he isn't; he's going to jail.

And then it was sirens forever as the black-and-whites swarmed the house like metal hornets with blue flashers.

And Harry said, You fucker. This is your call, and it's on your head.

Fine, Broker had agreed.

They put the cuffs on the man and took him into the station and booked him for assault.

The next day they were handing out traffic tickets on University Avenue when the call came in. Diane was back in Ramsey ER in a coma. That morning a judge who suffered from haughty extremes of robes disease and who tended to be lenient about domestic abuse and who was impressed with Summit Avenue addresses had let the dentist out on bail. He had gone directly back to Harry's house and beat Diane with a claw hammer he'd found on the back porch. Harry had been using the hammer to repair a loose rain gutter. By the time they got to the hospital, she was dead.

This time a different judge refused bail for the unrepentant dentist.

Six months after Diane Cantrell was married, she was back in the Lutheran chapel; this time she didn't see the light filtering through the stained glass. She didn't smell the pyres of flowers.

And Harry met Broker at the church door and said, I don't want you here.

It changed Broker's life. His dad had always figured he'd go to law school after tiring of the police. His mother wished for something more whimsical, something to develop the intuitive talents she saw in her son.

Broker remained a cop. But a detached and then a remote kind of cop. He told himself he'd sought out the deep undercover work to anticipate crimes before they happened. Then his current wife, Nina, came into his life. She looked at his undercover routine and said, What are you hiding from, anyway?

Broker and Harry tried but failed to put the friendship back together. They both left the St. Paul department. Broker went to the BCA; Harry to Washington County. Broker departed on his undercover pilgrimage. Harry found refuge in excesses of hard work and binges of drinking and gambling.

And every time they met it was instant time machine—they were back in that living room on Summit Avenue. Their voices were civil and professional, but their eyes were locked as if their hands were poised three inches away from their holstered pistols and each was waiting for the other to make the first move.

So the story passed by word of mouth, and it wasn't written down or reported, and some people said that Harry had put it all behind him. Others were convinced that Harry had never recovered from the events surrounding Diane's murder and it was only a matter of time before he took revenge on Broker.

And Broker understood that it was Harry's style not to be in any particular hurry.

Chapter Six

Broker drove the ten miles from Marine on St. Croix, where Milt had his river house, toward Stillwater, the Washington County seat. He was heavier by thirty-eight and a half ounces of steel slung in a nylon hideout rig behind his right hip. John was right. If Harry had gone off the deep end, it could get nasty. So after he showered and shaved, he loaded the Colt .45 Gold Cup National. Then he put on faded jeans, cinched the holster to his belt, and pulled a loose gray polo shirt over the pistol's bulk. Scuffed cross trainers and a pair of sunglasses completed his casual attire.

Never a big fan of sidearms, he had always preferred to deal with trouble inside the reach of his arms. But he was fond of the .45 for its usefulness in close as a steel club.

Broker breathed in, breathed out. *Don't get ahead of yourself. Take it one step at a time. Stay professional; it's a job.*

Bullshit. It was Harry.

He turned off 95 to bypass the business district and eased on back streets to the Law Enforcement Center at the south end of town. He parked in the visitors' lot by the front door. The red brick building housed the sheriff's office and the jail and looked like one half of a deserted shopping mall. The other half was the county offices next door.

Inside, John was waiting in the lobby in front of a framed map of the United States on which all the Washington Counties in the continental forty-eight states were indicated by police uniform shoulder patches.

A husky six footer in a gray suit stood next to him. A young guy.

"Broker, meet Lymon Greene," John said.

Greene's style was strictly in your face. For starters, he made a strength contest of the handshake. Broker endured the viselike grip without commenting.

"You have a first name?" Greene asked in that cop tone that implied, *You have a first name, asshole?* Except Greene projected a slight aura of stiff straightness that suggested he didn't use words like *asshole* a whole lot.

So Broker didn't respond to that slight either. They were not off to a good start. There was the fact that Greene was barely thirty years old and was obviously caught in the rapture of indomitable youth. He wore his hair cropped in a tight black skullcap. His brown eyes smoldered with a carefully masked contempt for Broker that conveyed: *geezer, retread, crony.* And, complicating Broker's gut-level aversion to Greene's persona and style, was the fact that Greene was a black guy. Actually less black than light wicker tan. But, at any rate, a black guy.

"Clearly this is a match made in heaven," John said in a dry voice. "C'mon, this way, you two."

After a brisk tour through administration, Broker emerged with a badge and a sizzling new laminated picture ID. John held up a .40-caliber pistol, a holster, and a box of ammunition.

Broker refused the weapon. "I never qualified with the forty.

Never could hit squat with a handgun anyway." He tapped the bulge on his hip. "Got my tamer right here."

Lymon smiled and said, "Forty's a sweet weapon. I could take you to the range, check you out."

Broker remained silent, but John Eisenhower winced as they went down the hall to his office. Sergeant Maury Seacrest, Lymon's supervisor, waited impassively next to the office. He had a mound of hard gut pushing over his belt, and sticking out under his gray 1950s flattop were extra-large ears, which had earned him his nickname.

"Hey, Mouse, how you doing?" Broker said, extending his hand.

They shook. "What's a big dog like you doing in our quiet little town?" Mouse grumbled with the barest smile. A drinking buddy of Harry Cantrell, clearly he disapproved of this day's work.

Lymon watched suspiciously as Broker greeted his supervisor. "You guys know each other?" Lymon said.

Maury's and Broker's eyes met, looked away. For a new guy, Lymon didn't know how to keep his mouth shut. They went into John's office and sat down. Broker noticed that John still had the same two Norman Rockwell pictures on the wall. The same chemically treated plastic card on his desk with a thumbprint and the invitation: *Test your stress level.*

Without preliminaries, John shot a question to Mouse. "As of this minute, who knows we got a saint's medallion on the crime scene?"

"The four of us; Joey Campbell, the Stillwater mayor; his police chief, Arnie Bangert; and Tim Radke, one of Arnie's patrol cops. He was the first copper on the scene," Mouse said.

"And that's how it stays until I get back in town. I'm bringing Broker in as Special Projects to do a little poking around. He reports only to me. So he wants anything, you guys give it him," John said.

"That's clear enough," Lymon said.

John pointed his finger at Lymon. "Watch it."

The phone rang; John took the call, then rolled his eyes. "Sally Erbeck," he said, "you must be psychic; I was just thinking of you. What's up?"

Mouse leaned over and whispered to Broker, "Sally Erbeck, *St. Paul Pioneer Press* reporter. Now it begins."

"Nothing much, Sally," John said. "It's pretty quiet out here in Sleepy Hollow. A couple cows got out of the barn, but I saddled up the boys and we rounded them up. Sure. See ya." John hung up the phone. "Just routine checks; she hasn't caught wind of the dead priest yet, so the troops are staying mum."

"I don't know," Lymon said, narrowing his eyes.

"What?" John protested. "I don't have an official cause of death yet. Sure, he had a bullet in his head, but he could have died of a heart attack. Get with the program, Lymon. Now, Mouse, what's our fallback position?"

Mouse shifted in his chair and spoke in a monotone. "The Church is in crisis; priests are being targeted; some guy shot one in Philadelphia a little while ago. We got a climate of scandal that could attract nutcases. This Moros wasn't around long enough to put down roots here. So maybe it's somebody striking from his past, or somebody with lots of grievances just lashing out at the Church in general. They throw in the saint's medal as misdirection, to twist our crank."

"We don't want to go anywhere near that yet," John said. "Try again."

Lymon took a turn. "Moros was alone; it's a fairly remote location. And there's been a rash of church break-ins the last month in town. Satanist graffiti, stuff like that."

Mouse shook his head. "Aw, shit, that's those little high school creeps with the green hair who wear black. I don't buy this vandalism-goes-wrong theory."

"It's not bad for a start," John said. "Okay, we need a minimum press release to cover our ass. The stress is on minimum."

Mouse shrugged, looked at Lymon. "How old was Moros?"

"Forty-three."

"'A forty-three-year-old male was found dead in Stillwater last night,'" Mouse said.

"Sounds great," John said as he checked his watch. "It is now nine-thirty. I board a plane to Seattle at twelve twenty-five. Have the Comm Center ship that out at eleven-thirty."

"So when the media calls and asks about the dead priest, what do we say?" Lymon asked.

"*We* say jackshit," John said. He pointed to Mouse.

Mouse shifted in his chair. "You say we're investigating, and we'll keep them abreast of events as they develop. They need anything more detailed, they should get ahold of me."

"But you're in federal court all week in St. Paul," Lymon said.

"Exactly," Mouse said.

"Okay, c'mon, guys." John made a hurry-up gesture with his hands. "You know why we're here. Broker is going to get us a read on Moros's background, but mainly he's going to take Harry off the table, so ah—well, Mouse, where is he?"

Mouse folded his arms across his chest. "Got me. He don't answer his phone. But he's probably home sacked out, sleeping off a hangover. I reckon he's been hitting the bottle steady since you took his badge. If he's not home, you could try Annie Mortenson's; she's his on-and-off lady friend, but she won't give him the time of day if he's been drinking, so he probably ain't there. I'd check every bar and casino within a one-hundred-mile radius."

"Great," Broker said.

"You asked." Mouse shrugged, took a folded sheet of paper from his jacket pocket, and handed it to Broker. "I'll check around and put the word out. All the other poop's there; addresses, phone numbers, the witness next to the church, the secretary who found the body. You can reach Mortenson at home or try the library; she's part-time there."

Lymon squared his shoulders, came forward in his chair. "Harry had contact with the priest. Why not turtle up, go out to his place, and bring him in for questioning?"

John waved his hand in a downward motion. "Don't provoke him if he's drinking; he could bounce weird. The last thing you want is to play guns with Harry. You got that, Lymon?"

"What did I say?" Lymon said.

Mouse scowled. "We don't know he had contact with Moros. We know he asked around and cleared an anonymous tip."

Lymon smiled, shook his head. "You guys all stick together, the over-forty club."

"C'mon, Lymon; you gonna arrest him because he called you a name? Where's your probable cause?" Mouse said.

"At least we should test his hands for nitrates, to see if he fired a gun in the last twenty-four hours," Lymon said.

"Enough," John said sharply. He turned to Broker. "See why I need a certain touch? None of these guys can think straight about Harry."

"Aw, bullshit," Mouse said.

John sighed. "Okay, Mouse; get it off your chest."

Mouse shrugged. "We're running scared. Bringing Broker in on Harry is too much gun. Sends a bad message."

John smiled tightly. "Says *you*. I say we eliminate Harry up front. No more embroidering his name into the Saint legend. Plus, the guy needs help; let's sock him away in treatment." John glared at Mouse. "You want to take him to treatment?"

Mouse shook his head. "Fuck that!"

"So that's it. Stonewall until I get back in town," John said. They all stood up.

Mouse said, "We'll keep it low profile, talk to the congregation..."

"All six of them," Lymon quipped.

Broker nodded. "I'll touch base later this morning after I call on Harry."

Lymon stepped closer. "You know, you might need backup going out to Harry's. I could..."

"Take off," John said sharply to Lymon as he took the young detective by the arm and walked him to the door. Then he turned to Mouse. "When it gets right down to it, Broker is going to need a hand with Harry."

Mouse shook his head. "Sure, but I'll do it under protest. I don't go for strong-arming him into the hospital."

"See what it's like here?" John said to Broker. "I got a mutiny."

"So hang me," Mouse said. "Harry breaks the law, I'll put him down. But all Harry did was mouth off to Lymon. I ain't defending it, what he said, but all he did was say some words." Mouse paused and said to Broker, "What you and him have in the past is your business." Mouse turned and left the room.

"I'm going to be real popular around here," Broker said. "And what's Lymon's story? The dude is barely housebroken."

"It's a brave new world, buddy. Lymon is pretty typical of the new breed. Smarter than most. He went straight from high school in the suburbs to college to patrol in Park Rapids. You remember in St. Paul, the first thing they had us do at rookie school?"

Broker shrugged. "Sober up?"

"You know what they do now? They put gloves on them and stick them in the ring. Most of these kids have never been hit in their life. Then they take them to the morgue to see their first dead body."

"Fuck me dead," Broker said. When he and John went through rookie school, 90 percent of their class was ex-marine and army grunts back from a shooting war.

"And you gotta watch what you say these days. There's age discrimination, there's sexual discrimination . . ." John wagged an admonishing finger and raised his eyebrows for emphasis. "There's racial discrimination. And there's a need to be generally sensitive. For instance, Lymon is pretty serious about his family and going to church."

"Gosh," Broker said.

"That's better. Now, here's my cell; I'll be monitoring it full-time in Seattle." John handed Broker two cards. "Give your cell on the second one." Broker scribbled the number and handed the card back. Then John asked, "Who are you going to approach at the archdiocese about Moros?"

"I thought Jack Malloy," Broker said.

"He'd be my choice," John said.

"I'll call him right now," Broker said and reached across the desk, picked up John's receiver and dialed information, got the number for Holy Redeemer in St. Paul, called it, and asked for Jack Malloy. He told the secretary it was urgent. The voice on the line said that Father Malloy was not available this morning. Broker covered the receiver with his hand and said, "Playing golf." He requested a sit-down with Malloy as soon as possible. He used the word *urgent* again and left his name and cell number.

When he hung up, John said, "Make nice to Mouse; he'll come around and fill you in."

"Yeah, right," Broker said. "Sounds like Lymon was part of the scene that got Harry in trouble."

"Harry comes into the unit stinking of booze, and somehow Lymon picked up the Mr. Coffee before he did, so Harry yells, 'Who gave this nigger cuts to the front of the line?' Bigger than shit in front of half the squad."

Broker shook his head. "Vintage Harry."

John pointed a no-nonsense finger. "I'm thinking when Harry

sees I sent you after him, he's going to blow his top. Everything's going to come out. You push him hard on the Saint. But then he goes inside, in-patient, four weeks at the CD ward at St. Joseph's. No treatment, no badge, no gun. You got it?"

"I got it," Broker said.

"I mean, you get Mouse to help you, and you walk him into the hospital to the admitting desk, and you don't leave till he has a little white plastic patient ID strapped on his wrist. And be careful; I don't think Harry's a threat to the public safety in general . . ."

"Just to me," Broker said.

"Well, yeah."

Chapter Seven

Broker had never been to Harry's home, but he knew roughly where it was and he had Mouse's instructions. It was the only house on a small unnamed lake in the middle of eighty acres of fallow farmland off the Manning Trail north of town. To get there, he drove past other parcels Harry had sold off and which now sprouted new homes in developments named Oak Grove Marsh or Pine Cone Ridge.

Wearing Diane's death date engraved in 7s on his arm, Harry hit Las Vegas, Atlantic City, the bigger casinos in the Midwest—he gamed across the board: blackjack, poker, slots.

And since her death he just couldn't seem to lose no matter how hard he tried. Ten, twelve years ago he'd started investing his winnings in farmland outside Stillwater just ahead of the housing boom.

Getting closer, Broker mulled over the standard lecture about the foolishness of gambling and how it usually ended with stating the exception that proves the rule: Of course, some people do win.

Harry didn't have to be a cop. He certainly didn't need the pen-

sion. Broker figured he liked to pack a gun and have the authority
to pull people over and stick a badge in their face. Possibly he kept
the job just to spite John Eisenhower, who had tried various ways
to get him to move on.

Broker consulted the directions, pulled off Manning, and drove
down a gravel road hemmed by red oaks and overgrown fields.
The dull space inside where he carried Diane Cantrell's death
began to ache. So what was it going to be? Manhandle a blubbering drunk to Detox?

Or High Noon?

Maybe it was being back in touch with the pent-up momentum
from all the years of wary hostility, worrying about Harry. Maybe
it was just being back in harness. Whatever it was, Broker was
leaning forward, working an edge.

He came to a plain mailbox with the name *Cantrell* handwrit-
ten on it in slanted block letters. He turned down the gravel drive
that snaked off into the woods.

Halfway down the drive he hit the brakes and pulled sharply to
the side of the road going into a turn.

Twenty yards ahead, in the belly of the turn, a silver Acura TL
type S skewed at an angle, the left front fender punched in against
the trunk of an oak tree. Broker glanced at the sheet Mouse had
given him. The make, model, and the license matched. Harry's
personal car. The passenger-side door was sprung open. Broker
stopped his truck, got out, and approached cautiously, circled, saw
that the driver's-side door was dented, striated with impact, and
jammed. The air bag had deployed.

He checked the road, the surrounding brush. No sign of Harry.

He leaned into the interior through the open passenger side and
saw a few dribbles of what looked like dried blood on the driver's
seat and smeared on the air bag.

Dried. It would be hours old.

He then studied the crash site and saw how the locked wheels had carved deep trenches in the gravel when Harry lost control overdriving the turn.

Broker looked back in the car. Like a drunken red flag, the keys were still in the ignition. On a hunch, he reached in and twisted them, to engage the electrical system. The digital clock on the dashboard blinked on and off, repeating the same number over and over: 6:42. Then the clock flickered, went dim, and then opaque.

He left the keys in the car and carefully inspected the road leading away from it. Squatting, moving slowly on his haunches, he searched for a blood trail.

A careful minute later he found a small ant war seething over a pizza crust. He returned to the car, leaned inside, and carefully inspected the smear on the air bag.

It had a dried anchovy stuck in it.

Okay. The carnage appeared more involved with cuisine than bloodshed. He got back in the truck and drove toward the house, parked, and got out.

Harry lived in a modest, comfortable rambler with stout vertical cedar planks for siding and a broad wraparound cedar deck. The door to the three-stall garage was open. A fishing boat sat on a trailer in one stall; the other two parking spaces were empty. Broker walked up and looked in the boat. It looked as if it had never been used.

He left the garage, went up the steps onto the deck to the door, which was also open. He peered in through the screen. Quiet. Empty. He rang the bell. Then rapped on the doorjamb.

"Yo? Anybody home?"

Getting no answer, he walked around the house on the deck. A good-size lawn in need of cutting inclined down to the lakeshore. There was a small dock with a rowboat tied off on a piling; a picnic table and a Weber grill sat on a patio. Several bullet-scarred cast-iron targets in the shape of pigs lay on the picnic table. Another was propped up on a stand. Broker estimated it was fifty yards from the picnic table to the house; extreme pistol range for anyone except an expert.

He turned toward the house and looked into the windows. In the living room, he saw a flat white Broadway Pizza box lying on the carpet next to the couch. A sliding patio door led from the living room to the deck. Like the front door, it was open. This time Broker slid back the screen and stepped in.

"Hey? Anybody home?"

He walked a quick circuit of the house and found clothes hung on doorknobs and strewn in the hallway. He stepped over a pile of damp towels and entered the bathroom. Little wads of crumbled toilet paper littered the sink, dotted with blood. A wisp of bloody fingerprint marked the mirror glass of the cabinet door. A disposable Bic razor lay in the bottom of the sink.

The garbage can overflowed in the kitchen; dirty dishes piled the sink. The refrigerator contained nine bottles of Pabst, a piece of cheese green with mold, and three slices of pepperoni pizza on a plate.

Harry's contradictory patterns were evident in the littered house; underneath the surface debris the fundamentals—the carpets, counters, bathroom tile—were scrupulously clean.

The bedroom had rumpled sheets, an overflowing ashtray, an empty Scotch bottle. . . . His eyes stopped at the framed wedding picture on the bureau. Diane. Harry. And Broker. Another woman whose name he did not remember. The maid of honor.

He turned away from the bedroom and went down the stairwell to the basement, which looked like the nuts-and-bolts aisle in Home Depot. Shelves went from floor to ceiling and were thick with a variety of cardboard and plastic containers. Except these boxes weren't for nuts and bolts; they held primers, powder, bullets, casings, and reloading dies. There had to be thousands of rounds of ammo here, in every conceivable caliber.

In the old days in St. Paul, Harry was famous for experimenting with pistol loads and trying them out on stray dogs.

A broad workbench spanned the area, with four reloading presses bolted to it. Two gun safes sat along the wall next to the shelves. Perhaps as a clue to Harry's current state of mind, the heavy doors on both safes were ajar.

Broker did not profess to know a whole lot about firearms. But he knew there were reloaders and there were serious shooters, and then there were wildcatters like Harry. And he knew that the small orange press on the right side of the bench was for sizing lead bullets and that the RCBS reloader next to it was for precision loading. These devices identified Harry as ultra-hard-core.

Broker walked up and perused the stacked boxes of reloading dies on the shelves. His eyes stopped on a box that read 338/378 K T. He vaguely understood this was a maverick caliber that was not commercially produced.

Curious, he went to the gun safes and looked in the first one. It contained all shotguns. He went to the second and saw a dozen rifles in the rack. His eyes immediately sought out the longest one; sleek and black with a distinctive muzzle brake perforating the end of the barrel.

This had to be the .338. Harry would have painstakingly assembled this rifle himself.

One look at the target knobs on top of the big Leupold field scope, and he was sure. The range finder was dotted in increments of 100 yards out to 1,200.

Broker lifted the big rifle and ran his palm along the custom fiberglass stock. He saw the Can Jar trigger with the two-ounce let-off and the bulky safety switch from a 1917 Enfield, the highly modified Enfield action.

This was Harry's idea of a good time. Go out on a calm day and punch holes in a pie plate at 1,000 yards. He'd always filled the sniper slot in the SWAT team. That's what the Marine Corps had trained him to be. And that's how he'd spent his time in the war.

Broker eased the rifle back in the safe and pushed both the doors until they clicked shut.

He went back up the stairs and returned to the living room, stooped, and inspected the pizza box. A yellow VISA receipt lay among a debris of chewed crusts. He recognized Harry's scrawled signature. It was dated 18:04 yesterday afternoon. Three empty bottles of Pabst were strewn at the foot of the couch along with a TV remote.

If the clock in the Acura had indeed jammed upon impact, that gave Harry thirty-eight minutes to make it from Broadway Pizza in downtown Stillwater to his driveway. Entertaining Lymon Greene's suspicions for a moment, Broker speculated that Harry could have driven to St. Martin's on the way home, parked his car, climbed into some kind of disguise, gone into the church, shot the priest, got back in the car, continued on home eating his pizza with one hand, steering with the other—and put his car into a tree. It was theoretically possible.

Darin Kagin's silent chattering face flickered on CNN at the edge of his vision. The TV had been left on, the sound muted. Broker reached over and tapped the remote button. The TV zapped off with an electronic sizzle.

He looked around one more time. No Harry.

He picked up Harry's phone and dialed Anne Mortenson's number from Mouse's instruction sheet. No answer. Then he tried the public library number and was transferred to the reference desk.

"Anne Mortenson?"

"Yes?"

"This is Phil Broker with the Washington County Sheriff's Department. I'm looking for Harry Cantrell. Can you help me?"

There was silence on the line for a beat, two. "Yes, he called this morning and asked to borrow my car." Her voice was level and direct.

"And?"

"Pardon me?" Anne said.

"Did he borrow your car?" Broker said.

"Yes. His broke down. So I drove over and picked him up. He dropped me off at home; it's only a few blocks to work."

"Did you happen to see his car?"

"Ah, no. He met me at the end of his drive by the mailbox." For the first time there was a slight waver in her steady voice. Concern, like a dropped stitch. "Is this official or personal?"

"Welll . . ." Broker drew the word out.

Anne's voice regained its strength. "It's official, I imagine. Harry is under a cloud. It's about his drinking."

"Okay, you're right. I need to find him."

Anne cleared her throat. "When he's been drinking, I usually don't encourage that behavior in any way. But on Wednesday mornings Harry visits his mother in the Linden Hills nursing home. I made an exception for that."

Broker hid his dismay. Initially, she had sounded smarter than that. "Linden Hills near downtown, on Green Street."

"That's it. He brings her flowers. She doesn't recognize him anymore, but she recognizes roses. That's Alzheimer's for you. He left here over an hour ago. If you hurry, you might be able to catch him."

Broker pulled a pen from his chest pocket, poised to write on Mouse's instruction sheet. "I need a description of your car."

"Yes, it's a new Subaru Forester, red, mono color, no cladding.

The S model." Anne gave him the plate number. As he wrote it down, she thought out loud, "Do you think maybe I made a mistake?"

Broker didn't want to give her a straight answer. "The sooner I find him, the better," he said. Then, after a quick thank you, he hung up and dashed for his truck.

Leaning forward in his seat, he pushed the Ranger over the speed limit, ran stop signs, and passed on the shoulder. Broker came into town hot and swung into the nursing home lot. He scanned the aisles of cars. No red Forester. He went inside, stopped at the reception desk, and inquired.

A nurse walked him down a hall into a private room. An elderly woman sat up behind a tray that was positioned across the bed. She was very involved in staring at a bouquet of roses.

"Every Wednesday morning Harry brings her flowers," the nurse said.

"How long ago did he leave?" Broker asked.

The nurse led Broker back into the hall and chatted with another nurse. She turned to Broker. "He was in and out, just making a delivery. So it was quite a while ago."

Back in the parking lot, Broker raised his eyes to the canopy of elms and cottonwoods where millions of leaves hung absolutely still, pressing down. His body suddenly crossed a threshold, and his sweat came all at once. Mopping his wrist across his brow, he stared across the hills, at the gingerbread facades on the houses, the quaint steeples, the river, the bridge.

Missed him.

Chapter Eight

Broker hated offices, so he moved fast through Washington County Investigations—a grid of gray cubicles with six-foot privacy walls that housed General Investigations, Fraud, and Narcotics. Art Katzer's empty office and a receptionist's desk were located at the head of the room. Interrogation rooms lined one wall; more cubicles made up the other.

He was looking for Mouse.

Several cops stirred around desks in white shirts and ties. They wore round leather backings with five-pointed county stars on their belts, along with holstered .40-caliber pistols. They were mostly older, mostly developing bellies. This being the far reaches of the Twin Cities' eastern suburbs, they were all white.

Several took a sideways look at Broker, then dropped their eyes. John's outsider.

Mouse's bulk was unmistakable at the end of the room next to the coffeepot. Their eyes made solid contact on the order of an eight-ball break shot.

"I got something for you," Mouse said.

Then the phone on Broker's hip rang. He picked up and heard Jack Malloy's voice. "Is this personal, or are you working?" Jack asked.

"Can you stay put? I need a sec," Broker said.

"You are working," Malloy said.

"Yep. For John Eisenhower."

Broker came up to Mouse and took him by the arm and walked him through the security door into the hall. He held up a finger to shush Mouse and turned back to the phone. "Victor Moros was a caretaker priest at St. Martin's in Stillwater. Are you with me so far, Jack?" Broker said.

"Yes, we heard this morning that Moros died. But the details are coming very slowly."

"Are we cool, Jack? Like way off the record here?"

"You're going to have give me cause, but we're cool."

"Good. Then I can tell you that the details are slow in coming because he was shot to death last night, in his confessional."

"Oh, my God—*here* . . ." Malloy's voice staggered. It was silent on the line for a moment, and Broker didn't need paranormal powers to divine what Malloy meant when he blurted: *here*.

"It gets a lot worse, Jack. We have to keep this strictly between us," Broker said. "You still with me?"

"Sure."

"He had a St. Nicholas medallion stuffed in his mouth," Broker said.

Jack Malloy groaned. "Jesus, Mary, and Joseph—the Saint. Great, so now it's really come here. We've had charges made, threats; but not a death. The press . . ."

"No press; not yet. We're sitting on the case. But I need a fast read on Moros's background, and it has to be absolutely discreet."

Malloy exhaled, steadied, and said, "I'm on it. Meet me here, at the rectory, at ten tomorrow morning."

"I'll be there."

Broker hung up and turned to Mouse, who was pushing the last crumbs of a doughnut into his mouth. "Okay—he's not home; his car was piled up against a tree in his driveway."

Mouse chewed, swallowed, and looked around for a place to get rid of his foam coffee cup. Broker took the cup from his hand. The door to Investigations snapped open; a young cop started out into the hall. Broker handed him the empty cup. The young cop looked at Broker, then at Mouse, and went back inside.

"And I talked to Annie Mortenson. She sounds way too straight for our boy," Broker said.

Mouse nodded sagely. It was a look he cultivated and played well with his battered features, weary blue eyes, and his bristly gray flattop haircut. "I figure Annie's his last resort; he keeps her around for formal occasions. She knows which fork to use, like that. So I figured this is a case where you go to the last resort first."

"Well, he got her to pick him up and lend him her car to take roses to his dear old mom who's in the nursing home," Broker said. "Except he'd already split from the nursing home by the time I got there."

"Down deep, when it comes to a dog like Harry taking flowers to his mother, even a sensible woman will melt into your basic enabler," Mouse said.

"His place was open, so I went in and looked around. He's got enough guns and ammo in his basement to rearm the Taliban," Broker said.

Mouse squinted his way into something like a smile. "Okay, so he's a hazard to navigation. Maybe he should be off the streets. Just so happens I found him."

"Goddammit, Mouse, why didn't you—" Broker said.

Mouse raised a finger to his lips, then pointed to the door to

Investigations, which appeared to be open a crack. He shook his
head. "Cops. Snoopy bastards," he whispered. "Worse gossips
than junior high girls."

They walked down the hall, left the sheriff's office, and stood in
the lobby. Mouse yanked his thumb back toward the unit. "I run
the north team; Harry runs the south team, right? Harry's lead
detective used to be Benish, who got transferred to Fraud. But
they stay in touch.

"So Benish comes up to me an hour ago and says, 'Tell Broker
that Harry is playing cards at Ole's Boat Repair.' He also says
Harry don't see the need to rush going to treatment. It ain't like
they're going to move St. Joseph's in the next two weeks."

Broker allowed a faint smile. "Sounds like Harry. He figures to
use every minute of his suspension to party. So he knows I'm on
the job and about Moros and . . ."

"Sure; if Benish didn't tell him, there's half a dozen other people who could," Mouse said.

"So where's this Ole's?"

"Take Highway Ninety-five south toward Lakeland. About
two miles this side of the slab, on the east side of the road there's
this sailboat repair shop that went out of business."

Broker squinted, placing the location. "The slab" was cop talk for
Interstate 94. "Yeah, okay. Tell me about the game," Broker said.

Mouse shrugged. "No sweat. It's a regular game in the back
room. No actual bread on the table. It's all chips and markers.
They settle up someplace else. Some hustlers cruise by and give it
some flavor; but nothing heavy, they all know who Harry is.
Mostly it's local guys with leisure time who like to rub shoulders
with mildly criminal types. Harry is a regular; he uses it as a listening post."

Broker and Mouse stared at each other for several beats.
Finally, Broker said, "It's too easy."

"Yeah," Mouse said.

Broker extended his hand.

"What?" Mouse said.

"Gimme your cuffs. Just in case."

Broker sat for several minutes in his idling truck as the A/C hummed up to speed and put a sheet of artificial cool between him and the day.

Okay. C'mon. Let's do it.

He left town and drove south on Highway 95. It had been more than a decade since he rode with a pair of manacles hanging from his belt. The thought of a take-down grapple to the pavement in this heat . . . Broker shook his head, leery. The fact was, he assumed the worst. It smelled like a setup; Harry making an overture like this, setting a time and place.

He stared out the windshield, and the day glared back. Crazy-making hot. The cars and trucks went by like brightly painted blisters. Even buttoned up in air-conditioning, he could feel the sweat puddle on his scalp.

Carefully, he reviewed the last time he'd seen Harry. At the Washington County Fair, last summer. A sweltering night perfumed with animal barns and sweat and cotton candy. Broker had been with his daughter, Kit, standing in line for the pony ride when Harry walked up.

He'd just looked at Broker, tried to smile, and said, "I heard you were married. Cute kid."

So they attempted to get a conversation going, but their small talk hobbled like stragglers through the no-man's-land yawning between them. When Harry awkwardly started to tousle Kit's reddish hair, Broker instinctively reached over and pulled her out of his reach.

"Must be reflexes, huh?" Harry had said. So the time machine had kicked in and they were back to it. They'd exchanged poison looks while his daughter unconsciously wrinkled her smooth broad forehead, soaking up the ambient hostility.

Harry half-turned as he was walking away. "You never had anything to lose before, did you, Broker?"

Broker once had heard a counselor describe alcoholism as a progressive disease, implying that just because you stopped putting alcohol in your mouth, it didn't mean the condition was cured. It continued to grow inside like an invisible vampire. Take a drink after ten years, and the vampire sitting on your chest was ten years older and stronger than he was the last time you saw him.

Broker figured the thing he had with Harry was like that.

He came up to his turnoff and spotted the building. Weeds grew in the broken asphalt of the parking lot. Fading blue lettering spelled Ole's Boat Repair on dirty white cinder block, and the showroom windows were boarded with plywood. An ancient sailboat was beached, unmasted and rudderless, on a trailer. The tires on the trailer were flat.

Broker drove around back and saw a dozen cars, SUVs mostly, and a brand-new shiny red Subaru Forester with a license plate that matched the numbers and letters on the clipboard on the seat next to him.

He parked, got out, and encountered the deeply locked-down feeling that was Diane waiting for him in the heat. Dark hair worn in a flip. The soft breathy voice.

Did you see her? She looks like Jackie Fucking Kennedy with tits. Harry's studied reaction the night he met her.

Years ago, the sensation would close off the light and last for whole days; now he processed it fast, working through the doubt and remorse to a bedrock determination.

He could never bring himself to say he'd done the right thing.

But he was confident he'd done what he had to do. So he took a deep breath through his nose to steady himself, walked up to the back door, and knocked.

The door opened a crack. A tubby guy with senatorial white hair and a melanoma golf tan peeked out.

"You have an invite? This is strictly an invitations-only party," the guy said.

"Phil Broker for Harry Cantrell. I need to talk to him," Broker said.

The guy squinted. "Oh yeah?"

Broker shifted his weight irritably from foot to foot. "Hey, c'mon. Get Harry out here."

The guy turned and called into the dark air-conditioned interior, "Harry, there's this guy here says . . ."

A deep, slightly slurred, but amused voice boomed, "Yeah, yeah, my fucking process server—bring him in."

The guy at the door thumbed Broker to enter.

Broker stepped inside and squinted. He was in a huge deserted workshop with a concrete floor and half-torn wooden racks. An industrial-strength chill churned from a dripping wall-mounted A/C unit. Stratas of cigarette and cigar smoke stacked up in a shower of light. It came from an oblong pool hall light that poured down on a round table covered with a green felt tablecloth.

Six men sat around it among a clutter of cards, chips, ashtrays, and drinks. Six or seven other guys lounged at a side table that held platters of sandwich makings, an ice bucket, some bottles. An old couch, some chairs, and a refrigerator rounded out the decor. Mouse had accurately called the crowd; ten years ago, in their late thirties, they'd probably taken some chances; now they looked as if they wanted to sit down a lot and mainly talk. Most of the guys at the card table were culturally correct, drinking from plastic bottles of spring water.

"Well, well, well," Harry said. He sat behind an ashtray, a whiskey tumbler, and a big pile of chips.

Same old Harry. He went five eleven, weighed around 175, and was fifty years old. As Broker came across the room he recalled that Harry always looked slightly smaller than he actually was. The illusion was created by the fact that Harry's clothes always fit him so well.

Today he wore gray stonewashed jeans and a green golf shirt. But even dressed in a white bedsheet Harry would still evoke a man-in-black persona. It was the thick dark curly hair, the sideburns, and the promise of dangerous excitement cocked in the slouch of his hips. His face was slightly flat, with Cherokee cheekbones and a chin that matched his brawny bone-prominent hands. The three red 7s were engraved on his tanned right forearm.

Harry had a Lucky Strike dangling at a sporty angle between lightly clenched teeth. But his eyes betrayed his jaunty smile, looking about as easy as two chunks of indigo dye melting in tomato juice. A clip of toilet tissue was nailed to his chin by a rusty dot. He blinked and raised a hand to knuckle at a runny nose. He was busted inside. Stuff was leaking.

"Is this guy here to play or what?" someone said.

Harry's eyes were fever brilliant but so very empty as he said, "Nah, he don't gamble with money, but he'll sure as fuck gamble with your life."

Chapter Nine

"Cash me in," Harry said, pushing back his chair. One of the guys came over from the side table, began counting chips and entering numbers in a small notebook.

Harry stood up, studied Broker, blinked several times, and tried to stand erect, but gravity was toying with his internal bearings. Harry was listing to port in Ole's Boat Repair.

He smiled. "So John gave you a badge and a gun and everything, huh? My own official escort to the booby hatch."

One of the guys said, "Aw, it ain't so bad; I been to St. Joseph's."

"I been there twice," someone said.

"The groups are fucked, though. They don't let you smoke anymore. Gotta go outside," someone else added.

Broker gauged the patter, which was along the lines of a reluctant but firm farewell. He shifted his weight, kept his hands at his sides. Waited.

Harry put his right hand behind his head and massaged his neck, stretched, turned, and looked at Broker.

"Look at you. Nothing ever gets to you, does it? You just keep going like the fuckin' Energizer Bunny. Why is that?"

"This isn't the time," Broker said.

"I mean, don't it ever bother you?" Harry said. Then he raised his hands in mock surrender. "I know, I know, it's not the time." He waved a hand in a cavalier farewell, turning toward his poker buddies, who came forward to gather in a group. Then he stopped, snuck a quick look at Broker, and said defiantly, "I want to finish my drink."

Broker shrugged. "Sure, what the hell."

Harry leaned over the table, picked up the glass, and raised it to his lips. But instead of downing it, he left half an inch in the bottom and hoisted the glass as if to say, See, I'm in control. He placed the glass down on the table with an emphatic thump and called out, "Well, guys; this is it."

A chorus of send-offs ensued, handshakes, a few hugs even though Harry was definitely not the hugs type.

As he started for the back door, Harry paused and grimaced. "Christ, kidneys are shot. I gotta take a leak."

Broker made a stymied spontaneous gesture with his hand which someone in the crowd captioned accurately: "You gotta go, you gotta go."

Harry walked quickly toward a door inside of the room. As he pulled it shut, the gang of guys moved forward.

"Is he gonna lose his job over this?" one asked.

Broker shrugged. "Nah, it's not exactly routine, but in-patient is covered by insurance."

"Can he still, you know, hang out and play cards?"

"I suppose he could drink Sprite," someone speculated.

It suddenly occurred to Broker in the course of this amiable little chat how the card players were forming a circle around him, a cordon as it were. Surrounding him shoulder to shoulder.

"Wait a minute," Broker said, starting toward the door through which Harry had disappeared. The group, amoebalike, oozed along with him and separated him from the door.

Broker feinted left, shouldered hard right, burst through, and yanked open the door. *Shit.* It led to a hallway running the length of the building with an exit door going out the side.

He sprinted for the exit door as a scornful voice sang out, "Ha, you sucker. He's gonna get his whole two weeks before you pry the bottle from his cold dead hand."

Out the door fast. Then not so fast as his adrenaline floundered, the heat sapping his energy like quicksand. *C'mon. Move.*

Harry? There he is, crouched behind the wheel of the Forester, swearing and banging his shoulder at the door. Running toward him, Broker saw what he was swearing about. In his haste, Harry must have slammed the seat belt and buckle into the door well. Now the door was jammed shut and he couldn't start the car because the door wasn't all the way closed. And he couldn't get the door open.

Seeing him coming, Harry yanked and banged harder on the door, and, as Broker came within arm's reach, Harry broke the door free. As he disentangled the belt and leaned to turn the key, Broker thrust his arm into the half-open window and grabbed at the wheel.

Harry was giggling like a boy playing a game. "Let go, motherfucker." The engine quietly purred on, and the car started to move in a fitful circle because Broker was cranking on the wheel with his right hand as he ran alongside.

"Stop the car, Harry!" Broker yelled.

"Anybody but you; shit. I'd make the trip with Lymon Greene before you. John should have known . . ."

"HAIR REEEE!" Broker yelled, seeing the side of the building loom up and letting go of the wheel just before the front bumper, headlights, and grille crumpled into the cinder block.

The Forester did a quick steel-crunching rhumba motion, the

air bag engulfed Harry, and then the car settled. Almost the second it stopped moving, Harry scrambled out from behind the air bag and pushed out the door. He staggered over to where Broker was in a pushup position, getting up from the boiling asphalt. From the corner of his eye Broker saw the poker players coming out the back door. And something else. During the shock of hitting the pavement, his pistol had jerked from the holster and was lying about three feet from his head.

Harry stopped and shook his head. He had a crazy bewildered grin on his face. He said, "Shit, man. That's twice in twenty-four hours I been kissed by a fucking air bag." Then he saw the pistol lying on the asphalt. His grin broadened to show wolfish canines, and he said, "Gee, and I thought you didn't like handguns? I thought killing people one at a time bored you. What was it you racked up in Quang Tri City back in seventy-two—something like six or seven confirmed kills? Course, by then they were scraping the bottom of the barrel, sending down half-trained fifteen-, sixteen-year-old kids . . ."

"Harry, back off," Broker said, getting up.

"More like child abuse than a war. Hell, I mean, *we* wasted all their *real* soldiers by seventy-one when I was there," Harry said.

Limping slightly, Broker retrieved the pistol, secured it back in the holster, and pulled the shirt over it.

"You all right?" Harry said.

"No thanks to you, asshole," Broker said.

"C'mon. It was fun," Harry said.

The poker guys were now assembled around the Forester.

"You saw the fucking squirrel, right?" Harry said.

"What's that?" they asked.

"When the tow truck gets here, a couple of you will be witnesses and mention a squirrel ran across the lot, and I swerved to miss him, and I hit the wall."

"Got it."

On full alert now, Broker waited at Harry's elbow while the call was made. Harry handed the keys over to the guy who kept track of the game in his little black book, along with instructions about where to take the car. Then he said to Broker, "Don't suppose you want to stick around till the truck gets here?"

"No, Harry. Right now let's get you separated from your support group here," Broker said.

Harry adopted a slightly wavering stance, eyed Broker, and said, "You used to have more hair, didn't you?"

"C'mon. Let's go."

"Okay, okay. Aw, shit. One last thing." Harry grimaced and slowly raised his cell phone. Entered a number. Waited. "She ain't home, got the machine." He paused, took a breath, and adopted a contrite tone. "I have some bad news, Annie; got in a small car wreck. I'm okay, but your Subi sustained a little front-end damage. I'm off to the lock ward at St. Joseph's to take the cure so check with Stillwater Towing. I told them to take it to the dealership in White Bear Lake." He gave the number for the towing company and then said, "I'm real sorry."

Harry tapped the phone off, inhaled, exhaled. "I suppose now she'll be pissed. Aw, I never got much past the missionary position with her, anyway." Then he fished a Lucky from his pocket, and a pack of book matches. Slowly, Harry tore out a match and drew it along the striker.

Broker could hear the individual teeth rasp in the friction as the match ignited. The flame was almost invisible, blending into the dense amber air. Harry took two quick drags, then flipped the cigarette away, tucked in his shirt, smoothed his belt line, and turned to Broker.

"Okay, okay. I suppose I can't put this off any longer, huh?"

Broker pointed to his truck. "C'mon, Harry; get in out of the heat."

Chapter Ten

Broker eased the Ranger from Ole's driveway into traffic on Highway 95. He actually felt better after the physical exercise of preventing Harry's escape. He felt a kinetic hum in his muscles. He was smiling as he waited for the A/C to kick in.

Harry came down with a fit of shaking and filled the cab with a meaty scent of sweat, alcohol, and Mennen's aftershave. Sweat dripped down his brow and streaked his cheeks. His eyes flitted. His nose began to bleed.

Broker reached over, opened the glove compartment, took out a small box of Kleenex, and handed it to Harry, who wadded some of the tissue and stuck it in his nose. Suddenly he looked like a sick kid. He said, "It had to be you."

"That's a song," Broker said.

"Yeah, an old one," Harry said.

Abruptly, Broker pulled to the shoulder in a spray of gravel. When the truck stopped, he rested his weight forward on his forearms against the wheel and slowly turned his head. "So what's it going to be? More fun and games?"

Harry shrugged. "What I meant was, John sent you to rub it in."

"Maybe a little," Broker said.

Harry shook his head. "Got to be more. John can be mean—but he ain't petty."

"You tell me," Broker said.

Harry's smile struggled to arrange his unreliable facial muscles and failed. Some blood dripped from his nose and streaked his neck. He reached for another Kleenex and said, "You'd like that, get me talking about the Saint, wouldn't you?"

"Yeah we would," Broker said. So Harry knew about the medallion along with everyone else.

Harry fumbled with his pack of smokes, and the shakes raced down his arms and spasmed in his fingers. Trying to extract a cigarette, he snapped it in half. More carefully, he took another one out. Then the book of matches defeated him. His agitated fingers couldn't manage the flimsy cardboard match and striker. Broker took the matches and gave Harry a light.

Broker hit the window controls to vent the smoke; the glass hissed down, and the lava air pushed in. The smoke just hung in place. He glanced at the matchbook, which had a red-and-blue Toucan on it: Treasure Island Casino. He put the matches in his chest pocket.

"Okay," Harry said, "one of the guys at the game told this joke. There's this couple on their way to get married, and they get in a fatal car wreck.

"So they're up in heaven at the Pearly Gates, and they get to talking, and when St. Peter shows up they ask if they can get married in heaven."

Harry puffed on the cigarette, blew a clot of white smoke into the muggy air.

"St. Peter says he isn't sure; he'll have to go check. So he leaves, and they wait and wait a couple of weeks. While they're waiting they began to speculate—like getting married in heaven has a terminal feel to it. If it's really forever, what if it doesn't work?

"So they're talking this over when St. Peter finally gets back. Yes, he tells them, you can get married in heaven. That's great, they say, but we were just wondering, If it doesn't work, can we get divorced in heaven?

"St. Peter is drag-ass tired, so he loses it and shouts: Give me a break; it took me a month to find you a priest up here. How long will it take to find a lawyer?"

"Funny," Broker said.

"And relevant," Harry said. He flipped the cigarette out the window and tried to hold Broker's eyes in a direct gaze. "You were going to be a lawyer; what happened?"

Broker looked away from the sputtering light in Harry's eyes, back at the road, and said, "I don't get the St. Peter joke."

"Yeah, you do. John's got a dead priest with a medal in his mouth. Christ, I know the Saint case better than anybody, but John's shipping me to the alky ward." Harry shook his head. "And at the last minute he sends you in like a shock treatment to see if I'll give something up. Is that a cry for help or what?" Harry's forced laughter degraded into a coughing fit; he gagged, leaned out the window, spit several times, fought off the dry heaves, and flopped back into the seat.

"So who's the real sick fuck in all this?" Harry said weakly, his face turning pale. He began to shake. His eyes darted. "I know it sounds bad, but I need a drink."

Broker put the truck in gear, stepped on the gas, and pulled back onto the road. "Just how bad you want a drink?"

Harry, trembling in the tropical heat, hugged himself. "That ain't funny."

Broker studied him from the corner of his eye. John had said push hard. "Why don't I grab a couple bottles; you and me go park under a cool shade tree, have a little chat," Broker said.

Harry stopped hugging himself to raise both hands and scratch at his cheeks. "No shit. Feels like I got fire ants under my skin," Harry said.

"Drown 'em in Jack Daniel's."

"C'mon, Broker, don't fuck with me, I know what you want. *Kung biet, toi dinky dau*," Harry said, reverting to Vietnamese slang.

"So it's the hospital; well, I'll just have to come visit. Out at the VA I hear they have people sit with guys who are drying out with the DT's; keep them from chewing their lips off," Broker said.

"Name, rank, serial number. C'mon, driver, take me to St. Joe's. I ain't afraid," Harry said.

"We're on the way," Broker said as the signs for Interstate 94 came up. He hit his turn indicator. A straight freeway run to St. Paul.

"Wait, I can't go in like this," Harry said. "Can we swing by my place? I need to pack some clothes, a razor, a toothbrush for Christ sake."

"Okay," Broker said. A little more time to sweat couldn't hurt. He drove past the freeway entrance, checked his mirrors, and swung a fast U-turn. They traveled in silence, came up on Stillwater, angled off to miss the business district, and skirted the town. After about ten minutes Harry's bout of shaking eased off. He leaned forward and ran his hand across the leather surface of the contoured dash.

"So this is the new F-150, huh? Got the Triton 4.6 LV8 engine. Lot of horses under the hood." He shook his head, stabbed a finger at the steering column. Lookit that. Story of our lives."

"How's that?" Broker said.

"The speedometer goes up to one hundred twenty." Harry pointed out the window. "And that speed limit sign says fifty-five." He flopped back on the seat. "Says it all right there. Living our lives with one hand tied behind our back."

Harry smoked another cigarette, and Broker drove over the speed limit. Finally, Broker turned off and was going down Harry's driveway. He slowed to a stop next to the scarred tree where the Acura had been.

"Tow truck must've come. I'm keeping them in business," Harry said, turning to Broker. "There *was* a squirrel, you know, I swerved to miss him . . ."

"I came out this morning. I figured you were eating pizza while you were driving," Broker said.

Harry sat up, more alert. "Not bad. So you went in the house?"

Broker said, "The door was open. So I went in and saw the receipt from the pizza place."

"You went in my fucking house," Harry said with a sag in his voice and his shoulders.

Broker interpreted Harry's fixed stare into the middle distance as resignation, passivity. "Yeah, like I said, it was open. You bought the pizza at six oh four. The clock on your car was stopped at six forty-two. That gives you time to stop off at St. Martin's on your way home. At least one of your colleagues thinks we should test your hands for nitrates."

Harry forced a shaky grin. "Lemme guess. My good buddy Lymon. Except after I bought the pizza I pulled into that car wash place in River Heights Shopping Center, gassed up, and put the car through the car wash. Paid for that on my VISA too, so there'll be a record. Doesn't give me much time to go around killing people, does it?"

Broker put the truck in gear and drove on to the house. They got out and went inside. Harry picked up the pizza box from the living room, stuffed it in the garbage, and tied the drawstring bag. "Gotta get this out, or I'll have critters in this heat."

After he took the garbage outside the door, he walked through the house as if he were looking for something. He went out on the deck and pointed to the deck chairs. "Gotta bring in the cushions; just throw them in the living room through the patio door."

Broker was leaning over to pick up a chair cushion when he heard Harry pushing around in the stack of magazines and newspapers on the side table next to a chair . . .

And the short hairs on Broker's neck rose up . . .

In that frenzied slow motion that wraps sudden danger, he watched Harry's hand come up gripping a stubby, nickel-plated .357 revolver.

Broker tried not to freeze as he processed the information. *Gun coming up, pointed at me.* His reflexes were engaging *so* slowly, his hand swinging back, but like underwater, reaching for the Colt under his shirt. *How dumb . . .*

Harry extended his arm and pulled the trigger. Broker winced at the sound, felt the whiskers of gunpowder brush by his face. A loud metallic clank echoed in back of him. Turning, he heard the lead pig target crash to the top of the picnic table fifty yards away, down in the yard.

"And this little piggy had none," Harry said as he swung open the cylinder and dumped the empty casings in his hand. Harry grinned. "I knew this thing was out here somewhere. Had you going there, didn't I?"

Yes, you did.

Harry sorted through the magazines and pulled out a nylon-zippered pistol case, put the revolver and the brass inside, and zipped it up. Then he gathered up the cushions, magazines, the pistol case, and turned toward the patio door. "Course, now it won't do any good to test me for nitrates, will it?"

Broker, aggravated, shook his head; *Harry and his freaky tricks.* He was so aggravated that, as he reached to get the last deck chair cushions, he broke one of his basic rules—which was never turn your back on someone who is potentially dangerous . . .

WHAM!

Harry sucker punched him from behind, and Broker's vision popped to static to black and his knees turned to water.

"She would have been forty-four this March, you fuck," Harry said.

Broker collapsed forward on the deck.

Chapter Eleven

He'd been struck behind the right ear, and the pain didn't register until after his chest hit the decking. His breath went out in a whoosh, and he struggled to take in another breath as Harry's knee slammed between his shoulder blades, driving him down hard.

Now he felt the pain, and he was amazed at the flimsy clichés that formed in his numb mind in the first seconds.

This is it.

This is so dumb.

Finally his mind got traction: *Fight . . .*

But Harry wasn't wobbling or slurring his words now. His trained hands efficiently removed Mouse's cuffs and the pistol from Broker's belt. Before Broker could react, metal circled his left wrist, and he saw Harry's hand clamp the other bracelet to a sturdy upright strut in the deck railing. Broker tried to shake off the shock and brace to push himself up with his other hand, but Harry's knee kept him pinned down. That's when Harry took the badge off Broker's belt and snaked the truck keys and the cell phone from his pocket.

The weight moved off his back, and Broker heard Harry's shoes scrape across the deck into the house. Alone, he attempted to focus and take a breath. After he drew a few deep breaths, he raised his free right hand and felt the lump behind his right ear. His fingers came away clean. No blood. Harry had hit him with an expert stunning blow, probably with the pistol case.

It was like lying underwater in the heat; slowly, awkwardly he flailed to his knees and yanked the handcuffs against the rail. The steel rattled, but the wood did not budge.

Harry returned carrying a fifth of Johnny Walker Red Label Scotch in one hand and an ice-cold slice of last night's pepperoni pizza in the other. He put the bottle down on the deck table and pulled a hammer from the waistband of his jeans. It wasn't a regular carpenter's hammer but an ugly, two-headed, short sledge. Broker recognized the type (he'd used one like it landscaping); it was heavy enough to drive pole barn spikes into railroad ties. Harry dropped the hammer on the table. Then he kicked the one remaining deck chair that had a cushion back beyond the radius of Broker's chained reach and sat down.

He chewed some of the pizza, swallowed, and took a generous slug from the whiskey. Despite his throbbing head, Broker noticed the round white plastic thermometer hung on the wall next to the patio door. The needle was stuck at 102 degrees. *How could the guy drink the warm alcohol in this heat?* He got his answer almost immediately as he watched control suffuse back into Harry's face and warmth trickle into his hollow eyes.

Broker didn't know a whole lot about the pathology of alcoholism, but he suspected that Harry had progressed to a point where unintended consequences could ambush him every time he drank. Broker watched the rage and sorrow slosh back and forth in the wreckage of Harry's eyes.

I kill you—I kill you not.

Harry studied Broker's predicament and said, "You're really miscast in this role, you know."

Broker rubbed his head and said, "What did you hit me with?"

"The gun case. Didn't hit you that hard," Harry said.

"How miscast?" Broker said, sounding casual, but his eyes stayed fixed on that hammer.

"This dead priest isn't your kind of thing. You're not an investigator. You're more the shock troop type. You go on missions after targets. That's what John did; he sent you on a mission . . ." Harry smiled. "After me." Harry tapped his forehead. "Old John is a pretty smart motherfucker, I'll give him that."

"He sent me to take you to the hospital."

"Yeah, right." Harry opened a palm and floated it out to broadly indicate the scene on the deck. "So why ain't we at the hospital?"

Broker blinked several times, but nothing worked right. Harry blurred in and out; there was a white-water rush in his eardrums.

"I'll tell you why," Harry said, "because you and me—we got a dialogue, that's why."

Broker's frustration broke through and showed when he impulsively yanked at the handcuff and only succeeded in hurting his manacled left wrist.

"You remember I asked you earlier, why didn't you go on to become a lawyer? I mean, you're way too smart to be a fucking cop. You never answered me," Harry said.

Broker felt the sun beat down like a spotlight. "You know why," he said. But his voice was hoarse, and his teeth were clamped tight.

Harry put his hand to his ear, cocked his head. "What-sa matter? Lose your voice? Louder."

With considerable effort Broker forced himself not to say the words that were on his lips. He had been about to ask Harry what he was going to do with him. No way he'd give the drunken bastard the satisfaction.

"Well?" Harry said.

Broker's concentration failed, and he actually laughed because he was remembering the first line in his favorite book when he was a child: "Odysseus was never at a loss." He'd tried to live his personal Odyssey that way. Now here he was chained and helpless, and the subject was all about loss.

He rallied and met Harry's hot blue eyes and gave the honest answer. "I couldn't go to law school after what happened to Diane, you know that. I had to try to . . . stop people like that."

Harry's face turned killing ugly as he lurched up from the chair. "Stop people?" he said incredulously. "We don't *STOP* people. We *catch* the twisted fucks *after* they . . ." He lashed the air with clawed fingers. "I tried to *stop* somebody, and you *stopped* me."

Harry reached over and wrapped his hand around the handle of the big hammer. He raised it slowly, and Broker could see the tendons in Harry's arm strain with the weight. Slowly, Harry pumped the hammer in the air.

Broker had lost the fight inside where his heart broke loose in a panic gallop. He resolved to construct a box around the fear, keep it contained, keep it off his face. His mind assembled the image of his daughter's face, and the idea was so painful that he thrust it away.

Give him nothing.

Nothing.

So Broker looked beyond Harry and pinned his eyes on the heavy foliage of two giant cottonwoods that grew along the lakeshore. He tried to locate himself in the variety of leaf and shadow, the shapes; mysteries, eternities of green . . .

"Why do you think you're chained up there like a damn dog, huh?" Harry yelled as the hammer moved in small piston circles, gathering momentum.

Broker couldn't keep the tree thing going. He turned back to face the hammer. "Fuck you. If you're going to do something, do it," he said.

Harry leaned closer. "Feel helpless, maybe? Like she did. One minute she's safe in her kitchen, the next that sick fuck husband of hers comes through the door; the same sick fuck you and me booked into jail the night before, right? Except now he's out, and he's got a hammer. A hammer. You ever really think what that was like?"

Broker felt a tic of nerves pry at his face, and he wanted to tell Harry it was sadness, grief, whatever—but not fear, goddammit. *Not.*

But he couldn't control the deep soak of fear sweat that gushed from his pores. Or the rush of rapid breathing. Out of sheer animal reflex he lashed against the manacle. The indifferent steel chain rattled but held fast. Then, finally, the survivor reptile part of his brain reminded him that Harry was standing too far away to actually hit him with the hammer. Harry was carefully staying beyond Broker's stronger reach.

"I just want you to answer me one thing," Harry said.

Then Broker watched Harry's clenched-teeth rage go slack. He staggered slightly and blinked several times. His nose started to bleed again. He wiped at his nose and said, "If it happened all over, would you stop me again?"

Harry straightened up and dropped the hammer to the deck. "You don't have to answer me right now. Think about it. I thought about it a lot." He dropped his chin to his chest, and then he rallied and his head came up and his eyes burned. He raised an accusing finger and jabbed it at Broker. "I could kill you easy."

Breathing heavily, Harry grimaced and snapped his fingers. "Just like that. And I very well might."

But Harry made no further move toward the hammer on the

deck. They glared at each other for several beats. Then Harry exhaled, took another pull on the bottle, and said, "Okay, listen up. John took my badge and my gun, so, just for kicks, I took your badge and your gun. Plus your keys, so I'm going to leave in your truck. You get your cell phone so we can talk. I got the number off the display." Harry placed the cell down on the patio table well out of reach.

"Talk?" Broker almost choked on the word.

"Yeah—you and John Eisenhower'll never catch the Saint in a million fuckin' years."

"Harry—I don't know a lot about this stuff, but you could go into alcohol shock and die. You should get some help."

"No thanks, I still ain't got over the last time you helped me."

Broker, who had struggled so mightily not to show fear, completely submitted to anger. Red-faced, smashing the handcuff against the unyielding redwood strut, he shouted, "Harry, you wacko, think what you're doing!"

Harry gave a fitful misfiring laugh and said, "Save your strength and, ah, don't go away." He left the porch, and Broker strained to hear him moving inside the house. He heard him go down the basement stairs, then after a few minutes trudge back up and go out the front door. The door on Broker's truck opened, then slammed shut. The front door to the house opened and closed. More sounds inside, up and down the hall.

Then Harry came back out on the deck and said, "Okay, what it is—I'm leaving the hammer so you can knock the rail apart and get out. And I saw the clipboard in the truck, with Mouse's handwriting on it. Don't tell Mouse what's going on between us here, 'cause then I won't help you."

Broker decided to give another push. "You're just loaded, running your mouth. You don't know shit."

Harry raised his hand and tapped his forehead. "Ah, psychology. Sorry." He held up the handcuff key. "Look—I'll leave this in the mailbox. I'll call you tomorrow. Meanwhile, you find out if the dead priest deserved it."

"Deserved it?"

"Yeah, like Dolman. He deserved it." Harry walked to the patio door, turned, and hefted the hammer. "See, if the Saint's doing God's work, as it were, I don't see any reason to interfere."

Harry extended the hammer. "This is between you and me, right?"

"You and me," Broker said.

Harry tossed the hammer. Broker snatched it cleanly with his right hand.

Then Harry said, "Course if the priest is clean and the Saint ain't doing God's work, then we'll . . . see. I ain't really decided yet." He reached in his front pocket, eased something out and held it in his fist, and said, "On the other hand . . ." Harry raised his closed hand palm down and opened his fingers.

The bullet clinked on the deck between Broker's shoes. It was about the length and diameter of his ring finger. Harry turned and disappeared through the patio door.

Broker listened to Harry leave the house, get in the truck, start it, and drive away. His knuckles tightened around the slick hammer haft, dripping sweat. He drew a bead on the piece of wood that held him prisoner and swung.

It took a minute to smash the stout redwood strut from the deck rail. Broker slipped the cuff off the shattered wood, snatched up the bullet, got to his feet, went in the house and down the basement stairs.

Harry had left the second gun safe open. Broker looked in the safe to confirm what he already knew: Harry's favorite long black rifle was missing.

Chapter Twelve

Broker got out of the cab and paid the driver. Then he took a moment to compose himself, run his hand down his sweat-soaked shirt, tuck in the anger and humiliation. He rubbed the red raw marks on his left wrist, tested the lump behind his ear for blood and found none.

He glanced around. The world looked deceptively unchanged. Except now Harry was seriously out there in it. Broker knew the stories about drunks who blacked out and continued to function like sleepwalkers for days, operating on pure reflexes.

Broker squeezed the thick .338 round in his pocket. Harry had some pretty advanced reflexes. As he walked toward the law enforcement compound, LEC, for short, he considered the unique potential for havoc in Harry, the blacked-out sniper. Well, John would be happy now that Harry was on board, as it were.

He buzzed himself through the security door with his ID card. Then he buzzed into Investigations and looked around for Mouse.

"He had to go to court," Lymon Greene said. "What do you need?"

"A car. I had some trouble with my truck," Broker said.

"Sure, let's go down to the motor pool," Lymon said. On the way out the door he stopped and took a set of keys from a cabinet and tossed them to Broker.

They walked down several staircases and some corridors and came out in an underground garage. Lymon led him to a tan unmarked Crown Victoria and said, deadpan, "Harry's car."

"Great," Broker said. He immediately opened the trunk, saw the first-aid kit, some equipment related to processing traffic accidents, a Kevlar vest, and what he was looking for: the .12-gauge Ithaca pump shotgun and two boxes of .00 buckshot.

"So how'd it go with Harry?" Lymon asked.

"Harry's just fine. Look. You got the church keys?" Lymon nodded that he did. "Okay, I want to see the church and then talk to this witness. So call him and tell him I'm coming," Broker said.

"Sure. I was just curious. What did John mean, we don't want to play guns with Harry . . . ?"

Broker stepped closer and placed his hand on Lymon's shoulder. "Lymon, pal, let's take a little history test. Who was Carlos Hathcock?"

"Don't play games, I asked you a straight question."

"All right. I'll tell you. Hathcock, like Harry, was a marine sniper. Ninety-two confirmed kills in Vietnam."

"I don't really get around to the History Channel that much. Too many Geritol commercials."

"Harry had forty-five kills. But then Harry was only there half as long as Hathcock," Broker said.

The jaw muscles maneuvered around under Lymon's smooth skin, but he decided not to say anything.

Broker said, "Okay, look—you gotta help me here. I'm real limited when it comes to small talk, paperwork, and offices. You follow me?"

A complex coolness descended on Lymon's handsome face; part inexperience, part age, some implicit racial baggage. Broker, smarting from his encounter with Harry, didn't give a shit.

"Okay, I get it; I'm in a movie with Tommy Lee Jones and Clint Eastwood. I've heard about you, you know," Lymon said.

Broker studied the younger man. "Yeah?"

"Sure. You know how, after nine-eleven, there was all that talk on TV about the CIA not having unsavory types on their payroll who could penetrate terrorist networks. That's kind of like you, isn't it?"

"Is it?"

"Yeah." Lymon carefully twisted his lips along a fine line of irony. "You're what they call Human Intelligence."

Broker tapped Lymon on the chest. "Meet me at the church."

He drove through town in Harry's car, catching traces of Harry's aftershave wafting off the fabric upholstery. His head throbbed, and the air-conditioning, cranked on full, hadn't taken hold yet. The heat squatted on the day, pressing down. And pushing up. You could almost feel the humidity summoning the crabgrass and burdock up into gaps and voids. The toughest weeds had green muscle enough to crack the heavy slabs of city sidewalk.

Like murder maybe. Just waiting for the right climate to rear up and bust through. Broker pictured this big nasty weed bursting right out of Harry's chest.

He was losing his distance. He was personalizing it. *Damn, it was hot.*

After a wrong turn, Broker found the church. There was no good place to die violently, but St. Martin's, abandoned and over-grown, would be way down on anybody's list. The cops had kept the scene quiet. There was no stark yellow crime scene bunting to advertise what had happened here.

Just Lymon Greene, who waited at the entrance looking like a deacon in his gray suit, shined shoes, white shirt, and quiet maroon tie. He stood next to a scrawled, six-pointed pentacle graffiti vandals had sprayed in black on the flagstones in front of the door.

As Broker approached, Lymon moved to unlock the door and said, "There's a small rectory around back where Moros lived; you want . . ."

"Wait," Broker said and nodded toward the rundown house across a vacant lot from the church. A scruffy broad-shouldered man sat in the shade of the narrow porch. Watching.

"Is that Tardee?" Broker asked.

"That's him; he's waiting on you," Lymon said.

"Okay, open it up," Broker said. Lymon opened the heavy wooden door. Broker inspected the lock. It would fasten when he pulled the door closed. He didn't need the keys to lock up.

"Thanks," Broker said. "Now I want to be alone."

Lymon began to say something like, Why the hell did you bring me out here? But he thought better of it and went toward his car. "I'll be back at the office," he called over his shoulder.

Broker had brought Lymon out in the heat so Tardee could see them together. It would help establish that he was a cop—because he was traveling a little light in the credentials department. *Because, you moron, you let Harry take your badge and gun.*

Broker watched Lymon's blue Crown Vic lurch away down the unpaved street. Then he turned, studied the arched stone entryway, and stepped into the church. The raw limestone, old oak, and coarse stained glass closed around him. The temperature dropped. It was cool like a mausoleum. Or a morgue.

He walked into the dank interior and found his way to the confessional. The crime techs from the BCA lab had left both doors wedged open.

First he looked into the penitent chamber and saw the kneeling rest, the shattered wooden grille through which the penitent would announce himself to the priest.

Bless me, Father, for I have sinned.

God's work. That's what Harry had said. *Was the Saint doing God's work?*

If pushed on the subject, Broker considered himself a serious but skeptical pilgrim who traveled without a declared belief in God. His eyes traveled over the altar, the old-world statues and pageantry. The roots of this power went back to imperial Rome; absolutely the longest-running show in the world. It occurred to him that if he were seriously trying to find God, he sure wouldn't start in a building some men had built.

Whatever.

He moved a few steps and looked into the priest's side of the confessional booth. A misshapen tape outline described where Victor Moros had lain in death. The bloodstain still looked damp in the middle. That was the humidity. Neither sweat nor blood were drying as they should.

Harry was right. Broker had never acquired the investigator's instinct to absorb telling detail from a crime scene. But even he could see the direction of bullets through the shattered wood grille, the bits scattered into the room. The killer had fired through the screen. The killer had been talking to the priest.

This was no burglary gone bad. This was personal. Or psychotic.

His eyes settled on the bloody carpet and the abstract taped image of the dead priest. *So did you deserve it?* Broker pushed sweat off his brow with the back of his hand and felt a throb of pain originate in the bump behind his ear and radiate through his head like a thought that Harry had put there.

The hell with this. Better to talk to the living.

He walked out, pulled the door shut behind him, went through a side gate in the sagging wrought-iron fence, and crossed a vacant lot snarled with weeds and wildflowers. Ray Tardee's house was a single-story wood-frame 1890s shotgun; living room, kitchen, bedroom.

Tardee sat in a slant of shadow on his front porch sipping a can of Pig's Eye.

He was in his midfifties, big shouldered, with not much belly. He wore a leg brace on his right foot, and even on this very hot day he wore motorcycle boots, grimy jeans, and a stained T-shirt from which the sleeves had been sliced out. His thick fingers and palms were intricately whorled in black lines, cured and callused in grease and gasoline.

Closer in, Tardee had shaggy brown hair, wispy mustache, and chin whiskers. The fading eagle, anchor, and globe of a Marine Corps tattoo graced his left forearm, and he wore a thunderbird beadwork wristband below the tattoo that suggested some Native American action in his confused bloodlines. Unmoving, he watched Broker come up his overgrown sidewalk.

"You Ray Tardee?" Broker called out.

"Sorry. I'm the fucking sphinx. I ain't suppose to talk to nobody about nothin'," Tardee said.

"Broker, Washington County Investigations. We just called you."

Tardee put down his beer can and folded his arms across his chest. "The sheriff said I ain't suppose to talk to nobody about nothin', and that's exactly what I'm doing," Tardee repeated.

"Right. Sheriff Eisenhower told me; but he's out of town, so right now you're talking to me."

"All right. Let's see some picture ID."

So Broker took out the brand-new ID that Harry had neglected to take off him. Tardee scanned it and grumbled, "Yeah, okay; I saw you at the church with that Selby Avenue Sioux."

Tardee studied Broker to see if he picked up on the racial slur. Broker got it. Back in the old days, before gentrification, when Broker had walked a beat in St. Paul, Selby Avenue was the main drag of the black ghetto.

"You got enough skin to get on a tribal roll?" Broker asked.

Tardee squinted.

"Ojibwa?" Broker asked.

"Net Lake."

Broker nodded. Net Lake was a poor rez, not blessed with gaming revenue. "Tough shit for you, no casino," Broker said as he came up on the porch and sat casually on the rail. "So did you know the priest?"

Tardee shrugged. "Mexican guy. He wasn't from around here. I saw him in the yard once, putting down sod. I told him it was the wrong time of year to lay sod, that September would be better for the roots to take."

"You talk about anything else?"

"Yeah, he said it was hot. I agreed."

"And that's it?"

"Pretty much. I already been over this." Tardee slipped his hand into his back jeans pocket and pulled out a business card. "With . . . Lie-mond Greene. Investigator." Tardee grinned, showing decayed teeth. "Kinda makes you believe in progress, don't it?"

"Say again?" Broker asked.

"Lymon Greene is progress, see. I asked him where he grew up. In fucking Golden Valley west of Minneapolis. He's a new one on me. I've known some splivs, in the cities and in the crotch. But Lymon, he's my first square black guy."

"Square, huh? Not hip like you and me?"

"There it is."

Broker endured a moment of sun-induced dementia. Suddenly,

he didn't want to be here. "Like for instance, Lymon would never rough somebody up, you know, just because they're a lowlife piece of shit. He probably never even says the word *shit*, huh?"

They regarded each other like natural enemies, and their eyes agreed it was too hot to pursue it. Tardee shifted his feet. "You know, the sheriff and I had this talk about this little situation I got coming up."

Broker raised his face and took another long drink of too much sun. Working the deals was high on the list of reasons he had quit police work; herding the rats through the sewers with sticks and carrots, keeping them out of sight.

Broker blinked and shook his head again. "Yeah, that was real smart, Ray; selling a bag of grass to an undercover cop."

Ray scratched his belly and grumbled, "Shit, man, it was self-defense; that fuckin' undercover narc was on his knees begging. Dude was undoing my belt."

"Sheriff says you got priors. You're over the line. That's a commit to prison."

"Fuckin' guidelines," Ray said.

"Yeah, but maybe we can get them to go for a departure from the guidelines."

"The sheriff didn't say maybe. He said be quiet about the woman in the Saints jacket going in the church, and he'd get me a deal."

"What I want to know is, could it have been a guy dressed like a woman?" Broker said.

"She looked like Robin Williams," Tardee said.

"What?"

"Yeah, remember that movie *Mrs. Doubtfire*, where he dressed up in that padded costume and the wigs and shit? That's exactly what she looked like. A fucking shim."

"Shim?"

"A she and a him. An in-between."

"How tall?"

"Too tall. About five eleven, but walking funny, like a kid in high heels. Like she was in built-up shoes. And, ah, she had a big ass."

"How so?"

"Too big. I'm good on asses, but I'm *better* on pussy. See, I got hit in the war, and they put this steel plate in my head." Ray thumped his skull. "Ever since, I got no sense of smell whatever; I can eat *anything*." Ray grinned broadly and let his tongue loll inside his smile.

"I'm impressed. So was there anything about her big ass that was distinctive?"

Ray grinned. "Yeah, it was too big for the rest of her. And she didn't move like someone who had a big ass. She moved like someone who had a pillow stuffed in the seat of her drawers."

"So it could have been a guy dressed up like a girl?"

"Could of been, but probably not, unless you really want it to be," Tardee said carefully.

Broker let it go; he was getting personal again, trying to make it be Harry. He thanked Tardee and left the broken porch. As he walked toward the car, he heard Tardee whistling behind him. He was a good whistler. The Fat Tuesday lilt of "When the Saints Go Marching In" was unmistakable.

Chapter Thirteen

Easing from North End gravel onto city pavement, Broker remembered the book of matches he'd taken from Harry. He fished the square of cardboard from his chest pocket and rotated it in his fingers like prayer beads.

He was starting to formulate a plan.

He flipped open his cell phone, thumbed out Mouse's card, and punched in his number. Mouse answered on the third ring.

"So what are you doing?" Broker asked.

"Driving back from federal court in St. Paul. They recessed on me. How'd it go with Harry?"

"Not so hot; Ole's was a setup," Broker said. "He talked me into dropping by his place on the way so he could pack a bag. And he . . . slipped out on me."

"Slipped out on you," Mouse repeated carefully.

"Where can we meet away from the shop?" Broker said.

"Is this, like, getting real fucked up?" Mouse said.

"Where, Mouse? I want to talk."

"Okay, since you're supposed to have all kinds of bread stashed away, you can buy me a drink at Club Terra in fifteen minutes."

"See you there."

Club Terra would not have been Broker's first choice. It was a supper club with a log cabin exterior across Highway 36 from the Washington County Government Center, so it did a brisk business with county workers. But he needed Mouse to level with him on Harry. So he drove to the restaurant, went in, and got a table just as the place was filling up with the late-lunch crowd. Mouse came in a few minutes later.

The weather was getting to Mouse. After being in court he'd exchanged his suit jacket, shirt, and tie for a baggy cotton polo shirt that covered his pager and holster. The shirt stuck to his ample belly in dark patches of sweat.

"Some weather, hey; and, ah, you look like shit," Mouse said.

"Christ, Mouse; half the county is here. I wanted to get away," Broker said, suddenly self-conscious.

"Stay cool. You wanted to get down and dirty, right? This is the place."

A waitress appeared. They refused menus. Neither of them had an appetite in the heat. Broker ordered ice tea. Mouse ordered iced coffee.

"Harry says he'll help," Broker said.

"Really?" Mouse said as he took a toothpick out of his chest pocket, put it in his mouth. "So where's my cuffs?"

Broker reached back under his shirt, took the handcuffs off his belt, and slid them across the table.

Mouse inspected them and said, "There's pieces of woody shit ground in the grooves here."

Broker didn't answer, so Mouse ran his practiced eyes over Broker and stopped on the raw red marks on his left wrist. Then Mouse said, "You know, you're, ah, wearing your hair shorter than you used to."

"Yeah?"

"Well, it makes it easier to see things on your scalp, like, for instance, the black-and-blue goose egg behind your right ear."

"Shit." Broker pursed his lips.

Mouse raised his iced coffee, sipped, put it down, and said, "You gonna tell me, or do I have to torture it out of you?"

"I turned my back on him," Broker said.

Mouse shut his eyes, grimaced, crossed his arms over his wide stomach, then raised his right hand and propped it under his heavy chin. "My fault. I shoulda come with you."

"No you shouldn't have. It's personal; this part at least." Broker pointed behind his right ear.

"You saying there's more?" Mouse squinted and leaned across the table.

Broker nodded. "Harry and I have this heavy private agenda we have to work through, right? But apart from that he wants to stay in touch. I think he feels left out."

Mouse shook his head, but he couldn't entirely hide the admiration in his voice. "Fucking Eisenhower. When Harry's drunk, he blames you for his wife's death. Some people think he's basically sworn to kill you; so John puts you next to him 'cause he thinks there's some weird chemistry between you two that's going to make him spill his guts."

"Kind of scary, huh? A man with a deviant mind like that being the sheriff in the fastest-growing county in the state," Broker said.

"So, did Harry tell you anything good?"

"He told me that if the Saint isn't"—Broker hooked the first two fingers of both hands and struck quote marks in the air— "doing God's work, he might help with the catching part."

"Like he really knows something."

"There it is," Broker said. "Of course he'd been drinking."

"Of course," Mouse said as he rolled a toothpick across his

mouth, fiddled with his napkin, and tapped his fingertips on the tabletop.

An ex-cigarette smoker, Broker recognized the symptoms of the craving. In fact, he was starting to feel the nervous hankering toying powerfully with his insides. He made a mental note to buy some cigars, sort of as a tobacco methadone fix against the heroin lure of cigarettes.

"He said that, huh?" Mouse said. Then he inclined his head and directed his eyes across the room. Broker followed the direction of Mouse's gaze, through the crowd. Three people were moving from the reservations desk behind a waitress, going toward a table. Two men and a woman.

Perhaps in thrall to status, they wore suits in spite of the heat— a blazer and skirt for the woman. They were too young and fit-looking to be normal county apparatchiks.

"Look like lawyers," Broker said.

"Uh-huh. County attorneys, actually," Mouse said.

Upon closer inspection, Broker saw that the two men were not remarkable. The woman, however, put out serious candle power. Black-framed glasses magnified a friction in her eyes that could ignite fires. She had very short razor-cut black hair and a sinewy athleticism. The calf muscles in her tanned legs clenched at every step.

"Stillwater girl," Mouse said.

"Say again?"

"My dad used to say you can always tell a Stillwater girl by her legs. From going up all the stairs on the hills."

There was only one female assistant prosecutor with a reputation for that kind of physical intensity. "Is that Gloria Russell?" Broker asked.

"Oh yeah."

"And?"

"And, well, you know—the Saint case was this real nightmare; it went through the county like an emotional plague. People quit; people went on medication; some people had affairs. Old Gloria hit for the cycle; she turned in her resignation, only they threw it back at her. She went on medication, and she had an affair."

"She did, huh?"

"Oh yeah. A real double-scream-back-crawler. You know, Harry never once denied he was the Saint. He'd sort of smile and he'd say, 'Well, somebody has to carry out the garbage.' But the one thing he'd always deny was . . ." Mouse inclined his head at the assistant prosecutor.

"You mean . . ." Broker said, craning his neck now to get a better look at her.

"Big time," Mouse said as he curled his left index finger into the hollow of his left thumb to make a circle. Then he inserted his right index finger into the socket and pumped it.

Broker raised his hand and flipped it over, palm up. "So connect some dots for me," he said.

Mouse twisted his lips in a sour expression. "Hey, I gotta work here in this glass house. John E. brought you in to throw the stones."

"Mouse, there's a dead priest with a Saint's medal in his mouth."

"Yeah, yeah." Mouse made placating gestures with his palms. "So what do you want?"

"You going to help me with Harry, Mouse? You were playing hard to get this morning."

"That's before you got hit in the head and maybe handcuffed. Harry's a great guy when he's sober, and I love him. But he can be dangerous when he's drinking. I mean"—Mouse carefully looked Broker in the eye—"he could kill somebody, right?"

Broker nodded. "Yep. If he's drunk and you get in the way of the wrong mood swing— Harry could kill you."

Mouse leaned forward and squinted. "Cut the shit, Broker; it's the Mouse you're talking to . . ."

"Okay, Harry could put one right here." Broker tapped his forehead.

Mouse nodded. "So you want us to put a Bolo on him for whatever it is he did to you, which you ain't saying? Drag his ass in?"

Broker caught a whiff of cigarette smoke gliding from the bar and all these vampire air sacs in his lungs sat upright in their coffins. "Nothing so obvious," he said. "Picture somebody chasing him down the street and he's blacked-out drunk. He took one of his favorite toys when he left his house—the one with the target knobs on the scope that's registered out to twelve hundred yards. He could climb up in a building, and it could bounce strange."

"I hear you," Mouse said.

"Or less dramatic, he could seriously disappear, and we need him. So we use him and then we trap him."

"And drag him off to the hospital in a net like a wild animal." Mouse grinned.

"Exactly," Broker said. "Remember what you said about checking every casino in a one-hundred-mile radius?"

"That was a joke," Mouse said, a little alarmed.

"No joke. Can you do that? Quietly, like, don't let your buddy Benish know. Fax Harry's picture around to the security officers. I mean, we're talking about a high roller who's drunk, who looks like a skinny Johnny Cash, who has three red sevens tattooed on his right forearm. How hard is that?"

Mouse nodded. "Maybe I can do that. I know a retired state patrol copper who runs security in the Grand Casino up in Hinckley. Maybe he can flog the network."

"We might get lucky. If I was Harry crashing and burning on my last hurrah, I'd hang in the casinos where it's dark and cool

and anonymous," Broker said as he stared across the room at
Gloria Russell in profile. She leaned forward, chatting intently
with her colleagues. Her teeth flashed in a smile like crisp punctu-
ation. She looked incredibly healthy and vital, as though she
breathed better air, took better vitamins.

"Okay, I'll get on the casinos." Mouse took a last swig at his
coffee and set the glass down. "When do you talk to the archdiocese?"

"Meet my guy in the morning," Broker said.

Mouse nodded. "When you get back, we'll sit down and run
everything we've got on Moros. You, me, and Lymon."

Chapter Fourteen

Maybe everybody was invisible down deep.

Or were they just hiding what they were thinking?

All the people she passed during the day. People she knew, went on break with. Even the man she'd let into her body. She couldn't really see the pictures moving in their minds just behind their eyes.

Windows to the soul?

Hardly. More like the two-way mirror in the hard interrogation room. You could see out at them, but they couldn't see in. They looked at you and saw their own reflection.

But they knew you were there, watching.

So more like—windows to the game.

Angel was through with games.

She was playing for keeps.

And right now she was daydreaming in the heat. Driving from Herberger's Department Store up on 36, she passed a digital sign on a bank marquee. The time, then: 102 degrees.

The heat made her light-headed.

Floaty.

So get serious.

Specifically, this afternoon she would be playing for keeps with Aubrey Jackson Scott. Aubrey was a freelance photographer. He lived in a river cottage on the St. Croix north of Stillwater. He was divorced. He drove a 1995 Accord. He had no police record. Just the one complaint.

A neighbor couple had griped that Aubrey invited their eight-year-old daughter into his house to give her a new bathing suit. They suspected, but could not confirm, that Aubrey had taken photos of her when she put the new suit on.

A Washington County deputy had talked to the parents. He'd signed off when he learned that the child refused to give back the suit. County, understaffed, had let it slide.

The back-and-forth facts didn't really matter. What mattered was that Aubrey's name was number two on the list.

Angel parked her car, gathered her shopping bag, and went into her apartment. Just as with Moros, she took time to prepare herself mentally. She sat down in her living room and stared at the face in the picture framed on the bookcase across the room.

You told me I had to be strong.

Then, methodically, she laid out her gear: the latex gloves, the medallion, and the wig. She kept two pistols in her desk drawer. She loved the .38. Its heft and bulk. But it was a revolver, and when she'd used it the first time she was damn near as scared as that creep Dolman when she heard it go off. She'd turned the volume on his sound system way up, and still she worried people would hear.

So this time around she'd decided to do a little research on-line that took all of ten minutes.

She typed HANDGUN and HOMEMADE SILENCER into Google.com and got hundreds of sites.

The book she bought with her sister's VISA card cost fourteen bucks and was titled *Homemade Silencers Made Easy*. Used automobile oil filters were the favorite home item recommended by the right-wing crazy who wrote this slim volume. But Angel couldn't see lugging around a dirty, oily hunk of metal in her purse.

Uh-uh. Angel preferred something clean.

Like a twenty-four-ounce plastic Mountain Dew pop bottle. No complicated threading device. Just a big plug of duct tape attaching the bottle to the barrel housing of a .22-caliber Ruger Mark II target pistol.

She bought the Ruger at a chain-store gun department using her sister's driver's license—same height, around the same weight, same eye color. And she'd worn her sister's wig for the first time outside of the apartment.

In her sister's glasses, and the wig, the resemblance was uncanny, although her sister's face in the license photo was much thinner than her own. So the salesman had perused the license, taken her sister's name and social security number, and submitted them to a computer background check.

Two weeks later Angel was the owner of a new pistol, which—according to the author of *Homemade Silencers Made Easy*—was a perfect fit for the clumsy but effective pop bottle taped to its barrel housing.

And, as the visit with Father Moros demonstrated, the silencer system worked just fine. The main thing was she had to get in close.

Angel slipped out of her working clothes and her underwear. She removed the new bathing suit from the shopping bag, held it up in front of her, and pitched a sidelong glance into her full-length mirror.

Close would not be a problem.

Chapter Fifteen

Broker drove around the back of the LEC, parked in the underground garage, and took an elevator up to the sheriff's offices. Going into Investigations, he checked Lymon's cube. Empty. He ignored the sullen nongreetings from the other cops, continued down the row of cubicles. "Narcotics," he sang out.

"We got a hell of a going-out-of-business-sale on Ecstasy right now," a young voice replied.

"Where are you?"

"Other side of the cubes."

A young investigator stood in the aisle. He was dressed in filthy blue work trousers, a soiled T-shirt, steel-toed shoes. A pair of bulbous ear protectors was slung around his neck.

"What are you supposed to be besides bright-eyed and bushy-tailed?" Broker said.

The young cop shrugged. "Working a UC gig; right now I'm a tree trimmer. Got a chain saw and everything."

"You are . . . ?" Broker said.

"Pete Cody. Narcotics." Cody did not offer to shake hands.

"But I heard about you. You're the loneliest guy in the world, right?"

Broker was not amused. "How'd a shrimp like you manage to grow up instead of being beaten to death on the playground?"

Cody smiled. "Musta been all that mediation counseling, I guess."

Broker said, "You know anything about a guy named Ray Tardee?"

Cody shrugged. "Sure, one of our perennials."

"Who's prosecuting?"

"Russell."

"Thanks."

Broker went to an empty cube, sat down at the desk, got out the county phone directory, called the county attorney's office, and asked for Gloria Russell.

"Miz Russell took the rest of the day off," the receptionist said.

"Tell her Phil Broker, Special Projects on Moros, called. We need to talk ASAP about one of her cases, Ray Tardee." Broker gave his cell phone number.

Broker raised his voice. "Anyone," he sang out loud enough to carry over the cubicle walls, "is Gloria Russell married?"

"Happily?" someone asked back. That caused a few titters.

"Is she married?" Broker repeated.

"She *was* married. BH. Oh yeah. For sure." Several voices replied from the cubes.

"BH, Before Harry," someone added.

"Her life is currently complicated by a dietary situation. She developed this craving for chocolate. That's why she works out so hard."

Then a more serious voice overrode the guffaws. "Her marriage went in the toilet. She separated. She's getting divorced."

Broker mulled it over, drew it out: Miz . . . Russell. That tingle on his neck hairs brought him around. A blond, balding, horse-faced guy stood behind him. One of the white-shirt potbellies.

"Who are you?" Broker asked.

"Benish. Fraud."

"What do you want?"

Benish glanced around the barren cubicle. "We were wondering if you're going to set up in a cube, you know, hang family pictures? Or maybe you won't be here that long?"

"Benish, in your professional opinion, do I need a coffee taster?"

"Not my department. You need General Investigations for poisoning cases."

"Thank you, Benish."

"Have a good day, Broker."

A secretary in her early sixties manned the gatekeeper desk at the entrance to Investigations. She had a smoke-cured bingo parlor face, frosted hair, and the trim body of a ballroom dancer.

"Marcy, right?" Broker said.

"You got it," Marcy said.

"So where's Lymon?"

"Lymon's doing Goths."

"I don't follow."

"You don't have kids in high school?"

"No kids in high school."

"Goths are to the left of slackers and grunge," Marcy explained. "Goths wear black all the time, dye their hair green, and insert cuff links in their pierced tongues."

A voice sounded in back of Broker. "Lymon thinks they also worship the devil. And, in their spare time tip over tombstones, deface and burglarize churches—stuff like that."

Broker swung around. Benish continued, "So Lymon's asking the little Satanists if they've, you know, whacked any priests lately."

"So Lymon has a theory about the case," Broker said.

"Two theories. His first all-purpose theory is Harry did it. If that doesn't work, then his second theory is the devil did it," Benish said.

Broker turned back to Marcy. "Has anything come in from the BCA crime lab yet?"

"Not yet," Marcy said.

"Okay, I'll be in touch," Broker said, walking down the length of the room. As he keyed open the locked door, he heard Benish snicker, "*He'll* be in touch." He took the elevator and paced back and forth as it descended, then left the elevator and started for the garage thinking . . .

So, if you want to know what's really going on, get away from the guys with the suits and ties and the big guts who take the long lunches. Maybe it's time to check in with the flat-belly street grunts.

Abruptly Broker turned away from the corridor leading to the garage, went up a flight, and walked into the patrol division. He cut through the deserted muster room past rows of folding chairs and a lectern. A yellowed pistol target taped to the bulletin board featured Osama Bin Laden's bullet-punched face.

He went into an alcove off the muster room where a statuesque brunette patrol sergeant named Patti Palen sat at an administrative desk. She had a full-service belt strapped over her regulation beige-on-tan county uniform. An HT 1000 portable radio sat on the desk and hiccuped static.

"Surprise, surprise," she said in a grudging voice. "I heard you were in the area."

"Hey, Patti, how you doing? Yeah, I'm around for a few days,"

Broker said. "Thought I'd drop down here belowdecks and see how the galley slaves are doing."

"You never were any good at small talk, Broker. So what do you want?"

"Hey, how's your kid doing? It's Alex, right? He must be, what—twenty-three, twenty-four now?" Broker said casually, avoiding the sight of Patti's face tightening as his eyes roved the small room.

Seven years ago Broker bumped into Alex Palen, then seventeen, in an entry-level position fencing stolen televisions and VCRs in the electronics division of a biker gang Broker had a relationship with. He'd given the kid a break, steered him clear of a felony bust, and hounded him into the Coast Guard.

Patti drew in a sharp breath, composed herself, exhaled, looked up into Broker's eyes, and said, "Alex is doing just fine." Her gaze then moved off and became seriously involved with the linoleum pattern on the floor. "Why don't you cut me some slack and talk to somebody else."

"Nah, you owe me. So what's making the rounds, Patti?"

Patti exhaled again. "Harry Cantrell got suspended for coming in drunk. And we aren't supposed to know, but a priest got shot in St. Martin's and they found a St. Nicholas medal in his mouth. The sheriff worked it out with the union so Harry has to go to treatment or he loses his job." Patti took a breath. "So Investigations is down one body, and we got a Saint's panic coming on like a storm surge."

"Anything you left out?"

"Yeah, last I heard, you, of all people, were gonna take Harry to the hospital. So, is he in the hospital?"

"Not yet. Tell me, Patti— you think Harry is the Saint?"

Patti shook her head. "Me personally? No. The coppers are pretty evenly divided on this. There's a third that think he is, there's a third that think he isn't, and the rest don't really have an opinion."

"One last question: what's the story on Harry and Gloria Russell?" Broker said.

They stared each other down. Second by second Patti's face filled with gravitas until it weighed about a ton. "Some people say they were like crossed live wires on a tin roof from the minute they started working together on the Dolman thing. It got so bad, it deep-sixed her marriage and was interfering with her work. So she talked to John E. and got him to take Harry off the case. Replaced him with Lymon Greene." Patti sat deeper in her chair and folded her arms. "Which really pissed Harry off."

"Yeah, go on."

"Apparently, Lymon replaced Harry in more ways than one. According to this version, that's why Harry pulled his Mark Fuhrman number. You know, the famous N-word scene."

Broker lifted his eyebrows.

"I give you one last thing, and then you leave me alone. Okay?" Patti said.

Broker nodded.

"The only thing I know for sure is Gloria and Lymon spend lunchtime together lifting weights downstairs in the gym."

"Thank you, Patti."

"Fuck you, Broker."

Broker continued to the basement motor pool and was going down the lines of marked and unmarked cars when he encountered Cody, the narcotics cop, and his partner, both wearing the tree trimmer costumes. Cody was carrying a black plastic bag. Seeing Broker, he held up the bag and grinned.

"We're going through garbage. You want to join us?" Cody called out in a sardonic voice.

Broker smiled and kept going, got into Harry's car, started it up, and drove from the underground garage into the ash-white sunlight.

He turned south on Osgood, crossed Highway 36, and stopped at the Holiday station, went in and bought several packs of Backwoods cigars. Back in the car, he fired up one of the rough-looking stogies with Harry's casino matches. As the raw but calming smoke meandered from his mouth, he caught himself automatically doing a terrain field scan. A pre-cop habit from a shooting war. He was checking the surrounding area by breaking it into quadrants, then stopping, reversing field to overlap the last quadrant before moving on and repeating the process.

Broker shook his head. *What do you expect? Harry's going to follow you in your own truck? The one he stole from you?*

With the windows down and the cigar clamped in his teeth, he put the car in gear and continued north through Oak Park Heights, past the quaint shady residential streets. Then, off to the left, the Oak Park Heights Correctional Facility hid in a fold of open field. The maximum security prison was sunk four levels deep in the ground, like a buried battleship.

The worst dudes in the state were entombed here like bad canned meat. Ten years ago, Diane Cantrell's murderer was on his way here for his own protection—but they didn't move him fast enough, and he was knifed to death in Stillwater Prison. Washington County was host to the state's two serious prisons, Stillwater and OPH, located within a few miles of each other. The county could boast more killers and rapists per capita than any other jurisdiction.

He hadn't consciously planned this; consciously, he was just buying some smokes. But now he knew that he was following a need to get close to the origin of this whole thing. So he stepped on the gas and raced past clusters of large framed homes. Then he topped a rise and saw the strip malls and monotonous condo barracks of Timberry sprawled below him.

He pulled over, consulted his Hudson's street map guide, got his bearings, and drove on. Ten minutes later he was in more open country. Then he pulled into the entrance to Timberry Trails Elementary School, where he was surprised to find a line of yellow school buses along the entry road.

Summer school, maybe?

Eight- and nine-year-olds wearing red safety patrol belts were walking out the front door, taking up positions at the buses. Broker parked, stubbed out his cigar, and popped a Certs in his mouth. As he approached the school entrance, it was as if they'd opened a faucet. Children squirted out the front door in a blur of color and squeals. They sluiced past him wearing shorts and T-shirts.

He stood motionless as they swept past. Little nudges and tugs, like a happy rush of water. Open faces, innocent bright eyes.

Trusting.

He shook his head to clear out the sunspots and entered the building, crossed an atrium, and went into the administrative office. There was a basket on the reception desk containing red clip-on visitors' badges. Broker picked one up, weighed it in his hand.

The receptionist eyed him, smiling less and less the more she looked. "Are you a parent?" she asked.

"Yes," Broker said. "My daughter is in preschool." *In Italy.* Broker dropped the visitors' badge and took out the Washington County ID and showed it to the receptionist. "Maybe I could have a word with the principal?"

"I . . . guess . . ." The receptionist turned and called through a doorway, "Marian, we have a police officer here . . ."

The principal was a short, vigorous woman in her early sixties. She came to the door and sized up Broker. Her expression steadied down, but she continued to smile.

"Come in," she said. "Marian Hammond."

"Phil Broker." They shook hands.

"You don't look well, Mr. Broker. Can I get you a glass of water?" Marian said as she closed the door.

"I'm fine. It's the heat."

"No, it's the heat plus. I'm in the people business, and you look like trouble. May I see some identification, please," Marian said promptly.

Broker showed his new ID card.

Marian scrutinized the ID. "Okay, so why is a detective in my school?"

"I thought school was out."

"Special summer event day. Why are you here, Mr. Broker?"

"I'm a temporary officer assigned to clearing out old files. I have a few questions about the Ronald Dolman case."

Marian raised her hand to her throat as Dolman's name glided across the room like a dark-finned shadow. She dropped her hand and balled her fists. "What kind of questions?"

"The boy involved . . ."

Marian nodded. "Tommy Horrigan. He was six then; he's seven now."

"Is he still . . . ?"

"Of course not; his parents moved out of state, and they requested no forwarding address be given out."

"Okay. There's no nice way to ask this one. Was Dolman buried in the county?"

Marian was probably a grounded, compassionate woman. But she curled her lip, showed her teeth, and did not conceal the flash of disgust. "I'd have thought you people would know about that. Ronald Dolman was cremated, and his remains were thrown in the trash."

Chapter Sixteen

Brother, was J. D. Salinger ever full of shit.

Angel frowned as a mob of shouting eight-year-old boys rocketed past. Defiant, she refused to even wince when their churning bare feet pecked her with sand. She watched them tear along the crowded beach and yowl and smile goofy breathless grins when they trampled the sand castles that two quiet, serious-looking seven-year-old girls were constructing at the water's edge.

See, it's all right there. The rampant Y chromosome and testosterone.

Give me a break. No way boys could concentrate long enough to save anybody from running off a cliff. Much less find them in a field of rye. Look at them, tearing around. Probably, they'll go off somewhere and light farts. Little fuckers.

Holden Caulfield, no, thank you.

Angel carefully picked grains of boy sand from her well-oiled arms, dusted off her towel, and then continued to rub SPF 40 sunscreen on her legs. She wore a broad sun hat, which left her face in shadow, and wide sunglasses. The tight wig was a bother in all this heat.

But necessary.

It was a sweltering late afternoon, the beach at Square Lake was packed with people, and Angel was far from invisible. No, today she had slipped free from her constraining sports bra and let out a little cleavage. Usually, she would wear a one-piece suit, but today was an exception. Today she was showing some skin.

Aubrey Jackson Scott spent his afternoons on this beach, and since the heat spell fell on them like hot dishwater she'd observed him here several times. Now she thought she had a plan that might work. So she'd bought the new suit.

He appeared to be omnivorous and might like a gal who was hanging out here and there. Angel got the impression that his appetites strayed all over the pasture and couldn't be fenced in. He did kind of remind her of a goat.

And he was a borderline exhibitionist. Which was sad, purely on the basis of evaluating his body type. He'd clearly been in shape once and let himself go. About thirty pounds over the line. Aubrey wore the briefest of swimsuits, a European job a bit skimpier than a Speedo, which sometimes nearly disappeared in the dross of his belly, or skinnied up between the cheeks of his butt. Once in the last hour Angel had watched two teenage lifeguards put their heads together and consult in his direction, presumably about his appearance.

Angel could imagine their discourse: *Well, he hasn't done anything wrong yet.* Right. That epitaph had graced a lot of tombstones.

So they let Aubrey jiggle his overweight gut and rear end around the beach. With a heavy gold chain around his neck, he had to be the greasiest man Angel had ever seen. His body hair was matted in streaks. The man actually oozed. He looked as if he'd acquired his deep-fried tan from a full immersion dip in a vat of boiling fat at McDonald's.

Maybe he'd been discreet once, but he'd passed the point of control. Aubrey was definitely surplus population. Somebody had to come along with a pooper-scooper and remove him from the scene.

Letting it all hang out wasn't his only problem. From a distance of twenty feet, Angel watched Aubrey remove tobacco from the tip of a non-filter cigarette, then tamp something in the cavity. He lit up, took a deep drag, and held it in. She could distinctly smell the thick oily marijuana in the heavy air. She shook her head. The guy looked as if he lived in a cannabis haze of sensation. Men, women, boys, girls. You name it. He'd probably tried it with his vacuum cleaner.

But she wasn't capricious. She needed some proof that he belonged on the list. Angel took her work seriously; she was prepared to go pretty deep undercover to get her confirmation.

Aubrey kept a blocky digital Nikon camera in his gym bag. He'd whip it out and grab snaps when the opportunity presented itself. She watched his camera follow a six-year-old girl in a blue bikini as she walked into the lake.

He was close enough for Angel to hear the precise snap of the shutter.

Angel had been moving in on him for more than an hour. Unaware that she was getting closer, he trolled his watery brown eyes up and down the crowded beach. Looking for strays, maybe. Except he had not approached any children. Occasionally, he just took some pictures. Once he walked down the beach, past the roped-off swim area, and snapped a group of scuba divers when they came ashore for a break; then he talked to them and wrote something down.

Hmmm.

Chapter Seventeen

So much for the idea that Dolman's remains might be in the ground close by and that someone, like maybe his killer, might visit the grave. Harry was right. Broker was miscast in the investigator's role.

On his way back into town he turned on NPR and listened to a discussion on homeland defense. Somebody from the Pentagon was explaining how the beltway road nets around major cities had been designed by the Defense Department. If the cities were nuked, the beltways allowed military convoys to travel around them, not through.

On the theory that it was sometimes better to drive around, not directly through, problems, Broker decided to take a little road time to think. He turned on Highway 36, went west to 694, and lost himself in the traffic, speeding along on the freeway loop around the metro.

Instead of a nuked city, he was driving around Harry's question: would he do it again?

If it was your wife and your kid, would you do it again?

As he thought back over that lousy day, he told himself it had been a case of bad timing. He'd run a red light on Summit Avenue on his way to the dentist's house. If he had stopped for that light, by the time he arrived at the house the dentist might have been dead.

There would have been questions, sure. But Harry would have bluffed his way through. And even if he had been brought up on charges, Diane would still be alive. That's what Harry had meant when he told Broker to leave and come back in five minutes.

Broker had talked this over many times with his old partner, J. T. Merryweather. J. T. compared it to the war. It was friendly fire. It went with the territory. You always assumed that friendly fire would hit somebody else.

In the middle of this meditation his stomach growled like a reminder that life goes on. He hadn't eaten today. He pulled off at the next exit, went into a Perkins, and ate a late breakfast of sausage, pancakes, and eggs.

When he arrived back in Stillwater, he parked in the LEC front lot, went in, buzzed into the sheriff's office and the nearly deserted unit. Summer. Everybody found reasons to get out early. Lymon was not in sight.

Marcy flagged him and handed him a sheaf of paper. "Lymon's interview with the secretary who found the body," she said.

Broker took the report to the empty cube, sat down, read it, and stared at the telephone. Probably he should call Milt's voice mail to see if he had any messages. He smiled cynically. Nina calling from Italy, perhaps. All is forgiven.

First he entered the voice mail number. The recorded voice told him to tap in Milt's number, then asked for the security code.

Finally, the computer voice informed him he had one new message. He pressed 1 to hear it.

One new message left today at 1:34.

"Broker, this is Janey . . ."

Broker took a deep breath. Wonderful. It was old home week.

"I know this is sudden, but I really need to talk to you."

He thumped 3 twice, speeded up the message, deleted it, and sank back in the chair.

Janey.

Jane Carli Hensen, maiden name Halvorsen, Norwegian-Italian ancestry. Whatever she'd once been, now she was a stay-at-home mom. Her daughter, Laurie, would be six now.

Broker, Janey, and her future husband, Drew, had known each other when they all worked at the Minnesota Bureau of Criminal Apprehension. She was in public relations, Drew was a police artist, and Broker was a field agent who was seldom seen in the bureau's offices on University Avenue in St. Paul.

She probably still read two or three mysteries a week. In the old days investigators used to run cases by her and only stared at her legs as an afterthought.

She'd had flings with various cop types, including a long, serious one with Broker; then she married the quietest guy around, Drew, who quit BCA and became a successful commercial illustrator who specialized in children's books. Now she had settled into a monstrously gabled and turreted house on Stillwater's South Hill.

He remembered her standing in the grocery store. She'd looked hollow-cheeked, physically haunted. Excessively lean.

Sort of the way he looked, actually.

Broker shared the Norwegian connection on his mother's side. Given to dark edges, sometimes moody, possessing a thread of melancholy that tied his inner thoughts in a tightly controlled bundle. And always the potential for storms of repressed emotion.

Speaking of threads . . . it would be sensible to avoid Janey, because she used to have this knack for unraveling his little carnal loose ends and giving them a tug.

He stood up and lost his train of thought when he stared down the rows of deserted cubes at a bulletin board that hung on the wall. In huge rushed letters someone had printed: THE SAINT LIVES: HARRY 2, PEDOPHILES 0.

Broker was not amused. He went to the board, erased it, left the office, walked through the lobby and out the revolving doors to the parking lot. He took the Ithaca .12-gauge out of the trunk, stuffed in shells, racked the slide to put one in the chamber, set the safety, and tucked the shotgun in the passenger-seat foot well within easy reach.

In case Harry came flying out of the shadows.

He just wanted to go back to the river, eat a microwave dinner, drink a couple of beers, and put an ice pack on his head. And think of ways to get even with John.

And this was only day one.

Chapter Eighteen

Okay. Showtime.

Angel removed her sunglasses, tilted her hat low over one eye, and concentrated on making herself look like a poster girl for mindless sex. She willed a victim aura into her face; she imagined a neon sign blinking on her forehead: Beat Me; Fuck Me; Blow Your Nose in Me and Throw Me Away.

Angel could move real nice when she wanted to. She moved real nice across the hot sand, stood over Aubrey with one hand plopped on a hip. "Nice camera," she said.

Aubrey looked up, brightened, and spewed language like spatters of grease. "Hi. Dig you. You like cameras?"

Angel made her eyes enlarge with wonder. "Is that real, around your neck?" she asked.

Aubrey fingered his gold chain, shrugged, then curlicued his finger up in the general direction of her chest. "What about those. Are they real?"

Angel put on her best lip-drooping bored smile. "For me to know."

Aubrey was up on his knees now, eager; clearly, this was a guy who loved to connect. He fingered the gold chain. "You know how you test to see if gold is real?" he said.

"Not a clue," Angel said.

Aubrey grinned. He had excellent teeth, healthy gums, and a tongue that jerked around like it could use a shot of Ritalin. His face had been handsome once, before he got soaked in fat. It reminded her of someone.

He was saying, "You bite it." He winked. "See if it dents."

Angel folded her arms protectively across her chest but couldn't quite manage to stifle a grin. "You keep your teeth to yourself."

"So what's up?" Aubrey asked, the voice more reasonable. Curious. And distancing. "Do you always talk to total strangers on a beach?"

Angel shrugged. "Just thought I'd tell you . . . that stuff you're loading into the Camels. I can smell it clear down the beach. So can they." She jerked her head at the lifeguards. "I wouldn't be doing it in plain view if I was you."

Aubrey studied her. "What's your name, honey?"

"Angela."

He reached up and patted her calf. "Thanks for the heads up. Now, why don't you run along."

Feigning a vast indifference, Angel shrugged, turned, and walked back to her towel. *Okay, now don't look over there. Nothing obvious. Let him think. Let him look up and down the beach. Is he bright enough to realize that he's just talked to the nicest little piece of chicken at Square Lake today?*

Angel watched Aubrey stand up, dust off sand, and pull on a pair of baggy shorts. Then a T-shirt, flip-flops, and a long-billed cap. She almost approved of the way he folded his towel, taut square corners. He tucked the towel away, shouldered his bag, and started up the beach to her left and disappeared from the corner of her peripheral vision.

She was careful not to turn and follow him with her eyes. There were always other days. Maybe she'd come on too forward, walking over there and striking up a conversation. Maybe the dope angle wasn't the most effective gambit. Too overt.

Wrong.

A thick shadow fell across her legs.

"So Angela, what's your story?" Aubrey asked. He had circled around in back of her and come up on her right.

Angel lowered her eyes. *With more clothes on, he doesn't look half bad. In fact he has this cleft chin in his deeply tanned face that bears a resemblance to . . . what's his name? The actor who'd been married to Bo Derek. Or maybe it's his manner, which is less intense and is, well, curious.* "My story?" she repeated, working to make her voice self-conscious.

He laughed. "I mean, who are you and where are you from, you know . . ."

"Oh." Angel managed to raise a blush to her cheeks. "I'm a teacher; I teach in an elementary school up in Thief River Falls. It's summer vacation, so I'm down here visiting my sister in Stillwater and" —Angel raised a hand to her lips as if to stifle a giggle— "well, actually, she's pretty straight."

"How straight is straight?" he asked.

"Born-again, Evangelical washed-in-the-blood, baptized-in-the-Holy-Ghost straight." Angel arched her eyebrows and showed the whites of her eyes.

Aubrey squatted down on his haunches, his forearms braced on his quads. "So you're not exactly picking up on any dope smoke wafting through your sister's house?"

"You got that right," Angel said.

"Do you come down here much?"

"Not much. We're originally from South Dakota."

Aubrey nodded. "Where about?"

"Rapid City."

"Sure, Interstate Ninety. Mount Rushmore. I did a shoot at the Sturgis rally and in Wall, you know, tracing the famous bumper sticker back to the source: Wall Drug, South Dakota."

Angel nodded. "The Badlands. I find the Badlands distinctly creepy."

Aubrey bobbed his head in agreement. "Theodore Roosevelt said the Badlands look like Edgar Allan Poe's poetry sounds."

Looking impressed, Angel said, "That's sort of nice."

"Actually, I heard David McCullough say that on C-SPAN, he wrote a book about TR."

Suddenly Angel blurted, "John Derek."

"Huh?"

Angel became animated. "The actor. He's who you look like, I mean your face, here." Her finger drifted out and up and hovered, almost touching the cleft in his chin. It was very difficult for Angel to actually touch a man's body anywhere. The funny thing was, in her other life she had to contend with physical cravings that went in the exact opposite direction.

Aubrey grinned and slapped his stomach. "I should drop a few pounds, I know." He squirmed closer on his sandals and extended his hand. "Aubrey Jackson Scott. But they call me A. J."

"Howdy, A. J.," Angel said. She managed the handshake without grimacing, but just beneath her skin she imagined all the capillaries writhing like blue maggots.

"So . . . life's pretty dull around the old sister's house, huh?" A. J. mused.

In a self-conscious reflex, Angel let one of her hands wander up and fluff her hair, then she toyed with a curl near her forehead. And she thought how things had never been exactly dull around her sister's house. Actually, things at her sister's house had been terrifying, and very very sad.

His voice brought her back to the present. "So, ah, do you like to get high, Angela?"

"I've been known to imbibe," Angel said.

Encouraged, he sidled a little closer. "Tell you what. How about we go someplace and smoke a joint, then go to a nice dark air-conditioned sports bar and get a burger?"

"I saw you taking pictures of the scuba divers. Are you really a photographer?" Angel knit her brow and put a wary lilt in her voice.

"Hey, absolutely. I string for the *Pioneer Press* and the *Star Tribune*. And I do a lot of stuff for the weeklies in the valley."

"And you have, like, a studio and equipment and everything?"

"Of course." He reached in his bag and withdrew the heavy Nikon D1. "This is not exactly kid's stuff I have here."

And Angel thought, *Oh, I bet it is exactly kid's stuff, you greasy fat fuck.* But she smiled, lowered her eyelids, and said, "And so? What . . .you're going to invite me over to your studio under the pretense of taking my picture and get me stoned, huh?"

A. J. shook his head and held out his hands in a genial protest. "Hey. No pressure on this end. Don't believe in it. You want to hang for a while and smoke a number, fine. If you don't, that's fine, too."

"Well, I guess you don't look *too* much like Charles Manson," Angel said.

A. J. stood up and held his hand out to help her to her feet. "Okay, c'mon."

Angel put her hand out to him and shut her eyes tight when she felt his grip on her fingers. As he hoisted her up, she repeated to herself, *Just remember, kiddo, you're not here.*

She folded her towel around her sun lotion. She'd left her beach bag in the car for obvious reasons. He asked where she'd parked, and she pointed up the grassy slope in back of the beach. So they walked side by side through the picnic tables and barbecue grates and up the stairs made of green treated timbers.

Near the top of the steps he smoothly cupped her elbow, to steady her balance, and she did not recoil because she was almost totally invisible now.

Angel had seriously, desperately asked God to help her when she was eleven years old. She had called on God—she'd never say *Him* again, not ever—with all her heart. And God must have been somewhere else, or maybe God was deaf or asleep, because God had not done a single thing to help her.

So she had learned to make herself invisible, lying rigid with her wrists crossed over her heart like thin iron bars.

Sometimes she'd pretended she was the wall next to the bed.

As they walked to the parking lot and he continued to steer her with his hand on her arm, she moved smoothly with his touch. Hold up a mirror, you wouldn't see her. *Uh-uh.*

Gone girl gone.

Chapter Nineteen

Angel disliked being closed in, so she drove with the windows open, and the air slicked her skin like hot oil. She caught herself drifting, involved in the fact that A. J. owned a blue 1995 Honda Accord. Not exactly a flashy car but a dependable performer. The Accord had rated high on *Consumer Reports'* reliability chart, and also held its resale value.

But lately it had been losing ground to the Volkswagen Passat.

She reminded herself to get more serious and focus.

She leaned forward and gripped the steering wheel with both hands as she followed his car back toward town. Then she reached down for the fifth time and confirmed that the automatic, the silencer, the pair of latex gloves, and the medallion were under a towel in her beach bag.

The wig clamped down, trapping sweat, broiling her skull. Wearing the wig in this heat was like torture. But necessary. And apt. She let her hand glide up and twisted a finger in a light ginger curl. Then, softly, she stroked the wavy hair over her ear. Soft, the honey color of champagne.

It was her sister's hair, expertly crafted into a wig. She had helped harvest it to be made into this wig, when the doctors told her sister that chemo had moved from among the options to mandatory treatment.

She dropped her hand back to the wheel. Stay the course, Angel; that's what her sister would say.

So she continued to drive south, toward Stillwater, and on her right, the western sunset was almost biblical in its intensity. It must be the smoke from the forest fires in Colorado and Arizona that had been on the news. Fact of life.

Dirty air was the prettiest.

She could feel herself getting ambiguous about this A. J. He did not project anything like social impairment. She saw no hints of the thing she feared and hated more than anything else, which was sexual sadism. He was easygoing; he did not seem to desire control. The vibes she got off him suggested a debauchee, a libertine.

Intuition whispered that he probably enjoyed wine, food, and dope even more than sex.

She was drifting. She sternly reminded herself that the Nonexclusive Type Pedophile can be attracted to adults as well as children.

If there is no hard evidence, Angel, you will let him go.

A. J. Scott lived off of Highway 95 in a bungalow with a broad wraparound cedar deck that overlooked the St. Croix River. He had the sunrise over Wisconsin, but the sunset was shrouded by the bluff above the highway. By late afternoon his yard was patterned with shade. Coming down his driveway, Angel left the glory of the western sky behind and parked in woodsy gloom.

No sunsets but lots of mosquitoes. The house was crowded close in among pines and mixed hardwoods.

The nearest neighbor was two hundred yards away through the thick trees. Angel spotted a peek of yellow and blue, a plastic tube slide and a swing set. Perhaps that's where the little girl lived. The one who'd tried on the bathing suit.

Angel got out. She liked the location. She was concerned about someone seeing her car, and she especially didn't want anyone to get a good look at her. When she'd called on Father Moros, she'd been in full disguise. Today all she had was the wig.

She walked around to the driver's side of A. J.'s Accord, and as he got out, she pointed at the left rear wheel well.

"Just drives me nuts how it happens in the same place every time," she said.

A. J. cocked his head.

Angel explained, "See the boil of rust there on the rim of the wheel well? Accords, Civics, and Preludes; they all start to rust right there. It's a design flaw."

"I'm impressed; most people don't pick up on that kind of detail. You have a good eye," A. J. said.

Angel shrugged. "I owned a couple Hondas." She walked with him to the door.

A. J. raised an eyebrow. "A good eye is a preselection factor for being a photographer."

Angel nodded. "I remember this high school class. I liked the stuff we did in the darkroom."

He unlocked the door, and they went inside. A. J.'s house was built on two levels, into the slope. Entry was through the kitchen, which was clean.

"Mind if I snoop a little?" Angel asked.

"Go ahead," A. J. said.

She nosed around quickly. The clean, uncluttered counters met with her approval, as did the dishcloth carefully folded between the double sinks. The sinks themselves were spotless and smelled faintly of Clorox. The first level was like a loft; kitchen, dining area, bath, and laundry room cantilevered over the broad living room below.

Then she followed him down the stairway to the main level, which was one long airy space with a fireplace at one end. A door led to what Angel assumed was a bedroom on the other. A central patio door opened onto the wide deck. She could see a wedge of river between the trees. It was all very spare and orderly; minimal furniture, maximum hardwood floors, bare walls and windows. A computer desk was set along the wall by the fireplace with an equipment rack next to it. Long black canvas bags were stacked on the rack. A rolled-up scrim hung from the wall like a picture screen. Some spidery folded-up metal things leaned against the rack, like music stands. Probably for lights. But she didn't see any lights.

"You liked the darkroom, huh? Well, things have changed," A. J. said.

"What do you mean?" Angel was immediately wary. She reminded herself not to touch anything.

"I mean the darkroom. Like, where is it?" A. J. asked.

Angel shrugged. "But this isn't your studio, is it?"

"Pretty much." He swung his camera up on the strap over his shoulder. It was dense black and intricate with knobs, buttons, apertures, a heavy lens. She could tell it was very heavy, just the way he braced to raise it up. "Everything is internal now."

"Internal?"

A. J. pointed to the computer along the wall. "Like, in there. In the tube."

"No darkroom? No more chemicals and doing things with your hands, the shadow stuff . . . ?"

"Dodging." A. J. bobbed his head. "Yeah, I miss it; the little touch of witchcraft. But then this came along." He held up the camera. "Nikon D1 digital. Check this out." He pointed to a small gray window on the camera's thicker right side. "I press this monitor button, and the most recent shot comes on in this viewing window."

He smiled when he said that and moved closer so his hip and arm brushed her, casual but intimate. Angel didn't care; she'd completed her physical trick and didn't even feel it. He might have been touching a wall. And she'd made up her mind on this. She'd allow him in a lot closer to get a look into his computer files.

But then she stiffened. The picture that popped up in the monitor window was of herself, captured in miniature. That was her, all right, sitting on her towel at the beach. Perfectly framed and perfectly clear. The sonofabitch must have a long-angle lens. He must have taken her picture just before he walked over and started talking her up.

This was not good.

But she controlled herself and said, "A. J., I don't mind you taking my picture, but I'd like to know in advance; I don't care for this sneaky candid stuff."

A. J. placed the palm of his hand on his chest. "I apologize. Habit. What I do. But the thing is" —he smiled— "you can delete it; see the button here, next to Monitor . . ."

"How cute; it's got a little bitty trash can on it," Angel said, feeling more relieved and seeing her opening.

"All you have to do is press the delete. Go ahead."

Angel was reluctant to touch the camera. She did not believe that wiping surfaces reliably eliminated all traces of fingerprints. But this was not a time to introduce speed bumps. She put her index finger forward and carefully pressed the button with the tip of her fingernail.

"See," A. J. said.

A dialog box appeared in the middle of the picture in the monitor. ERASING IMAGES. Underneath it said YES, then a little hand pointing to a delete icon identical to the delete button she had pressed. She pressed the delete button again with her fingernail, and the picture disappeared.

She smiled and pursed her lips. "But how do I know that's the only picture?"

A. J. acted hurt. "You don't trust me."

"I don't *know* you."

Angel pronounced *know* with just the right suggestion of unfolding revelation. Encouraged, A. J. steered her to the computer table and said, "So why don't you just edit through all the pix I took at the beach."

"I can do that, like, just here? Now?" Angel appeared to be genuinely curious. The fact was she knew her away around Macintosh computers and Photoshop software. She smiled.

A. J. smiled back.

He didn't know she'd smiled because she felt she was getting warm.

A. J. removed the film card from his camera. "Four hundred bucks, one hundred twenty snaps." It was the size of a short, flat book of matches. He put the card into a slot in a mouselike pad. His screen saver—a goofy dog sailing after a bone—vanished, and his desktop appeared. Then a Nikon D1 icon came on. His fingers flew over the keyboard, and strips of pictures appeared.

"There you go," he said, "just scroll through them and see for yourself."

Warmer.

"Show me," she said. She put her beach bag down under the computer table within easy reach. Then she sat in the chair in front of the Macintosh and kept her hands primly in her lap.

"Just use the mouse to scroll. If you want to magnify, double-click on the checked box in the corner of the frame." His lips were close to her ear, and she could smell his breath on her cheek. His breath smelled like Tic Tacs. She recalled that the priest's breath had smelled exactly the same through the grille in the confessional.

"Can I ask you something personal?" A. J. said.

Angel prepared herself. *Okay. Here it comes.*

But he said, "You didn't go swimming, did you?"

"No. Why do you ask?" She was still sitting up straight, hands folded in her lap, reluctant to touch the keyboard.

"Because you're wearing a very expensive wig, and you didn't want to get it wet."

Angel turned and looked A. J. directly in the eye. "Tell me, do you think the first time you meet somebody is an appropriate occasion to discuss the Big C?"

Her words were a puff of fire. He immediately stepped back.

"Don't worry," Angel said with a brave smile, "it's under control. And A. J.? it's not contagious."

A. J. blushed with embarrassment. Before he could stammer a response, Angel spoke up.

"Now can I tell you something personal?"

"Sure."

"You *did* go swimming because you smell like weeds, and there's this sign when you drive into that park that says you could get swimmer's itch."

"Good point. Why don't I take a shower. You can browse around the computer. Just don't pull the card out of the reader, okay?"

Angel nodded. "Gotcha."

He turned and bounced up the stairs and went into the bathroom. The moment the door closed behind him, Angel reached into her bag and yanked on her latex gloves. By the time she heard water running in the pipes, she had closed out of the pictures A. J. had taken today and was racing through his card files.

No categories to help her. Just dates going back a month. Then maybe he refiled them, probably after burning them to a DVD.

She pulled up dates and scanned a few frames. It was routine newspaper filler—head shots, people at events, local-color shots. Minutes passed. Her fingers blurred over the keys; opening files, random scanning, closing them. She almost didn't want to find anything.

But then, of course, she did.

She scrolled down the strip of frames. This was some kind of fashion shoot because the subject was posed against a light blue background. She got up, went to the hanging scrim mounted on the wall by the equipment rack. Pulled it down and found a matching light blue. So probably these were taken here.

She returned to the desk and studied a picture of a blond teenage boy in a pair of jeans naked from the waist up. He was thin but svelte, with smooth little ab muscles. Some of the shots looked as if he was modeling the jeans, but in others he was clearly modeling himself.

Especially the ones where he had the fly unzipped. In successive frames the jeans were doing a hula down his hips.

Then she double-clicked on the frame where the zipper was three-quarters open and his not-so-little-business was half tumescent, just kind of ready to pop out of its crinkly nest of pubic hair like a just-opened present nestled in excelsior. Clearly, this was a gift waiting to be discovered. And if the boy's posture didn't convey the intended message, the expression on his face certainly did; the lower lip sagging, the tongue in motion.

Angel stared at the eyes. The way they absolutely owned the jaded intersection of violation and vulnerability.

Suddenly, she realized that the shower was no longer running. Upstairs, she heard him coming out of the bathroom. Bare feet slapping the hardwood floor, coming down the hall into the dining room. She dragged the mouse up to FILE and selected PRINT. Copies: 5.

Angel reached down, grabbed her beach bag, and set it in her lap. She slid her right hand in and curled her fingers around the pistol. The chair had casters. It was easy to push away from the computer, so he could see the image on the screen as he walked down the stairs.

She half wondered if he'd presume too much and come back down in a bathrobe; but, no, A. J. had on baggy shorts and a tank top. Halfway down the stairs he saw the picture on the screen, heard the printer coughing out the copies. He did not seem alarmed; more alert certainly, but mainly curious.

"What's going on?" he asked.

"I don't know, you tell me. I hit some keys, and this popped up."

"And the printer?"

"More buttons, I guess." Angel was willing to hear his argument but she could feel Athena forming in her bones, armored, of the piercing brow, implacable.

A. J. made a reasonable gesture with his hands. "I didn't invent Madison Avenue, Angela. So maybe I'm a little ahead of the curve, playing with the edges of child erotica. But ads have been published in the *New York Times Magazine* and in *Vanity Fair* that are a mere inch away from that."

"Looks more like about six inches to me," she said in a flat, deadly voice.

He misunderstood her comment because he grinned and said, "It'll be mainstream someday, so I'm getting ready."

"He's just a kid, for Christ sake," Angel protested.

"Really. Did you know how old the shepherd boy was who posed for Michelangelo's *David*? No? How about fourteen."

"So this isn't pornographic? This is art?" Angel felt the trigger along the pad of her index finger, the trigger guard eased against her knuckle.

"I don't see any sex act, do you? And the statutes are very specific on that. 'Clear and convincing' is the rule. 'Explicit' is the governing term," A. J. said.

Angel rolled back to the computer, reached out with her left hand, and selected another frame.

"Why are you wearing gloves?" he said in a challenging tone, and now the first thin quiver of alarm sounded in his voice.

"So my hands don't get dirty, asshole. Now tell me about the artistic content of this one." She clicked twice, and the boy was back except now he was unmistakably limbering up to masturbate for the camera.

"Get the hell out of here," A. J. said. In fast jerky steps he crossed in front of her, closed out the computer file, and turned off the printer.

"Right after you," Angel said as she came off the chair and started to swing the gun up out of the bag. For a second the Ruger snagged in the material.

A. J.'s trained eye took it all in immediately. He bolted across the room, through the patio door onto the deck. By the time Angel had the pistol free, he was tearing down the steps. As she came out on the deck, his bare feet failed him on the sharp gravel at the bottom of the stairs.

"Ow, shit," he yelped, grabbing one of his feet, hopping absurdly.

She was on him and walked behind his weird jumping, waiting until he made it off the gravel and fell on the grass. "C'mon, A. J.; you just can't take a joke," she said.

"What, what?" he said, pushing himself up, attempting to run. She tripped him, and he fell heavily and rolled over. That's when she decided to go for the belly shot.

Squeeze, don't jerk, the trigger.

The muffled *clap* sounded like applause as she fired point-blank from a distance of five feet and hit him low in the abdomen.

"My God," he gasped and pawed in disbelief at his belly.

Angel hovered over him, the pistol and its bulbous silencer in plain view. "Hold that thought. Now you get to find out. Is God or isn't God?"

He tried scuttling away, this painful, ungainly motion on his back. For a few seconds, he was aided slightly by the incline of his property, but after ten yards or so, Angel tired of the routine and swung the pistol on target.

Clap-clap-clap.

The small rounds tracked up his chest, and the last one apparently missed. Coming closer, she saw that her last shot hadn't missed. It hit him in the mouth, broke some teeth, and exited his cheek. He was still wet-gargling air when she stuffed the medallion in his wrecked mouth. She returned to the house, collected the printouts, came back out, and pasted one of the pictures over his bloody face.

She put the others in her beach bag. She made sure she had one that was daubed with his blood.

Then she placed the silencer against the soggy print of the boy stripper that was stuck to A. J.'s twitching face and squeezed again.

Clap.

She watched the physical systems shut down, muscle spasms, breathing; a few last convulsions and then stillness.

As she got ready to go, she remembered the lie she'd told him. About the cancer. In fact it was contagious. It's just that the doctors looked for the causes in all the wrong places. Angel knew where the disease came from. It accumulated inside some men's hearts, and, after a certain amount of time, it drained down and was absorbed into their sperm.

Angel absolutely believed that the cancer that killed her twin sister had been cultured in their daddy's body, that he had transmitted it into her sister's twelve- and thirteen- and fourteen- and fifteen-year-old uterus, where it rooted and matured into the malignant ovarian tumor that had eventually eaten her up inside and destroyed her body.

Her life had been destroyed much, much earlier on.

So, before turning toward the house, she shot A. J. Scott one last time in the balls just for spite.

Chapter Twenty

Broker drove back to Milt's with one eye fixed on the rearview mirror. Distracted, he didn't appreciate the blazing western sky, where it looked like North Dakota, South Dakota, and Nebraska had caught fire along with Colorado and Arizona. He turned off Highway 95 and braked his way down Milt's winding gravel drive, quadrant-tracking the dusk that filtered in through the trees. There were a thousand places up in this darkening bluff where . . .

He spotted the maroon Lexus 300 with smoke-tinted windows tucked in the oaks at the bottom of the drive about twenty yards from the house. Nobody said Harry had to be driving Broker's truck. So Broker pulled over, killed the engine, grabbed the Ithaca .12-gauge and approached the house at port arms with his right thumb on the safety.

All he needed was Harry staggering around, drunk and armed.

He felt the low, slanting sun come through an opening in the trees and hit his back. He saw his shadow stretch out, preceding him on the gravel drive. Stepping carefully on paving stones so he didn't make a sound, he came in close to the house and lost his

shadow in the larger shadow of the overhanging eaves. He flat-
tened himself against the side wall. Ever so slowly, he edged his
head around a corner just enough to get a view of . . .

Janey Hensen.

Chagrined, he clicked the gun on safe. She sat on the top step of
the stairs leading up to the deck, looking trim in a white halter,
denim shorts, and tanned skin. She wore no makeup and had her
hair pulled back in a ponytail. A fine layer of sweat shimmered on
her tan as if she'd just been misted with a spray bottle. She was
reading a book.

"Janey? What the hell?" He stepped around the corner holding
the shotgun awkwardly at the vertical in his right hand like a high
school boy carrying a bouquet.

Janey was unfazed. Always dry on the uptake, she batted
her eyes and said, "Jeez, Broker, I figured you missed the old days
but not this much." She stood up and brushed off the back of her
shorts. Maybe it was the sunset hamming it up like a Rodgers
and Hammerstein background out of *South Pacific*. Maybe it was
the businesslike way she dusted off her bum—but it struck Broker
that Janey still bore a resemblance to midwestern ensign Nellie
Forbush as played by Mitzi Gaynor.

He hefted the shotgun self-consciously. "Just putting it in the
house; just be a sec. Ah, what's this?" As he went up the stairs he
changed the subject by flicking his finger at the book she was
reading: *Living Terrors: What America Needs to Know to Survive
the Coming Bioterrorist Catastrophe.*

"Our own Michael Osterholm," Janey said.

Osterholm had been the Minnesota state epidemiologist.
"Yeah, I know," Broker called over his shoulder as he slipped into
the kitchen through the patio door. He quickly racked the side,

emptying the shotgun. He stuffed the shells behind a bag of corn chips on a counter, stashed the gun in the broom closet, and came back out. "I read it."

"After the anthrax scare?" Janey said.

"No, when it first came out." He smiled tightly. "Nina brought it home from 'work.'"

"And how is Xena the Warrior Princess?" Janey said.

"That's fair. She called you the Stepford Wife," Broker said. Nina and Janey met two years ago at J. T. Merryweather's retirement party. They chatted, ostensibly discussing the movie *American Beauty*. The way Broker remembered it, their words rattled back and forth like long elegant needles, probing for vital spots.

"Really? And we only met once. Do you think she got it right—me sitting in my Martha Stewart kitchen, tapping the mute button when the school shootings and Zoloft commercials come on CNBC in between stock quotes?" She inclined her head and said, "I heard you two separated."

Broker stared at her as if to say, What are you doing here?

She shrugged. "Drew took Laurie to T-ball, so I went out to the lake to work on my tan. I was in the neighborhood, so . . ."

"How are you doing, Janey?" Broker said.

"I'm morbid." She hunched her shoulders, let them drop, and then held up the book. "He suggests in here that a guy could walk into a big shopping mall with smallpox cultures in an aerosol doo-dad, set it up in an air-circulation duct, turn it on, and kill over one hundred thousand people." She raised her eyebrows. "You think that's possible?"

"I don't think Osterholm is into writing books for the money," Broker said.

Janey tossed the book on the patio table, spun, walked to the rail, leaned into it with both hands, arched her back, and kicked up one sandaled foot. "This is nice here," she said.

"Yeah. I'm watching it for the summer. The owner's a friend of mine. He's in Europe."

"Milton Dane, the attorney."

Broker didn't ask how she knew; he just smiled.

Janey turned, smoothed a hand along the side of her hair, and said, "You're too skinny. There's hungry, and then there's starvation."

"Pot calling the kettle." Broker caught himself getting involved in the motion of her upper arms as she raised her hands and fussed with the binder in her ponytail.

"And the short hair, it throws me," Janey said.

"You didn't used to smile so much," Broker said.

"It's the influence of the postindustrial service economy. We're surrounded by people whose jobs are being nice to people. It makes us smile more. When people worked in steel mills, they didn't say things like 'have a nice day.' "

Too many words.

She'd always surrounded herself with too many words, sharp words projecting like porcupine quills. "So you said you wanted to talk," Broker said.

Janey slouched against the rail, her eyes rolled up, and she said, "You never were one to dance a girl. No flirty chitchat to get things rolling."

"Rolling," Broker repeated, knitting his eyebrows.

"You know what I mean."

"Sure, small talk."

Janey smiled. "Never your thing. I understand completely. You were always into" —Janey creased her forehead and searched for the right phrase— "the eloquent silence of the hunter. It must be hard on you now, living ordinary life."

"It's hotter than shit. It's been a rough day. I'm getting a beer. You want one?" Broker said, heading for the kitchen.

"Sure."

He returned with two Heinekens. The cold green bottles immediately beaded in the heat. Janey took hers, sat in a deck chair, and inspected the drip of condensation that dribbled down the side. Very deliberately, she dug through the damp label with her thumbnail and flicked the ribbon of label away.

Then Janey dropped it on him: *Boom.* "Did you ever wonder why I married Drew?" she said.

Broker stared, momentarily unfocused, his mind paddling to stay afloat in the heat. "I was curious," he said slowly.

"He was the opposite of you. After you, I designed this man rating system—one to ten; solitary hunter to social gatherer."

"What's in between?"

"Most guys. No, that's not true. I never had a representative sample. I was up to my neck in law enforcers. Cops and prosecutors. Men with authority hang-ups."

Broker drew his right hand between them in a slow, level motion and said, "Drew is steady. A safe bet for the long haul." From memory, Broker re-created Drew's angular unlined face, his mild blue eyes.

Janey smiled tightly. "Make that *was.* Past tense." She raised her chin, which began to quiver slightly. "After what happened on nine-eleven, I heard people were supposed to take inventory, reaffirm their relationships, draw closer together. Well, Drew missed that particular point entirely, because he's seeing another woman, and he's not even being discreet about it." Then Janey began to spill big hot tears all over her white halter.

So he brought her a towel to wipe her cheeks. Then he brought her a glass of ice water and cleared the decks to hear about the other woman.

And he could empathize, to a point. He had visited the subject of the other man. The younger other man. So he assumed that Janey's other woman would be younger and bursting with wonderful unlived-in smells and secret places. She would be unwrinkled from lack of child rearing. She would have pert *Cosmo* snow cone breasts.

"She's this . . . *cow*," Janey seethed. "You know, with the big bovine brown eyes."

Okay, so not *Cosmo*. *Playboy* maybe. He listened patiently.

"Goddamn men and their midlife crises." Suddenly, she seized his left forearm, pulled him toward her, and looked directly into his eyes. "You could talk to him."

He retrieved his arm. "Janey, I'm a little busy right now."

Without missing a sniffle, she pointed to his left wrist, where he wore a bracelet of dark purple blood bruises from Mouse's handcuff. "You should put some ice on that," she said.

She got up, folded her arms across her chest, and paced.

"Twelve years of married life, for Christ sake. I thought maybe you could knock some sense into him? He always respected you." She gulped several rapid breaths, then sipped some water to steady herself.

Broker protested, "Drew never respected me. He thought I was . . . crude; a door ripper, lacking subtlety."

"Well, just what are my daughter and I supposed to do? It's not fair."

"I'm sorry." Broker's voice backed up to try again. He tried again, and all he could come up with was the same. "I'm sorry."

"That's all you can say is—you're *sorry*?" She tossed a hand in disgust, then swiped the tears away with the back of her hand and set her jaw. "Fuck a bunch of crying. I should never have quit working," she said in a dead-serious voice. They did not make eye contact as she stalked off the deck and down the stairs.

Broker watched Janey stride toward her car and get in. She

started the Lexus and lurched backing up, bumped a pile of fire-wood, and put a twelve-hundred-dollar scratch in her rear bumper. Finally, in a grind of gravel, she was gone up the drive.

Broker drank his beer and opened another; then he put some ice cubes in a dishrag and placed it against the bump on his head. Holding the ice with one hand, he washed down three 200-mg Ibuprofen. Then he lit a cigar.

He logged onto the laptop and checked his e-mail. NO NEW MESSAGES ON SERVER.

One-thirty in the morning the cell phone rang. Broker fumbled it to his ear and heard a disembodied voice caterwaul from way down in a whiskey wind tunnel: *"I came to believe I was power-less over alcohol . . ."*

"Goddammit, Harry," Broker shouted.

. . . .

Click.

Chapter Twenty-one

Scricchhhhh....

The rasping sound brought Broker stark upright. Skimming like a water bug, he'd barely made a dent in sleep.

Scricchhhhhhhh....

He eased up on the bed, holding the shotgun that was slick with his sweat, looking around. Another night without the A/C, thinking he could hear better with the windows open.

Scricchhhhhhhh....

It wasn't quite fingernails screeching on a blackboard. But it was close. He oriented quickly on the sound of cat claws raking across a screen door.

Ambush wanted to go out.

When Milt got involved with Hank Sommer's widow, he also inherited Hank's cat, Ambush, who was now Broker's responsibility for the summer. The cat was getting old, plump, fussy. She communicated her desire to go outside by pawing at the patio screen door, and now she had managed to get one of her claws tangled in the ripped wire mesh.

"Okay, just a minute," Broker mumbled as he rolled from the sheets and padded barefoot across the kitchen to the door that led onto the deck. He freed the stuck gray paw from the abraded screen and slid the patio screen open. Ambush strolled across the deck and disappeared down the stairs.

He looked past the deck. The river had acquired a muddy Nile-brown complexion under an overcast gray sky. He stood there naked for a while and let the malarial dawn drip over him.

The thought formed that the Saint was out there, waking up in this very same heat. And Harry, the midnight crooner. Unless, of course, they were, as a third of the cops in the county believed, the same person.

Onward.

Sweat trickled from his scalp, streaked down his check, dripped from his chin, and splashed on the oak floor. Running in this heat would be an exercise in hydraulics. He'd have to grow gills. It would be absolute madness. Sort of like the general atmosphere in Investigations at Washington County.

Harry could be out there, could have put him to bed. Could be waiting to get him up in the morning. He considered lugging the Ithaca along on the run. Screw it. Broker sat down and pulled on his Nikes.

Five minutes later, he couldn't tell where the air stopped and his sweat started. By the time he'd made it up the hill, he was back remembering his Camus from a literature class at the University of Minnesota—*The Stranger*, Meursault, on the torrid Algerian beach absurdly killing a man purely because of the heat. Broker completely understood the condition as he jogged into entry-level heat exhaustion. He crossed the road to catch some patches of darker humidity disguised as shade. He took a long look down the road at the steamy licorice waves rising off the black asphalt. He made his first really smart decision in the last couple of days.

He turned around and walked back down the driveway, skipped the plunge in the river, which was probably the temperature of warm spit, and went straight for a cold shower and a hot shave.

And he skipped making coffee; easier to grab some on the way into town. He did pay attention to the note he'd left under a magnet on the refrigerator, next to a snapshot of his daughter, Kit. *FEED CAT!*

He dumped about a pound of dry Chef's Blend into a large stainless steel mixing bowl and remembered to check to make sure the toilet seat was up so Ambush could get to water. Then he pulled on a pair of loose khaki's, a light cotton polo shirt, and loafers. He debated about the shotgun and decided to put it back in the trunk. Loaded. Okay. He had the ten o'clock meeting with Jack Malloy, pastor at Redeemer in St. Paul.

Heading south down 95, he hit an open stretch, so he put the souped-up Crown Vic cop package to the test, easing off the gas just shy of one hundred miles per hour. Going fast didn't change the fact that the morning air was turning to sticky gray vapor right before his eyes.

It was a little over half-an-hour drive time to St. Paul, so he figured he had time to stop by the Washington County government center for an unscheduled office call on Gloria Russell, ostensibly to get the deal machinery going for Ray Tardee.

In reality he wanted to get a close-up look and see if the Harry-Gloria-Lymon gossip really had legs.

He parked on the government side of the county offices, went in, and took an elevator to the attorneys' offices on the third floor. He showed his ID to the secretary and asked the location of Ms. Russell's office.

No, he didn't have an appointment.

Broker found the office and rapped on the doorjamb.

"Yes?" Gloria Russell spoke without looking up from the paperwork on her blotter. She sat behind her desk in a gray sleeveless blouse that complemented her short black hair. There was enough definition in the muscles of her upper arms so that a discreet puddle of purple vein rested in the hollow of her elbows and disappeared up either biceps. Her office space was Doric, basic, unadorned; just shelves of a law books and law degree on the wall.

"I'm Broker," he said. "I called you yesterday about Ray Tardee."

Gloria's tanned face came up like a bronze figurehead. Broker saw heat and danger but not a lot of warmth; Joan Crawford from 1940s noir. Not a bad face if it learned how to relax.

Lavender triangles of fatigue stamped the smooth tan below her lower eyelids. The eyelids quivered slightly. A faint stripe on the third finger of her left hand had almost completely faded into her tan. She took her heavy framed, black, plastic glasses from the desktop and put them on like a mask.

"Oh yeah, Broker. You're Special Projects on the dead priest," Gloria said. "John Eisenhower brought you in to spy while he's out of town."

"Nice meeting you, too," Broker said, giving her his best empty grin.

"I checked around. The book on you is BCA left you out in the cold five years too long. A lot of people think you migrated to the other side."

"Yeah, well; I just did a fast migrate back. Can we talk, or do I go down the hall and talk to Jerry?" Jerry Hassler was the county prosecutor.

"And you know Jerry going way back to when he worked in St. Paul, I know. You know everybody. The Old Boys' Club. That's why the sheriff sailed you in here on a sky hook." Gloria exhaled. "Fine. Come in, sit down, get comfy, and stay for about thirty seconds."

Broker entered her office and sat at the stiff-backed chair in front of her desk. A stand-alone picture frame on the corner of the desk faced the visitor's chair and held an enlarged block of type:

NO PERSON IN THE UNITED STATES SHALL, ON THE BASIS OF SEX . . .BE SUBJECTED TO DISCRIMINATION UNDER ANY EDUCATIONAL PROGRAM OR ACTIVITY RECEIVING FEDERAL FINANCIAL ASSISTANCE.

Broker thought about it and decided to jazz her a little, to see where it went. He pointed to the frame. "So are you really the dark side of Title IX? Funny, you don't look like that kind of feminist . . ."

"Really." Gloria inclined her head and raised her hand, a reflex to fluff hair that was no longer there. "And why is that, because I'm not ugly?"

"But, on the other hand, you could be an Amazon."

"Is there a difference?"

"Sure, feminists talk; Amazons do."

"You know this for a fact?"

"Absolutely. I married an Amazon."

Gloria managed a small grin on her drawn face and said, "That sounds like a good title for a weepy male memoir. So how'd it turn out?"

"She left me for a younger guy."

"Good for her."

He leaned forward. "We need Ray Tardee as a witness on the dead priest. John wants to deal him down to some light county time. No commit to prison," Broker said.

"No way. Tardee is a scumbag repeater who sells dope to high school kids. He's over the line on points. He's on his way to a new career as a wifey and pole smoker in Stillwater Prison." Gloria paused. "Unless you can tell me why you're pulling a news black-out on this priest thing." She pointed out her window, across a grassy plot at the LEC. "We're all getting calls from our favorite reporters. Everybody in our shop is real curious just what you have going." She leaned forward and said, "Motive? Suspect?"

Broker rubbed the bruise circling his wrist that was starting to look like a Maori tattoo. "You mean Lymon hasn't told you?" If Patti Palen down in the patrol basement knew about the Saint's medallion yesterday afternoon, this legal diva had to know too.

Gloria sat up straight in her chair. Her voice went dead formal. "Lymon Greene? No. As a matter of fact he hasn't."

"What about Harry—he tell you anything?" Broker said.

She narrowed her eyes. "I heard you were going to escort Harry to St. Joseph's, and somewhere things went . . . awry."

Broker couldn't put a fast comeback together and granted her the point. So he let his eyes wander past her shoulder to another picture frame on top of her bookcase that he'd missed when he first walked in the office. A small school picture of a smiling boy with freckles and a cowlick, maybe six years old. Besides her law degree, the picture was the only personal touch in the office.

"Your son?" he said, pointing past her at the picture.

"No. I don't have any children," she said. Then she stood up, turned, plucked the picture from the bookcase and put it in her desk drawer. Then she fussed with some papers on her desk, worried her lower lip briefly between her teeth, and said, "Look, I don't know you. And I don't like being dictated to by strangers. You have to give us a legitimate reason to back off on Tardee."

Broker raised his hands in a reasonable gesture. "John's orders. That's really all I can tell you right now."

She jabbed her index finger at him. "If—and it's a big if—Tardee helps you make a case, we might consider a departure from guidelines. So let's see the case."

"When the time's right." Broker stood up and extended his hand. "Thanks."

Gloria did not accept his handshake. Her face was gray beneath her tan. Her eyes were as flat as her voice. "Are we through?"

"Yes," Broker said, heading for the door.

"Broker."

He turned in the doorway.

"For your information: Mouse and Benish should mind their own business," Gloria said.

Broker gave a noncommittal nod, then walked from the office, went down the hall, and stopped at the receptionist's desk. "Tell me something," he said.

The receptionist sized him up, looked down the hall in the direction he'd come from, then back at Broker. Apparently, she was not a neutral when it came to Gloria, because she enunciated in a hard, level voice, "Maybe, baby, but I kinda fuckin' doubt it."

Broker was unperturbed. "The kid in the picture on Gloria Russell's bookshelf looks familiar. Who is he?"

"You're new, huh?"

"Yeah, I'm new."

"That's Tommy Horrigan; he was the victim in the Dolman case."

"You mean, alleged victim? Dolman was acquitted." Broker chose the words to get a reaction.

She responded with cold, controlled hostility. "Yeah, right."

Broker turned and walked from the office with what felt like a sheaf of daggers planted in his back. It looked as if the Dolman case had never stopped festering in the county, and now the dead priest with the St. Nicholas medallion in his mouth had ripped off the scab.

He took the stairs down, worked through the corridors, went out the door and hit the heat—*Jesus—the fuckin' heat actually throbbed, like the theme from* Jaws . . .

He hardly noticed a young woman who was smoking a

cigarette next to a square brick column. He was absentminded, thanking his friend John Eisenhower for dropping him into the middle of this nutcase mess.

A sudden movement to his left rear had him crouching, hands coming up. *Yikes.* She darted in front of him; her breath smelled of tobacco.

"Jumpy, are we? You know, if you're smart, you'll talk to me," she said.

Like most of the people who annoyed him these days, she was young; a little over thirty. Five-six or -seven. She wore loose white cotton pants, Chaco sandals, and an armless rayon blouse. The headband tied in her brown hair conveyed a certain fashion statement; it was July, so maybe she was showing solidarity with the Parisian mob that stormed the Bastille. She had brown eyes, freckles, and a spiral notebook in her hand. She would be attractive if you liked skinny reporters.

"Hi, I'm Sally Erbeck, with the *Pioneer Press.* You're Broker, special assignment on the dead priest, right? "

"Excuse me, you're in the way." Broker put his head down and walked toward his car.

"Hey, you . . . you've got a dead priest. I'm going with a lead that says he died Tuesday night in his confessional and foul play is suspected. You want to comment?"

"Better show me some ID," Broker said, still walking. He was halfway to the car.

"Hey you, wait—I'm the Washington County reporter for the *Pioneer Press.*" She whipped a laminated card from her purse.

"Never heard of you." Broker kept walking swiftly. He nodded at her identification. "And you can get one of those faked up anywhere. I saw it on the Learning Channel. If you're really a reporter, get a letter of introduction from your editor." Broker opened the car door and climbed in.

"If I was a guy, you wouldn't pull this shit! I'm gonna remember this," Sally yelled.

Broker popped the ignition and raced the engine. He cupped his left hand to his ear and leaned slightly out of the driver's-side window. "What?"

Then he rolled up the windows, cranked up the air-conditioning, stepped on the gas, and fishtailed toward the exit, leaving Sally Erbeck in a patch of burned rubber.

Chapter Twenty-two

As Broker drove west on Interstate 94, a bright migraine blue sky burned through the haze while, up ahead, the skyline of St. Paul levitated in a heat island bonfire. Crouched over the wheel in his air-conditioned bubble, he exited the freeway and drove into the downtown loop.

Holy Redeemer was just off Kellogg Boulevard, overlooking the river bluff, in the shadow of the Landmark Center. In keeping with Minnesota's basic law of nature—there are two seasons: winter and road construction—Kellogg was torn up for blocks in either direction. A maze of chain-link barriers and yellow tape blocked the adjacent streets. Broker had to park in a ramp and circle back through the west end of the downtown loop.

So he found himself on foot in the new St. Paul walking across snug, newly laid cobblestone streets. He passed by Hmong women in traditional embroidered tunics and Somali women wearing the hijab who had laid out vegetables and fresh flowers in outdoor stalls. He walked past caffeine addicts bent over their laptops outside cafés.

He tried to count the rings pierced into the ears of a youth on a scooter with orange buzzed hair. And he stared at slices of tanned bare midriffs decorated with navel rings as they swung by. Tattoos were on parade; they circled arms, they climbed bare calves like clinging vines.

As he walked across Rice Park, he discovered that the tarnished bronze statue of St. Paul icon F. Scott Fitzgerald had been surrounded by a lynch mob of bulbous, vacantly grinning cartoon sculptures: Charlie Brown, Lucy, and Snoopy. Charles Shultz was being celebrated as St. Paul's new favorite son. Charlie Brown was in; Nick Carraway was out.

But some things never change.

Up ahead, past the silly cartoon characters, Holy Redeemer's gray stone shoulders hunkered down between the face-lifted building and the commercial finery like a Roman linebacker—strictly playing defense these days.

Broker walked past the church and up the steps to the rectory, rang the bell, and introduced himself to the secretary who answered the door. The interior of the rectory was low lit, gray, and musty. Crossing the threshold, Broker felt like he was entering an American catacomb. When the door closed behind him, he was standing in 1956, and God was in his heaven, and the cars were still made out of steel.

"Father Malloy will be with you in a moment," said the secretary, a middle-aged woman whose dress and demeanor matched the quiet decor.

Broker sat on a hardwood chair flanked by large amber glass ashtrays set in metal pedestals. The carpets, walls, furniture yielded an underscent of cigar smoke.

"Hello, Broker," said Jack Malloy, coming into the vestibule, right hand outstretched. Broker rose, and they shook hands. In his youth, Malloy had evaded his calling to the ministry by hiding in the St. Paul Police Department. He and Broker had met in the patrol division.

Malloy's golf shirt stretched taut over his flat stomach. His grip was strong, his blue eyes direct. "You want some coffee?"

"Sure."

Malloy walked back into the rectory kitchen and returned with two mismatched coffee cups. He handed one to Broker.

"Do you really think the Saint has reappeared?" Malloy asked as he led Broker up a flight of carpeted stairs, down a hall, and into a study.

"We don't know. So we're taking it real quiet until John gets back in town. He had to go to Seattle. Death in the family," Broker said.

"I'm sorry to hear it; give him my regards." Malloy pointed to a pair of stuffed leather chairs. They sat and sipped their coffee for a moment.

Malloy's eyes became a little tight, the muscles working in his cheeks. "So the hysteria has arrived in Minnesota and killed a priest," he said.

Along with the 1950s decor and the tincture of tobacco, the rectory had sluggish, ancient air-conditioning. Malloy's words were floaters in the sodden air.

"You tell me. Did you know Moros?" Broker said.

Malloy shook his head. "No. But it's obvious that St. Martin's was not an ideal post. There was bound to be talk about any priest moved quickly into an obscure cranny of the Church these days."

"Right now WashCo is totally stalling the press on this," Broker said. "When they have to give up some information, they'll feather their way into it—tell them we're handling it as a burglary gone bad. Which is true up to a point since they're investigating along that track."

"So you think someone might call in to take credit?"

Broker shook his head. "I don't know. That wasn't the Saint's style."

"No, it wasn't. The Saint didn't leave a trace, as I recall," Malloy said.

"So, you can see . . . ," Broker said.

"Exactly. The imagery is irresistible: Saint returns to clean house when the bishops won't. Once you add the medallion to the mix, an entire scenario falls into place. High carnival on the archdiocese," Malloy said.

Broker put down his coffee cup. "Jack, somebody from Moros's parish in Albuquerque called in an anonymous tip. They told the secretary at St. Martin's he'd assaulted a girl."

"Yes, I know."

"You knew?" Broker leaned forward.

Malloy held up his hand. "Slow down. I did some checking last night. I have a buddy in the archbishop's office. We were classmates together in Rome, so we're pretty tight. He expedited Moros's transfer from Albuquerque. If the Saint is active again, he got the wrong guy. Moros comes up clean."

"Tell me."

Malloy nodded. "I don't have documentation. But I can get it. And so can you. This is what happened. Moros dabbled in painting. Murals mainly, but he was competent enough in other mediums to teach classes, which he did on a regular basis at his parish in New Mexico.

"Last April there was an incident in one of his classes. The students were junior high kids, and this particular day they were working in pastel chalk. At the end of class, they were putting their sketches away." Malloy paused. "You know anything about pastels?"

Broker shrugged. He thought vaguely of sherbet colors.

"Well," Malloy said, "they're real powdery. Unless you zap

them good with fixative, they get all over everything. One of the students, who happened to be a teenage girl very mature in the physical department, tipped her sketch as she was putting it on a shelf. The chalk dusted down the front of her blouse and jeans. So Moros was standing there, and without thinking he goes—'Oops, look out.'"

Malloy pantomimed sweeping his hand across Broker's chest. "Moros goes like this, to wipe away the chalk. There were witnesses who said it was pure reflex, like shooing a fly."

Broker winced, seeing it coming.

"Exactly," Malloy said. "The girl blushes, sobs, and runs from the room."

"Oh boy," Broker said.

Malloy nodded. "The next morning, the parents and their lawyer come banging on the bishop's door and it's, 'What's this Mexican Rasputin doing molesting my lily-white daughter?'"

Broker felt a wrinkle of sadness. He remembered the tape outline of the shape Victor Moros's body left on the carpet in the confessional. He had not even seen the crime scene photos yet. He did not know what Moros looked like. He could not put a face to the name.

Malloy continued. "So we have this great window into the current state of our culture—we have issues of hair-trigger litigiousness, of parental hysteria. And there's a robust serpent of racism slithering through the whole business."

"How'd he move out so fast?"

"Like I said, things are different. Moros wasn't assumed to be a sinner who needed a thrashing. His bishop didn't try to minimize or hide the allegations. There's policy. The bishop moved immediately to investigate; he called in the cops."

"Ah."

Malloy nodded. "It should be on file with Albuquerque PD.

They talked to witnesses who had a different interpretation of the event and decided that the charge was groundless. The bishop was all for fighting in court if need be. But . . ."

"The intangibles. The gossip."

Malloy nodded again. "Maybe Moros didn't want to wage a long battle to resurrect his reputation in what was an upscale Anglo parish. I think he left because he could never confront the racist whispering campaign. That's only a personal gut read."

"So how did he wind up here?"

Malloy pursed his lips. "Because God is a golfer. Moros's bishop and my bishop play golf together in Florida. A favor was requested; a favor was granted. And we parked Moros out at St. Martin's as an interim posting."

Broker shook his head. "What's the moral to this story? Don't dust spilled chalk off a teenage girl's blouse?"

The creases in Malloy's face ran deeper than Broker cared to contemplate, through a system of consequences that receded back through centuries, millennia, past mystery into eternity.

"So," Malloy said. "You may well have a sicko out there who has a twisted sense of humor. But, according to my information, the Saint's victim profile doesn't fit. We obviously have our share of bad apples, but Moros wasn't one of them. Even so . . ."

"Yeah," Broker said. "The appearance of it is still going to be a huge damage-control problem."

Malloy raised his hands, let them fall. "We brought it on ourselves. The sin of clericism, all the shady in-house solutions that are now coming out. The Church has taken a beating for six months on this; Cardinal Law running a protection racket for Shanley and Geoghan in Boston, Weakland resigning in Milwaukee . . . our very own sequestered coven of monks and priests at St. John's Abbey in Collegeville who've been accused of or have admitted to abuse. It's been . . ."

"Hot."

"Exactly. So—no leads at all?"

"We have a guy who lives next to the church who saw a woman go in before it happened. We're keeping him under wraps for now. And there was some fresh graffiti on the church, a Satanist pentacle. But that could be just creeps acting out. There's been a rash of church break-ins in Stillwater . . ."

Malloy raised his eyebrows.

Broker shrugged. "But our witness has the suspect wearing a navy blue Saints baseball jacket."

"That sort of puts it, like we used to say, right on front street. Okay, so what do I tell people?"

"Nothing for a couple of days. John has me working a long shot," Broker said.

"Hail Mary," Malloy said.

"Knock on wood," Broker said as he stood up. "Could you get a transcript of the bishop's investigation? It will be useful to have it in the file. I'll get our guys in contact with the coppers in Albuquerque."

"I'll see what I can do," Malloy said. "But I'm not sure about this secrecy about the medallion. I understand the need to protect your investigation—but there's a serious public safety question. Priests should be warned."

"I'd think every priest in America is already pretty security conscious right now," Broker said. "Like I said, John thinks we have a solid local angle. We might catch this guy before . . ."

"He kills another priest."

"Okay, you're right; but if we go public and put priests on warning, you get the media storm. For right now, let's keep St. Nicholas between you and me, under the seal as it were."

They walked out into the hall and were silent for a few beats. "I guess no one is really ever safe, are they?" Malloy said.

Going down the stairs, Broker said, "I was wondering. Isn't it unusual to have a Catholic church named after a guy named Martin? I mean after what happened in Wittenberg and all?"

Malloy shrugged. "The fact is, we have our own Martin on the books. He was bishop of Tours, in the fourth century. He was your kind of guy: the patron saint of the infantry. And horses and, ah, beggars and geese, I think."

They shook hands in the vestibule, and Broker left the quietly lit, ordered sanctuary of Malloy's living quarters behind, stepped back into the street, and walked toward the absurd mob of short, round cartoon characters in the park.

He put on his sunglasses, stared into the sun, and spoke aloud for no particular reason the first words to enter his mind: "Beggars and geese."

Chapter Twenty-three

Broker paced back and forth on the top level of the Victory Ramp smoking a cigar and combing through his talk with Malloy. The ramp had been full, and he'd had to park the Crown Vic on the roof. There wasn't a square inch of shade in sight.

Recalling the determined look on Sally Erbeck's face, he figured the medallion would be outed within twenty-four hours, if not sooner. The Saint was going to stage a return whether or not Father Moros was deserving of his—or her—attentions.

It was time to check in with John in Seattle.

He punched in John's cell number, got voice mail, and left his own cell number. Then he waited. Sweat stewed in his hair and trickled down his forehead. He made a note to get a hat.

Broker was getting down into the less tasty end of the cigar when his cell rang.

"So, where are we at?" John asked without preamble.

"Malloy says no way the priest was a child molester. But he was transferred from his last parish after he was cleared of *allegations* of child abuse. Malloy says the Albuquerque cops ran the investigation."

"But there's the appearance that Moros was a child molester."

"There it is," Broker said. "And the only people who had that information, besides the church secretary, were in Investigations: Harry and whoever else saw the complaint."

"I'll call Mouse, get him to run the phone logs to see if anybody else got tipped about Moros. And I'll have him liaison with Albuquerque. It's long shot, but maybe somebody followed Moros to Minnesota. You get Harry to the hospital?" John said.

"Not yet; he's still out there."

"Is he giving you a hard time?"

"Oh yeah. A regular barrel of laughs and crazier than a shit-house mouse. But he's hinting he knows something about the Saint."

"Good. Good. So, how are the troops holding up?"

"Everybody knows about the medal, the whole damn building, patrol and detectives."

"Uh-huh."

"Which means any minute the press is going to have it. Seventy, eighty cops can't stay mum on something like this."

"Actually," John said, "you might be surprised about that."

"You may believe in that blue-code-of-silence bullshit, but I don't," Broker said. "Yesterday some wit wrote on the unit bulletin board, 'The Saint lives: Harry 2, Pedophiles 0.'"

"So what? Gallows humor."

"Goddamn Harry. He's fencing with me."

"Keep reeling him in; he's the key."

"What if he isn't? Malloy has a point; if someone's targeting priests, they should be warned."

"It's local. It's in our shop. I'm not going to panic the whole state."

Broker thought for a few beats and said, "I don't think *panic* is the right word; more like *sensation*. If the Saint comes out of the closet people will come out in those baseball jackets cheering him on. So if you think you have a cop who is going around killing suspected child molesters, I wish you'd tell me."

"Who said it has to be a cop?"

"Say some names, John."

"I'd prefer to hear them from you."

"When the fuck did you start talking like Bill Clinton?" Broker said loudly.

"Push Harry, push him hard," John said and hung up.

Broker dug Mouse's phone number out of his wallet and punched it in. He got the voice mail. Goddamn, he hated talking to machines.

"Mouse, it's Broker. I talked to Malloy. I'm on my way in, about twenty minutes out."

Ten minutes later, Broker's cell rang. He flipped it open and hit the button. Not Mouse. Harry Cantrell sounded like he was calling from inside a pinball machine. Broker heard lots of electronic bells and jingles going off.

"So what do you think of Sally Erbeck, neat chick, huh?" Harry said.

"You put her on to me?" Broker said.

"*Au contraire.* I'd never rat a brother officer out to the yellow press, not me," Harry said with elaborate seriousness.

"Where are you?" Broker said. But he thought he knew; the electronic calliope music he heard in the background sounded like the intersection of five hundred slot machines.

"Uh-uh. The question is, where are you?"

Broker endeavored to comb the burrs of anger from his voice. Be cool, he told himself. *It's a game.* "Driving east on thirty-six, heading into town."

"You know the Civil War statue in front of the old courthouse on the South Hill?"

"Sure."

"Be standing in front of the statue at noon," Harry said.

"A meeting, Harry?"

"Silly boy, I want you where I can see you're alone. I'll call. Noon sharp."

"Make it at one. I have a sit-down with Mouse," Broker said.

"Okay, at one. Don't get smart on me. Be alone," Harry said. The connection went dead.

As he drove east on Highway 36, Broker entertained a fantasy replay of the last scene in *Easy Rider*. The black Ford Ranger would pull up next to him, and a leering Harry Cantrell would lean out the driver's side with a shotgun cradled in his elbow. Then, after he pumped four rounds of .00 buck into Broker's face, he'd drive away.

At 120 miles an hour.

Broker walked into Investigations looking for Mouse, who was in his cube on the phone. When Mouse hung up, Broker said, "We're still on, right?"

"Oh yeah," Mouse said. "John called. Sally Erbeck's calling every cop she knows in the county. The *Star Tribune* called, and so did Channel Four and Channel Five and Channel Eleven. Word's out we got a dead priest. They all asked the same question: was foul play involved?"

"And you told them?"

"We're in the initial stages of an investigation, and we'll keep them informed. They're closing the ring."

"Great. So where's Lymon?"

Mouse's battered face conveyed a perfect Gallic shrug. But he got up and motioned with a jerk of his head for Broker to follow him. Benish joined them. They stopped at Lymon's cube, which was along the outer wall and had a window that faced the lawn between the sheriff's offices and the government center.

Lymon kept his space orderly. Just one personal picture, an attractive light-skinned woman and a smiling toddler in a frame on his desk. Mouse pointed at the Levolor blinds on the window, which were tilted, the right side up at an angle. Then he summoned Broker forward to look out the window and pointed up at the government center.

"Third floor," Mouse said.

Broker scanned along the third floor windows and stopped on one that had its blinds tilted in a position similar to Lymon's. The county attorneys' offices were on the third floor, where he'd been this morning.

Benish stepped forward and said, "We've come to think of it as jungle telegraph . . ."

"Benish," Mouse warned.

But Benish went on. "Although now, since they have matching Palm Pilots, they tend to message each other. Like the ad says, there are times when text is better than talk . . ."

Mouse held up a key. "Why don't you cruise by the gym downstairs and tell Lymon it's time to meet."

Broker took the key and went down two flights of stairs, took a few turns, and opened the door to the gym. The room had blue cinder block walls, a blue carpet, and was too small for the thicket of stainless steel exercise stations. In among the crowded steel it was silent but not empty.

Lymon stood on one side of the room with a sheen of sweat on his smooth face. He was methodically lifting dumbbells in alternating biceps curls. Not showy, he wore gray wind pants and an oversized white T-shirt. Thick grids of veins swelled in either forearm as he slowly hoisted and lowered the forty-pound weights.

Across the room Gloria Russell sat at the pec fly machine, spreading her arms, aligning her back, and dragging her arms together, working her delts. She wore black spandex shorts and a black tank top. Broker could not see a hint of fold in the tanned belly above her waistband. Gloria's eyes bored into the middle distance, concentrating on the reps.

Tremendous fatigue streamed off both of them. Broker could almost see it, like smoke. Lymon couldn't miss Broker coming into the small area, but his eyes didn't register Broker's entry. In the zone, his focus remained fixed elsewhere; his lips continued counting reps.

Lymon's lips mimed *eight* as he lowered the weight in his right hand. Then he repeated the silent *eight* as he lifted the barbell in his left hand, and his eyes moved across Broker and fixed on a point in space about a foot off Broker's shoulder. No one spoke.

So Broker watched them progress gracefully through their compact jungle of iron and steel. After she finished with the pec fly, Gloria moved to the inclined bench press. She started with dime plates on the bar. Did a steady set of ten reps.

Lymon had finished the alternating curls and continued his biceps work on a barbell. But now he was no longer staring into space. He monitored Gloria, who had added a pair of nickel plates to the bar for her second set. On her seventh rep her arms began to tremble but she maintained her form and was able to pump out the eighth rep. The barbell clunked into the weight stand; she sat up and stared, catching her breath.

Broker intruded into the interval between sets and said, "Lymon, we have a meeting with Mouse."

"Ten minutes," Lymon said.

Now Gloria added another pair of nickels to the bar and locked her knees over the raised supports and lay back, resuming her head-down prone position on the inclined bench. She composed herself, carefully placed her hands, and lifted the weight. Smooth, concentrated; two, three, four . . .

At four she began to fall apart. She struggled.

Lymon was there instantly, hovering, adding a light tug with his fingertips. His spotting made the difference, and she completed the lift. In that second, as she braced her arms and prepared to lower the weight, their eyes locked.

Then, for the first time, they acknowledged Broker's presence. As a pair, they looked back at him. Broker thought they appeared romantic, arranged there together among the benches and the barbells, which was to say they looked young, beautiful, and haunted. They also looked guilty of something.

And doomed.

Chapter Twenty-four

Broker, Mouse, and Lymon sat down to talk. Broker thought it ironic that Mouse chose the soft interrogation room to have their chat, the room where victims were questioned gently. They sat in cheap but comfortable easy chairs. A short child's blackboard and a box of toys sat in the corner. Broker could clearly picture Harry interviewing Tommy Horrigan in this room a little over a year ago.

Broker related his off-the-record talk with Malloy, underscoring Malloy's obvious worry that someone was declaring open season on priests. Then he kept his mouth closed and listened.

Mouse said, "Okay, here's the deal. John's not back till Friday night. We have to stall the media going into the weekend. Then, on Monday John will hold a press conference. If we don't come up with anything by then, he goes public with the medallion. So . . . if the press gathers, we avoid the front door. I'm telling everybody to enter and leave the building through the basement garage. The call takers in Dispatch are screening all the media calls."

Mouse turned to Lymon. "Get on the horn with Albuquerque

PD and check out the family that accused Moros. See if they've done any traveling lately, like to Minnesota."

Lymon shook his head. "This is big," he said. "We should call in the state guys right now. If we have a new player out there who's going after priests . . ." He stared like a man watching a tidal wave coming ashore. "These back-channel games, meeting Malloy on the sly, chasing after Harry, they amount to gambling with people's lives."

Mouse said, "Go call Albuquerque."

Lymon narrowed his eyes but managed to keep his mouth shut. Without another word he stood up and left the room.

Mouse turned to Broker. "He's right, you know."

Broker nodded. "I agree about the gambling part. John's gambling this is local, and that Harry has been sitting on a solid lead. I'm gambling that Harry will tell me what it is before he sneaks up and skull-fucks me in my sleep." Then Broker reached over and thumped Mouse on his dense chest. "And Harry is gambling, because he called me thirty minutes ago, and I heard the goddamn slots banging in the background. So get on those casinos. He's driving in from one right now."

"How do you know?" Mouse said.

"Because he wants me someplace where he can see me for a meet. Not in person. On the phone."

"Hell, where? We'll stake it out."

Broker shook his head. "No way. This is Harry, remember. Anything looks out of place, he'll spot it. The last thing we want is a confrontation. Did you call your pal in Hinckley?"

"Called him and sent the faxes. It's being put in place. C'mon." Mouse motioned for Broker to follow him back to his cube, where he had a state map spread on his desk.

"Okay, I sent stuff to every joint in the state; that's sixteen in all. But we're concentrating on these." Mouse tapped place-names highlighted in yellow magic marker on the map that formed a rough circle around Minneapolis and St. Paul. "The *Grand Casinos* in Hinckley and Onamia, *Mystic Lake* in Prior Lake, *Treasure Island* in Red Wing, *Turtle Lake* in Wisconsin, and *Jackpot Junction* in Morton—but that's getting way out there."

Broker bit his lip. "It could work. We want to find him when he's half in the bag, distracted in a public place. We want him in a goddamn trance staring at a blackjack dealer. That's the way to approach him."

Mouse hitched up his belt, cleared his throat, and said, "Wonderful. This has become competitive between you two."

"Always was," Broker said.

Broker had forty minutes to kill before his date with the statue. He figured Harry needed a support system so he might turn to Annie Mortenson again. He drove out of the basement ramp, eased through the back streets, worked around to the west of town, came down Myrtle Hill, turned left on North Fourth, and parked in front of the Stillwater Library. From here it would be a quick hop up Third Street to the old courthouse.

The Carnegie library was one of Stillwater's jewels, with *A.D. 1902* chiseled over the door. Broker picked his way through kids' bikes that were strewn on the broad lawn like a snapshot from a happy childhood. He went inside, asked for Anne Mortenson at the curved front desk, and was directed downstairs to the reference desk.

Broker came down the marble stairs two at a time and saw her standing behind the desk in jeans and a maroon paisley blouse. She was younger than he expected, midthirties. His initial impression was: medium, in height, in looks, in intensity. Her brown hair was clipped in straight bangs across her forehead and fell on either side of her oval face in a lank pageboy. Her bookish brown eyes did not entirely conceal a dynamo of spinster energy that suggested her trim appearance would not change for the next forty years.

As he walked up to the desk, he sketched her quickly: She was independent, she owned a cat. She took long, solitary vacations and enjoyed them. She'd never marry. Men like Harry would always break her heart.

Broker came in fast with a stiff cop edge to shake her a little. "Anne, I'm Phil Broker. We talked yesterday about Harry."

She blushed slightly. "My poor car. How could I be so dumb? The dealership gave me a loaner, which I will never let Harry Cantrell go near, ever."

"Good. Because Harry's being difficult. It would be a mistake to offer him any kind of encouragement," Broker said.

She dropped her eyes, then recovered quickly.

Broker stepped in closer and said, "Are you and Harry . . ."

"Close?" She furrowed her eyebrows. "As in, do opposites attract?"

"Yes, that's exactly what I mean."

"Not when he's drinking." She said it clear-eyed and emphatically, and she was lying through her straight, even teeth. "It's a game with him, you know. Outwitting the sheriff. He thinks he can make a deal, get reinstated without going into the hospital. He doesn't believe in alcoholism. The only thing he believes in, as far as I can see, is winning streaks."

Broker picked up a slip of notepaper from the desk and a short, sharp #2 pencil and jotted down a number. "This is my cell. If Harry contacts you, call me," Broker said in his best cop voice. He turned and left without saying good-bye. But as he stepped back into the sun, he was smiling. Maybe he had learned something. Maybe Harry wanted to make a deal.

Thinking he might actually be getting a break, he drove up South Third and parked next to the old Stillwater courthouse, a graceful storied building with Italianate arches and a cupola on the top. He walked down the sidewalk and up the steps and across the grass to the monument set in the corner of the lawn by the flagpole.

Broker knew this place well.

He reached up and patted the weathered bronze replica of a Civil War soldier who, rifle at the ready, leaned perpetually forward, advancing to the attack. Eighty-four years of heat, snow, rain, and cold had mottled the statue's surface with pewter blues and grayish blacks and lacy green flourishes. Broker thought of the weathered metal as the color of history, like black-and-white photographs.

His dad had first brought him to this spot when he was six years old. He remembered only a fragment of what his father had explained to him. Mainly he had acquired the powerful impression that this was a statue of his great-great-grandfather Abner Broker.

Abner's name was one of hundreds recorded on the broad plaque behind the statue. The names represented Washington County men who'd served in Minnesota regiments. Abner had left his logger job in the north shore pineries, moved to Stillwater, and joined up with the First Minnesota Regiment in 1861.

He had caught the train right here in Stillwater to go to Mr. Lincoln's war to save the union and free the slaves. His journey included the rough afternoon of July 2, 1863, on Cemetery Ridge at Gettysburg, Pennsylvania. The regiment had charged an Alabama brigade and stopped them in their tracks. Only a handful of Minnesota boys came back from that fight, including a limping Abner. But they had bought General Winfield Scott Hancock the five minutes he needed to rebuild his collapsing line and perhaps save the country.

So, as six-year-old Broker would remember it, Grandpa Abner won the war.

Broker sat down, rested his arms on his knees, and watched black ants boil in the thick green blades of grass. He thought of the picture of Tommy Horrigan sitting all alone on Gloria Russell's bookshelf. What did Tommy have to associate with being six? For sure, something far less secure than swinging on the resolute unbending arm of Grandpa Abner.

His cell phone rang. He popped it on.

"So did the priest deserve it?" Harry said.

"No, Moros was hounded out of Albuquerque by gossip. The local cops cleared him," Broker said.

"That's what I thought. So you and John have a real problem . . ."

"Yeah?"

"Yeah," Harry said. "The Saint has returned with bad target information."

Broker shivered. Mocking the heat, a cold needle of adrenaline jabbed through his heart. "You know this *how*?"

"I keep this personal log of anonymous tips, stuff too flimsy to file a formal Initial Complaint Report. I clear them and delete them off my computer. But last week I found a pile of printouts in this drawer in a desk. Somebody had gone into my computer and retrieved my notes from the trash. Moros was on top of the stack." Harry paused a beat. "I always had a problem emptying my trash . . ."

"Harry?" Broker was on his feet, squeezing the chunk of Samsung plastic in his hand as if he could force Harry's voice back into the circuits. But the line was dead.

Chapter Twenty-five

Goddamn you, Harry—where are you?

Frustrated, Broker scanned the neighborhood. Just the still foliage of the trees and the shadows on the deserted streets. Harry probably wasn't on foot . . .

Moving now toward the car. What about Annie Mortenson? She had been lying about helping Harry. . . . But by the time he reached the car, he'd decided he needed more help than Annie could provide. Annie didn't really know Harry.

Harry had only wrecked Annie's car. But he'd wrecked Gloria Russell's marriage.

Ten minutes later, Broker was inside the government center, taking the elevator to the third floor. The receptionist, who had been hostile to him earlier, saw him coming, and her expression froze. Her eyes went wide, then filmed over, unfocused.

Broker had seen this response before, as a young operator in MACV-SOG doing fast ugly missions with the Provincial Reconnaissance Units. He remembered sweeping into Vietnamese hamlets, the villagers numbing their faces into empty smiles. Their eyes had escaped inward as fear bred the hope they could make themselves invisible.

When he slowed to take a good look at her, it struck him that she was a low-rent version of Gloria Russell. The same gym-rat tan. The same muscle tone. The same shortish hair, only hers was dishwater blond.

He continued down the hall and into Gloria's office.

A slender guy in a blue shirt and tie was talking to her. He had a sheaf of manila folders in his hand.

"Sorry, but I got to talk to Gloria," Broker said.

"Is this . . . ?" the guy said.

"Yeah, this is Broker," Gloria said.

"I can come back." The guy turned and left the room.

Gloria pushed a Washington County edition of the *Pioneer Press* across her desk. "You see the paper?" she said.

Broker shook his head.

She handed it to him and said, "The story stripped down the right side."

Broker scanned the headline: "Priest Found Dead in Stillwater Mission Church." Under Sally Erbeck's byline, the lead sentence read: "Foul play has not been ruled out in the death of Father Victor Moros."

"The gossip jumped buildings this morning. Now I know why you want to deal Tardee up; he saw a woman in a Saints jacket go into the church about the time the priest died," Gloria said. "You could have told me yesterday."

"I just talked to Harry," Broker said, evading her remark.

Gloria tensed visibly. "How is he?"

"Drunk. He has these two forward gears when he's drinking. One is lucid. The other is . . ."

"I know, dangerously crazy."

"So, can we talk straight?"

"Sure, Lymon filled me in. The priest was murdered in his confessional. He had a St. Nicholas medallion in his mouth."

"And?"

"And . . . you've determined that the priest was not a pedophile. So somebody is playing games with the Saint's calling card."

"You know what Harry says?"

Gloria raised one hand in the stiff, dismissive gesture Gena Rowlands made famous in *A Woman Under the Influence.* "By all means, lay it on me."

"Harry says the Saint is back with bad target information. He says somebody in-house has been retrieving his notes from the computer trash and has put together an erroneous list of child abusers."

Gloria was careful not to bristle too much. "Ah, Jesus. I'll make it simple for you. Harry Cantrell is brilliant but erratic. He had quite a juggling act going, but now he's dropped his balls, as it were. Now he's grabbing at straws. I know the man. We, ah, had a thing . . ."

"I heard."

"I broke it off. Hell hath no fury like an old macho scorned."

"He's teasing me on the telephone. He won't give me a name."

Gloria cocked her head. "Okay, let me tell you about Harry. Do you know how we initially got onto Dolman?"

Broker shook his head.

"Sometimes cops go out to schools and talk to teachers about reporting child abuse, what to look for, stuff like that. So a year ago last spring Harry goes out to Timberry Trails Elementary and talks to the staff.

"There's this one paraprofessional who's got this chest like a shelf, right? This dish. So after he gives his talk, Harry starts putting the moves on her. Naturally, being the snake that he is, he uses the elements in his talk as an entrée.

"And this lady has a pile of these storybooks at her desk that kindergartners have written about themselves, and Harry is paging through them as he's doing his thing. The kids draw self-portraits on the front of the books and write their names. The teachers help them with the text. And he comes across this book that looks different from the others. Instead of a happy smiley face, the face is all colored in. So he holds it up and asks, 'What's this?'

"And the lady answers, 'Oh, that's Tommy Horrigan; he always draws himself with his back turned.' Harry opens the book and reads things Tommy has written, 'The leaves are coming back' or 'Mommy plants tulips.' He sees that Tommy does not put himself in his story.

"So Harry asks to meet Tommy Horrigan, and the rest is history." Gloria shook her head. "Harry starts out trying to get laid and winds up detecting the trail of a child abuser."

Broker looked her square in the eye. "And you started out with Harry, building a case against Dolman. And you wound up getting laid."

Gloria pursed her lips, looked at the wall, and said, "You know, it really bothered me that a guy that old, with such lousy personal politics, could be so damn . . ." She mugged a smile, turned back to Broker, and said, "Is this what you came for?"

"You asked to have Harry taken off the case," Broker said.

"Had to. When I took on Dolman, my marriage was on life support. The *thing* I had with Harry basically pulled the plug. But it was interfering with the work."

"Enter Lymon," Broker said.

Gloria leaned forward. "Don't get distracted by the boy-girl and the racism. Bottom line: Harry has it worked around in his head that if he had stayed on the case Dolman would have been convicted."

Broker studied her. She came across as bright, candid, and brave; plus sinewy in her armless blouse and raven crew cut. She looked as if she belonged on the front of a Patagonia catalog, scaling a sheer rock face. *Gloria Russell conquers El Capitan over a long lunch.*

"Do you know what it was like, losing that case?" Gloria said. "I was so mad at first that I stormed out of the chambers. But then I realized I had to go back . . ."

She drew herself up, and Broker watched it come, a memory like electrodes clipping onto her body, sending electric current up the corded muscles of her neck, into her face, and burning in her eyes.

"Because . . . I left that little boy in there alone watching Dolman grinning and pumping the hand of his attorney."

She shook her head violently. "And we said we'd never leave him alone. We always said we'd be there to protect him."

Gloria was tough. Gloria didn't cry. She kept talking in a dead, level voice. But her body cried. It was like looking at a statue of grief and seeing the unmoving bronze eyes trying to water.

"We had to go back and *explain* to Tommy and his parents. How do you explain that to a six-year-old? Here we told him that we were going to protect him. . . . Christ, do you have any idea what we put that kid through? The physical examinations—our doctor, the defense's doctor . . ."

And Broker watched her dissociate with the moment and retreat into a private limbo. Gloria spoke as if to Tommy Horrigan. "We told you we'd get the guy who did those things to you. But we didn't get him. We didn't do our jobs good enough, and he got away."

In a purely visceral way Broker now understood why John had brought him in. Nobody who'd been close to the thing wanted to pick up this particular live wire.

"Worst day of my life," Gloria said.

Gloria caught herself and looked across her desk. "I don't have to be here carrying water in county, you know. I could be almost a partner by now in a legal money factory in St. Paul or Minneapolis, driving a Beamer, working seventy hours a week, and taking files on stressed-out vacations to wherever. I chose not to do that because I believe there's more to life than making money. And I believe in being involved in this system out of self-interest, to protect all of us from people who will take the law into their own hands."

"So Harry gets your vote for Saint," Broker said.

An expression of painfully acquired revelation came over Gloria's face. She said, "Just as I'm sure I get his. But *Saint* is much too kind a word. The next time you see Harry, take a good look at him. He's the face of the mob."

Chapter Twenty-six

"Majority of U.S. Bishops Have Protected Abusive Priests," declared the headline in the newspaper box at the front door to the county building.

Broker walked out into the heat with Gloria's parting shot stuck in his mind. Fuckin' Harry. He crossed the parking lot and kicked the Crown Vic's tires. Fuckin' Harry's car. As he flopped behind the wheel, his phone rang. He whipped it open and braced for another Harry mind game.

"Mr. Broker, this is Annie Mortenson; I've been thinking about what you said and we should talk."

"Where are you?"

"I'm at the library, but I'm through for the day."

"I'll meet you on the front porch in ten minutes."

Eight minutes later, after scalding his hands on the red-hot steering wheel, he met her on the library steps. They sat down side by side on a bench.

"Harry did contact me and asked me for a favor. Am I in any trouble?" Annie asked.

"No, no. What was the favor?" Broker said.

"He asked me to call you and give you this information anony-mously." She handed him a note written in concise Palmer pen-manship: *Broker's truck can be found in the vicinity of County Road 97 and Merril Lane today after 3 P.M.*

Broker took the note and tucked it in his chest pocket.

"Your truck isn't going to wind up like my car, is it?" Annie said.

"I hope not," Broker said as a shadow fell across them.

"Is this guy bothering you, Miss?" an amused voice said.

Broker looked up. The tallish man standing in front of him had calm, angular features and straight blond hair falling an inch over his ears. His powder-blue eyes ruminated behind wire-rim glasses.

Drew Hensen, Janey's husband, had always reminded Broker of Garrison Keillor's radio persona: congenial and wise in a cute way and several comfortable steps removed from the real world. Broker remembered him lanky in chambray shirts and faded jeans. Today the heat had him in a tank top and running shorts and flip-flops.

Taken by surprise, Annie put her right hand to her throat, then dropped it to the top button of her blouse. Self-consciously, she twirled the button with her fingers. "Drew? Oh no, we were just talking . . ."

Broker stood up. "Drew, how you doing?" They shook hands.

Drew shrugged. "Same old stuff, waging war against junk food and prime-time TV."

"You two know each other?" Annie said.

"Sure, we used to work together," Drew said.

"You two, really?"

"In another life. At the Bureau of Criminal Apprehension. I used to be a police artist," Drew said. "Remember, I told you."

"Okay," Anne said. Her eyes rolled back, placing a memory.

"It's been a while, though," Broker said, practicing small talk while he checked Drew out. The artist appeared totally relaxed and untroubled by any marital discord Janey had alleged. However, Broker did notice that, in his presence, Drew and Annie adjusted their gaze to avoid looking directly into each other's eyes.

"Janey tells me you married a soldier," Drew said with a sly smile.

"An Amazon hoplite, actually," Broker said.

"*Hoplite*. Now there's a word you don't hear every day," Annie said.

Drew smiled, warming to the repartee. "They burned off their breasts, didn't they?"

"The right breast. So it wouldn't get in the way drawing a bow," Annie said.

"Now I think they just burn off men's balls," Broker said, smiling pleasantly.

"Always the mellow fellow," Drew said. "So are you still on the job?"

"I'm filling in as a deputy for John Eisenhower, just for a few days," Broker said.

Drew nodded. "Sure. I know John. Are you, ah, working now?" He nodded toward Annie.

"No, we have an acquaintance in common. That's all," Annie said.

"Well, I gotta go in and set up this program," Drew said.

"He has this afternoon reading group for third graders," Anne said.

"Watch yourself, Annie. Broker worked deep undercover; he's a sneaky sort of guy," Drew said amiably.

"I'll be careful," Annie said.

"See ya," Broker said.

Drew waved good-bye and went in the library. When he was gone, Annie said, "Do you know his books?"

Broker nodded. "He draws these friendly monsters like Sendak, but in brighter colors. I read a couple to my daughter."

"He's very good," Annie said.

"Right. Look, Annie: keep in touch about Harry. Anything at all."

"I will."

Broker thanked Annie, accompanied her out to the street, and then they went separate ways. Briefly, he watched her walk down a line of parked cars and wondered who was worse for her, Harry or Drew. Then Broker turned away and went in search of his truck.

Not sure about the whereabouts of Merril Lane, he opened the glove compartment on a hunch and found a Washington County road map. He also found a black billed cap with a motto stitched in yellow across the crown: I Am Not Like the Others. And below, in smaller letters: 3rd Mar Div Force Recon. Broker consulted the map, and seeing that he was headed into the country— maybe for a walk in the sun—he put Harry's hat on his head.

Broker drove northwest of town toward White Bear Lake into rolling countryside. He passed acres of long, white slat fences and horse barns. Overgrown gravel driveways wandered into the brush with signs that said things like Excellent Development Site. He found the intersection of Manning and Merril and saw only rolling empty fields. Probably the farmers had them in the land bank. *In the vicinity of*, the message said. He continued down Merril, topped a slight hill, and feathered the brakes. In the distance an American flag tossed in a hot gust of breeze.

Nothing unusual there; more and more flags had popped up in the countryside since 9/11, flying from mailboxes or fence posts. This flag, however, was attached to a black Ford Ranger.

The truck was parked way out in a weedy pasture that was gated and fenced with barbed wire.

A tractor path meandered into the field, but the gate was padlocked. So Broker got out and climbed over the gate. After a few minutes walking through the knee-deep grass and thistles, and avoiding numerous cow pies, he was thankful for the hat because he had to walk toward the west into the lowering sun. As he crossed the field he saw that the truck had been parked with the hood facing east, the direction he was walking in from.

Clearly, this was Harry's idea of a joke. He took out his cell phone and held it at the ready.

About one hundred yards from the truck, he caught a powerful draft of manure fermenting in the sun. He saw a pile of it dumped next to the truck.

Uh-oh.

A dozen steps later, he realized that some of the smell was coming from inside the truck.

Harry, you . . . son . . . of . . . a . . . bitch . . .

Broker walked closer in and saw that the interior of the cab had been shoveled full of cowshit. A note was stuck on top of the crud with a downward-pointing arrow. The note said: *Badge and gun this way.*

There was no sound except the buzz of insects and the faint rustle from the flag when it caught and released a nudge of steaming air. Instinctively, Broker backed off and started to circle the truck looking for some sign, tracks maybe . . .

A flash of opaque gray stood out against the green of the grass and weeds. Approaching, Broker saw it was a plastic gallon milk container. It had been planted upended on a stout, sharpened sapling. Then it had apparently been pushed over. Dirt still clung to the stick's sharpened end.

With a definite pucker contracting between his lips, Broker saw that it had been discarded after it served its purpose. Its purpose was obvious from the three bullet holes grouped in a two-inch radius in the middle of the container.

Harry had taken a few practice shots. Then he'd left the target in plain view.

Broker thought about it . . . Harry's finger out there attached to a nervous system drowned in Jack Daniel's, caressing the trigger on the black rifle. A trigger with a pull so fine a sneeze could set it off.

So now what? Jump under the truck? Into the weeds?

He squinted to the west, because that's where Harry would have set up his firing position with the sun at his back, in that tree line about six hundred yards away. Broker raised his right hand in that direction, middle finger extended.

Then he turned and noticed that the side-view mirror on the truck was cranked out and had some tiny writing on it in Magic Marker.

He took several steps forward and read: *Smile! You're on candid camera.*

Broker watched his own eyes freeze in his face in the mirror. Instinctively, he understood that Harry had planted the flag on his truck to keep track of the wind direction. He could even appreciate the twist of elegance in the way Harry had set him up, looking at his face in a mirror at the precise moment the .338 slug . . .

The hot sizzle passed through the air where his shoulder and his neck formed two sides of an angle. Broker watched the image of his face explode in the mirror before he could react.

A tiny fragment of flying glass cut his cheek as he dropped to his knees in an involuntary reflex. Otherwise he was untouched. Most of the glass had been knocked from the mirror frame, and there was a small hole a little off the dead center.

Broker took a deep breath, turned, and fixed on the tree line about six football fields away. Far enough that he wasn't aware of having even heard the sound of the shot.

He just had to go see, so he got up, started walking toward the trees, and began to count his steps. 1, 2, 3, 4, . . . *damn it was hot . . .* 54, 55 . . . *used to be able to shed the heat . . .* 74, 75 . . . *Jesus, it can't get any fuckin' hotter . . .* 124, 125 . . . *when is this fucker gonna break? . . .* 290, 291, 292 . . . *shoulda brought some water, dummy . . .* 340 . . . *dehydrated for sure, gotta watch it . . .* 430, 431 . . . *not a kid anymore, at least you're still putting out sweat . . .* 510, 511 . . . *be careful, you could crap out in this field, just sink in these weeds . . .* 587, 588, 589. Dizzy, squeegeed dry by the sun, he staggered into the shadow of the trees and looked back. His truck was about the size of his hand. He checked the tree line carefully and couldn't find any sign of a person having been there.

He mopped sweat from his face, squatted down, and thought about it. Harry had perfectly positioned him for the shot, down to the direction of the truck, even the angle of the mirror. And Broker had made the obvious assumption: the firing position had been in these trees, the best cover in sight.

Exactly the misdirected conclusion Harry had wanted him to reach. Like an opponent putting out counterfire would assume. Harry, meanwhile, would be somewhere else.

He got up, walked through the narrow line of trees, and climbed the gentle hill behind them. His truck was now obscured from view by the foliage.

Then he found the props Harry had left behind on a low hillside.

A small sandbag lay on a hummock of dirt. The kind used for prone support on rifle ranges. Broker walked over and found a dug-out area where Harry had made himself comfortable. Five Lucky Strike butts were ground into the dirt in a little circle.

Squatting in the depression behind the hummock, Broker could clearly see his truck through a deceptive opening in the tree canopy.

Again plastic gleamed in the sun, bright transparent this time. Harry had left a liter bottle of spring water in the grass. Almost full. Like a diagram of insanity, the water bottle lay next to an empty pint of Johnny Walker.

Greedily, Broker twisted off the cap and drank the hot water in three long gulps. Only when he'd finished did he see the patch of bare dirt that had been scraped flat. Harry had used something pointed, a twig or pen, and had printed very legible uppercase block letters in the earth: *YOU FLINCHED!*

After he stopped swearing, Broker called J. T. Merryweather. Then he called Stillwater Towing. Then, as he walked back across the field to the gate, to meet the tow truck, he called J. T. again.

Chapter Twenty-seven

Angel glided at the edge of the group of parents who were putting down blankets and unfolding camp chairs on the grass next to a fenced-in baseball diamond. She wore a sleeveless blouse, clam diggers, and sandals as she sauntered across the steamy playing field.

Just another mom.

That's what the prospect probably thought.

Look at him, just the nicest guy. Gathering the kids around him on the sidelines. Hands and eyes. Six-year-olds. Boys and girls in yellow T-shirts and baseball caps. Tigers, *the script on the shirts said. Watch his hands and his eyes. The way they move among the young bodies.*

George Talbot was a T-ball coach. Thirty-seven years old. Mid-management at 3M. He was husky, jowly, with a heavy four-o'clock shadow and ruddy cheeks.

Watch his hands and eyes.

He had fast little eyes behind a constant smile. And quick small hands. Dainty hands. At odds with his thick muscular legs.

Angel scanned the parents. Maybe one of them had made the

call. Saw something. The complaint had been vague and anonymous. *Don't trust him around the kids. Something about the way he is with the children.*

The boys and girls were paired off and struggled to catch the soft baseballs in their oversized mits. And Angel was thinking that some parents could be playing dirty politics. *My kid isn't in the first lineup. My kid is always in the outfield. My kid isn't getting enough playing time.* So get the coach. So make an anonymous phone call. Smear him.

Look at him, hopelessly normal. Handing out batting helmets to the first kids in the batting order. Remember, not all men are bad. Patience, Angel; you must be sure. Very serious stuff. Got to be sure. And keep moving.

Her eyes scanned the playing field, the cars parked along the street. She was looking for I-am-a-cop antennae sticking up on an unmarked car. She had to be careful.

Nothing specific in the news about the dead priest. Not a peep about A. J. Scott.

No mention of the medallions.

They were getting tricky on her.

Have to be careful.

After the game George drove down Greeley and joined the kids and their parents at Nelson's Ice Cream Parlor. Hot, crowded around the flimsy plastic tables in the parking lot; the ice cream dripped. George wiped the spill from a boy's thigh. Close quarters, all sweaty and jostling. *Did the hand linger? Did the knuckles drift across the boy's crotch?*

Angel, watching from across the parking lot, could not be sure. *Reasonable doubt.*

Though accelerated, her system of fact-finding and punishment wasn't arbitrary. The more she watched George Talbot roughhouse and joke with his boys, the less certain she was.

Good touch or bad touch?

She was leaning toward not charging George.

Good touch.

She was thinking maybe George would get to live his ordinary comfortable life. She was thinking that if she knew George, she'd tell him to eat smaller portions and get more exercise.

The matter was clinched half an hour later as she trailed George home. He lived north of town, in an area so recently opened to development that the houses were on huge one-acre lots. The rules of rural vigilance applied here. Any car that came down this road would be noticed. Living out here, George could keep a loaded shotgun.

And the house itself was not friendly to approach; it sat three hundred yards off the road next to a small pond. Angel observed a golden retriever, tongue hanging out, race down the long driveway to meet George as he drove in. Going past, Angel saw a basketball hoop on the garage. Two girls, short, dark haired, playing badminton.

From the corner of her eye she saw the mom come out; George's soul mate with dark hair, also in need of exercise. Her last impression of George Talbot was that he'd changed his name. With his dark complexion and the animated way he and his wife talked with their hands and touched each other as he got out of his car, he could be Italian or Greek.

Angel continued down the road. Too open around the house, and to get inside she'd have to get past the dog. Angel didn't know how to neutralize a frisky seventy-pound golden retriever.

No way I would harm an animal.

Uh-uh.

And then it's summer; the wife and kids are around . . .

No, he presented too many problems for her minimal surveillance skills. And these problems make it easier to err on the side of reasonable doubt.

George Talbot, you are free to go.

• • •

Letting George off the hook left a void in her evening. So she went home, changed into her running duds, and hit the steamy streets. The heat buoyed her, carried her, had become the chrysalis for her mission. Like infection, it concentrated the poison and drew it to the surface. Now she felt it pooling all around her, in the humid dark, in her sweat, as her shoes thudded on the concrete.

And it was literally all around.

As she ran a circuit of streets at dusk, she watched the light drain out of the sky, to be replaced by an artificial light flickering from living rooms.

Murder kenneled in the television sets. Along with assault, rape, things blowing up; tits and ass on prime time.

Kids in there with their upturned faces getting fat eating munchies were learning that killing was just another point-and-click solution. When she was little, the boys played with toy guns and fought with their fists. Now the kids weren't allowed to have toy guns, and they shot each other with 9 mms.

Face it, Angel thought, *I am nothing more than all of you carried one step farther.*

I am as normal as breathing the electronically tinted air coming off all those video tubes.

Whatever.

Focus.

She was getting close to the end of her spree. She had to start tying up the loose ends. She made a mental note to do a little research on a certain someone. To find out if they were right- or left-handed.

Angel flung out her arms and thrust her chest forward, sprinted through an imaginary finish line.

Yes.

Chapter Twenty-eight

Broker talked to J. T. on his cell as he drove, explaining his predicament. J. T. mostly listened. Then Broker hung up and traveled the back roads south into Lake Elmo. Ordinarily he'd enjoy this drive; escaping the malls, the subdivisions, the freeways. The last few miles to J. T.'s farm, Broker traveled on a timeless two-lane county road. Just rolling fields broken up by tree lines and the silhouettes of silos and barns floating on the horizon in the haze of heat.

Pretty country, except Broker's eyes kept wandering to his rearview mirror, where he could see the face of the grinning driver of the red Stillwater Towing truck that had loaded his shit-afflicted Ranger on its flat tilt bed.

The sign by the mailbox said: Royal Kraal Ostriches. J. T. Merryweather ran about two hundred birds on one hundred acres. Besides the pens for the stock, J. T. had fields in alfalfa, oats, and corn. He had a big red barn and a comfortable farmhouse in the shade of a huge willow tree. Today the long willow branches hung like a limp hula skirt.

Broker directed the tow truck driver to unload the Ranger next to a manure spreader J. T. had parked by the barn. He paid the driver and watched the truck turn back on the county road and disappear.

Then he walked toward the toolshed in the lower level of the barn. He passed a bird pen, and several of the eight-foot-tall hens bobbed along in the heat; a gaggle of long legs, long necks, big popped-out curious eyes, and droopy gray feathers.

Broker selected two short-handled shovels and a hoe and stepped back outside. He was fighting the sinking thought that the whole truck cab was a write-off.

Goddamn Harry.

He went around the barn and spotted a green tractor hitched to a box kicker and the red rails of a hay wagon marooned out on an alfalfa field.

Then he spotted a golf cart scooting along the side of the field, heading in toward the barn. Broker waited in the barn shadow, priming the handle of the hand pump, then bending to the stream of cold artesian water and slaking his thirst. He straightened up and inhaled the heat-fermented malt from the bins of oats, the stacked alfalfa bales. He watched the barn cats scuttle through the stanchions of an old windmill tower.

J. T. Merryweather wheeled his golf cart up to the barn, got out, walked toward Broker, and flung an arm at the sky.

"Farmer's nightmare: burned on top and wet on the bottom. Not a good day to have a hay crop cut and lying in the field. Goddamn humidity is 83 percent. Just won't dry out." Broker followed J. T.'s gaze, squinting up at the orange smear in the haze.

J. T. wore a black Stetson, was six feet tall, and was cooked black on black by the sun. He was field-hand lean, leaner than he'd been in years. Farmwork and fresh air agreed with him more than the desk he'd used as a captain running St. Paul Homicide.

His face was large and generous, but his tight brown eyes had always preferred the mysteries of the sky to the predictable people beneath it. So he took early retirement and started up this farm.

They shook hands.

Broker looked around. "Where's Denise and Shammy?" J. T.'s wife and daughter were not in sight.

"Denise took Shammy to the Cities, club team tournament."

Broker nodded. The daughter practiced basketball like a religion.

"Okay, let's go have a look," J. T. said. He couldn't suppress a grin.

"Not funny, goddammit. Look at that." Broker jabbed his finger at the shattered mirror.

"Six hundred yards, you say." J. T. mulled it over.

"More like six hundred fifty. I walked it off," Broker said.

"The man always could shoot," J. T. said.

Broker dug in his pocket and showed J. T. the .338 round. "He gave me this as a taunt when it all started, like I told you on the phone. The drunk sonofabitch could have killed me!"

J. T., who, like Harry, had a basement full of reloading presses, took the rifle bullet from Broker and turned it over in his fingers. "That's a 378 Weatherby Magnum necked down to 338. Weatherby's a low-end elephant gun. Basically this shell casing is too big for the bullet, got way too much powder behind it. I'm surprised the whole mirror frame didn't explode. And if he would have clipped you anywhere around the head, we wouldn't be having this conversation because your head would be this fine red mist floating over a strawberry bog in Wisconsin."

"Spare me the hymn to gun freaks, okay?"

"Just saying . . . he hit what he wanted to hit. Six hundred yards is an easy shot for a guy like Harry. He's just fuckin' with you."

J. T. tossed the bullet back to Broker, who caught it, stuck it in his pocket, and turned toward his truck.

Grumbling, he opened the passenger door, and the full aroma of the sun-ripened cow dung rolled over him.

J. T. spotted the badge-and-gun sign, the arrow pointing down, and began to howl.

Broker ignored his glee and started shoveling out clots of manure. J. T. went around to the other side with the other shovel. "Eureka," J. T. crowed as he gingerly lifted Broker's .45 on his shovel. A moment later they found the badge.

J. T. brought out a five-gallon can full of kerosene and dumped in the gun and badge. He turned back to the truck. "Forget the shovel. Get on the horn and call your insurance agent; call it vandalism, whatever. You're going to have to replace everything, the seats, the dash. I doubt you'll ever get the smell out."

"Can't hire a couple farm kids to scrub it out, huh?"

J. T. snorted. "Shee-it. They are no more farm kids. Average age of the American farmer is fifty-seven." J. T. toed the dirt. "You know, I was you, I'd think of changing trucks. You don't have a lot of luck with Fords."

"Oh yeah?"

"Yeah, two years ago August, Popeye kicked your last Ranger to junk; now this," J.T . said.

True, J. T. had made the mistake of driving Broker's truck into a pen with Popeye, his four-hundred-pound aggressive stud. Popeye had pulverized the truck with kicks and damn near killed J.T. when he made a break for it. Now Popeye was gone. J. T. had sent for the fatal ride on the big truck.

"It ain't like you're on a fixed income," J. T. said. "What do you think about the Toyota Tundra?"

Broker waved his hand in a disgusted gesture. They left the truck and took the can of kerosene over to an outside workbench next to the toolshed. J. T. went in the shed and came out with two wire brushes and a handful of small glass jars.

Broker fished out the badge, unpinned it from the leather backing, and hurled the round hunk of leather at the nearby burning barrel. No way the leather would ever clean up. He scrubbed at the badge with the wire brush.

Meanwhile J. T. methodically took the .45 apart and put the various pieces in the glass jars. He took out a Leatherman tool and patiently began to remove the smallest screws.

"Whoa. I'll never be able to get that back together," Broker said.

"I'll give you a loaner," J. T. said. When he had the pistol totally disassembled, he poured clean kerosene into the jars.

They scrubbed their hands under the pump with Boraxo, then went over to the picnic table in the hot shade of the willow. J. T. went in the house and came out with a frosted pitcher of iced tea. He took out his pipe. Broker reached for a cigar, then, still hot and shaky from his walk in the sun, decided not to.

J. T. lit his pipe and poured iced tea. He took a sip and stared at the dusky waves of heat rolling over his fields. "Got a call this morning. Bubble Butt Reardon's dead. Dehydrated. Heat stroke. Just like Corey Stringer. Cutting his lawn . . ."

"Aw, Christ." Broker stared at the cold glass of tea in his hand. Reardon had been a notoriously overweight St. Paul detective.

J. T. lifted his iced tea. "Push fluids."

"Amen."

After a moment J. T. said, "You know, I never believed that bullshit about Harry being the Saint. Harry is a compulsive planner. That's his training. Look how he set up that shooting gallery for you today. At the very least, he would have waited a year till all the fuss over the Dolman trial died down." J. T. clicked his teeth and grimaced. "But I believe he's capable of letting it slide if he did know who the killer was. John E. is right-on in that respect."

"You worked with him, after I left St. Paul," Broker said.

"Yeah. In Homicide, before he split for Washington County."
J. T. laughed. "And I kinda felt like Sidney Poitier playing Virgil
Tibbs in *In the Heat of the Night*. You know, harnessed to red-
neck Rod Steiger. Harry was just this impossible bigot. But he was
up front about it."

"You didn't get along."

"Didn't like each other from the jump—and said so. But we
functioned because we respected each other, you follow?"

"He's good; give him that."

"Look, he's an asshole. But he's our asshole so he's worth sav-
ing," J. T. said. "But Harry all the way sober? I don't know if
we're ready for that."

"This ain't funny, J. T. Look what he did to my truck."

"I told you, man. You got bad luck with Fords."

"Harry is a menace, J. T.; don't sugarcoat it."

"True, he's hard to take. I wouldn't want him around my family," J. T. said. "I certainly wouldn't want him talking to my
teenage daughter. But I'll tell you a dirty little secret: if my kid was
in Columbine High School that day, you better believe I'd have
wanted Harry to be the first cop on the scene."

Chapter Twenty-nine

"The heat index has exceeded one hundred ten degrees for two consecutive days," said the announcer on WCCO AM radio. "In Minnesota, the heat wave has now claimed seven lives."

Including Bubble Butt Reardon.

Broker clicked the radio off and drove back to the river through the gorgeous, and now lethal, sunset. When the sun went down, the heat just changed color from light to dark.

Broker had accepted J. T.'s offer and now had an old reliable 1911 military-issue .45 stuck in a borrowed holster on his hip. He had a badge, minus the leather backing, that smelled of kerosene.

He parked, went into Milt's house, and put his belt, the pistol, his wallet, pocket change, and cell phone on the kitchen table. Then he went outside to the garbage cans, stripped off his clothes, and threw them away. Back inside, he slapped a fresh battery in his cell phone and took an extralong shower.

Then he walked with a towel around his waist, opened a beer, and checked his e-mail box, which was empty. On impulse, he called his folks in Devil's Rock.

"Hello," Irene Broker answered.

"Mom, it's me."

"Phillip, how nice of you to surface and check in . . ."

"Ah, how's Dad doing?"

"Your father and your uncle Billie went out on the big water at dusk, after steelheads."

"He's feeling okay, then?"

"Seems to be. Of course, I had to remind both of them to wear their life jackets."

"What's the weather like up there?"

"Beautiful. Seventy-two, with a nice northwest breeze. How's it by you?"

"Don't ask."

"I won't. And there's no word about Nina and Kit on this end. You should make some inquiries," Irene said tartly.

"Don't start, Mom."

"I'm sorry. I'm sure you've got it all under . . . your control issues."

"I love you, too, Mom."

Broker hung up, finished his beer, and opened another one. The phone rang, and he braced for Harry. Except it was the house phone. He picked up. Not Harry.

It was Janey. "Broker, it's not real good here right now. Could I have your cell phone number, just in case I have to reach you when you're not home?"

"I'd prefer not to get involved in your . . ."

"Broker, for Chrissake, I got a kid to worry about here."

He gave her the number. She thanked him and hung up. He took his beer out on the porch and lit a cigar. Impervious to the smoke, the mosquitoes came out of the dark like a shower of darts. He went back in and turned the TV in the kitchen to the Weather Channel.

He tried to get interested in a newsmagazine show about global warming. He was told that 1995 was the warmest year since global records started to be kept in 1856. Then the weather lady told him there were reports of Eskimo hunters falling through the arctic ice as a result of global climate change. That did it. He thumbed the remote to kill the TV, then went through the house, closing all the windows. He flipped on the air-conditioning, opened his fourth beer—two was his usual limit—turned off the lights, and lay down on the bed with his cell phone for company.

Broker fell into an exhausted sleep as the slowly cooling darkness closed in on him.

After the ring and groping with the cell phone on his chest, a thoroughly drunken voice came out of the dark. "This is Harry, where am I?" The dark sounded like a roar on Broker's end.

"Harry?"

"*Tai sao! Tai vi! Tai vi sao!*" Harry belted out the Vietnamese slang loud as he could.

"What's that, the wind?" Broker asked.

"Fuck yeah, man," Harry yelled. "Going through my hair . . . a hundred twenty miles an hour, I shit you not." The line went dead.

Broker was up, pacing. He considered making a pot of coffee, but then he wouldn't be able to get back to sleep. Another beer maybe? Christ, Harry was driving him to the bottle. He decided no beer. Instead he opted to brave the mosquitoes, go out on the deck, soak in the heat, and smoke another cigar.

Outside, he watched the running lights on a boat ease down the channel. The inky air hugged in close and suddenly evoked a sharp memory of the mosquito-repellent-soaked, very filthy, plastic stock of an M16 parked against his cheek.

Night after night.

The cigar started to taste like bad history, so he threw it away, went back inside, and settled down at the kitchen table. He concentrated on Ambush the cat. Ambush reclined patiently on the linoleum a foot away from a tiny space between the refrigerator and a cabinet. Ambush was absolutely motionless, covered in thick gray fur. She wasn't complaining about the heat. She smelled a mouse.

She was working.

So Broker sat with her until . . .

Rinnngggg . . .

Broker was getting so he could activate the cell with his eyes shut.

"Ha! You pooped your pants today," Harry said.

"Damn near. You this keep up, somebody's going to get hurt," Broker said.

"Count on it," Harry said. "And by the way, don't get too attached to my hat."

Broker could hear a new hivelike, much lower roar in the background. A very busy bar or a casino. Then Harry launched into a drunken monologue: "So three years ago, when the head of Investigations opened up, I thought I was a shoo-in to take over the unit. But John had other ideas; he brought in Art Katzer from St. Paul. I was upset and said so to John's face. It went downhill from there . . .

"Then I got onto Tommy Horrigan and started zeroing in on Dolman."

"And zeroing in on Gloria," Broker said.

"We hit it off, what can I say? Any rate, I'm doing interviews, building a file, and Katzer comes over and tells me John thinks it's a good idea to give the case to the new guy."

"The new guy was Lymon Greene."

"Yeah." Harry paused. "He took Dolman. I should back up here and admit I made a few wisecracks about Lymon when John brought him on board."

"Wisecracks? You mean, like: Gee, lookit this shiny new quarter?"

"No, ah, more like: John's lost his nerve, knuckling under to all this diversity bullshit."

"Were they overhead?"

"Oh yeah, and reported back to Katzer and to John. I got a letter of reprimand in my file. So when I bitched about giving my case to a rookie detective, they thought it was more of the same." Harry paused for a few beats. "The problem with saying something dumb is that it causes people not to hear when you say something smart."

"Like?"

"Like that Lymon was not seasoned enough to handle that kind of case. For starters, working with Gloria threw him for a loop. They struck these weird sparks from the beginning. I mean, everybody figured Gloria was a closet lez until I came along and turned her out. Suddenly, she starts lifting weights; hell, before that, she would barely acknowledge you, wouldn't shake your hand, like she couldn't bear to touch you or something," Harry said.

"I thought she was married."

"Oh yeah, right. Her husband was this PC bookend; guy wasn't even there. A fucking English professor at Macalester College. Any rate, they do Dolman. I came up with three kids I thought were violated, two in the neighborhood and one in his class at school. But the school kid, Tommy Horrigan, was the most credible, so they went with him.

"We had Dolman cold. I'd found a trunk full of kiddie porn in his house. I'd found Polaroids of the kids with their pants down. But Dolman thought he was smart. He cut the faces out of the pictures. But Tommy had a birthmark on his thigh. And that should have been the lock. Plus that kid took the stand, and he was a rock; I'll give that to Lymon and Gloria. The kid was prepared. And the scumbag defense attorney couldn't shake him. Not directly. But the defense attorney saw something. This one juror. White male, fifty-two years old. This fat guy who probably hadn't seen his pecker in ten years.

"It was subtle, but Mouse and me picked up on it; facial expressions, body language. This guy flat resented Lymon. It was textbook. I mean he hated seeing Lymon sitting next to Gloria. This was back when Gloria had this long black hair and looked like fuckin' Snow White. It was that goddamn simple.

"The defense kept calling Lymon back to go over procedures. Keeping him on the stand. I went to Gloria, and I told her to put Lymon down in the weeds, keep him out of court. But she wouldn't hear it, coming from me; she went the other way and kept Lymon by her side.

"So the jury stayed out for three days, and there was the one juror who wouldn't budge from not guilty. This puke didn't even see that little kid. All he saw was this black guy working with this white woman. It's subjective, but that's my take on how Dolman got off."

"And you probably didn't keep this perceptive observation to yourself."

"Nah, I had a few drinks and talked it around. It got back to John and he had me on the carpet and tore me a new asshole. Threatened to suspend me. I had to attend goddamn diversity classes. So I buttoned up and stuffed it. I had this equal and opposite reaction. I buttoned up too much. 'Cause, thing is, the day the verdict came down and Dolman got off, I followed Lymon and Gloria out of the courtroom. Lymon was hustling her out of sight because she was so pissed. I mean volcanic. I caught up with them in this empty office and . . .

". . . I swear to God, man, he was restraining her, and she was grabbing at his holster and she was saying, 'That creep will never be around kids again. I'm going to blow his fucking head off.'

"I never told that to anybody until right now. See, I figured they wouldn't believe me, all the stuff I'd said about her and Lymon already.

"And two days later, somebody did just that. Put twelve rounds in Dolman's fat face. And they left a St. Nicholas medallion in his mouth. Okay, so finally I get put on a case. I worked the Saint with the BCA.

"I remembered what Gloria said after the trial, so just to run out all the grounders, real quiet so as not to draw any attention, I checked on her and Lymon's whereabouts the night Dolman got whacked. And you know what? They were together. And not any place that could be verified. They were together in his car, driving the freeways, talking."

"What are you getting at?" Broker said.

"Gee, I dunno. Maybe somebody should, ah, check where Gloria was the night the priest got whacked," Harry said.

The connection went dead.

Chapter Thirty

Friday morning dawned with an arsenic yellow haze and hit 102 sticky degrees by 9 A.M. Another no-run day. Broker drove into town trying to take J. T.'s long view on Harry: just round him up and get him off the streets, sober him up, and then seal him in a cabinet like a fire ax. Maybe hang instructions around his neck: Break Glass in Case of Emergency.

Investigations was empty, except for Benish, who sat glumly watching his phone.

"Where is everybody?" Broker said.

"They just found a body north of town."

"Another one?"

"Nah, this is superweird." Benish straightened up and stared at Broker. "Don't you have a radio in your car, a computer?"

"Sure," Broker said, grinning. "I just never turn them on."

Benish shook his head. "Any rate. This guy had a heart attack, and dogs got to him is what I heard. Kinda grisly, a real eye-fuck special. Now everybody's piled on to get a look, and I'm stuck waiting on a must-get call." Benish jotted an address on a slip of paper and handed it to Broker.

Dogs?

Broker took the address, headed out the door, and got back in his car. For a moment he studied the Mobile Data Terminal grafted onto the dashboard like an unplugged R2D2. He picked Harry's hat off the passenger seat, the one that announced "I Am Not Like the Others," and placed it on top the computer.

Then he drove down Main Street, through downtown, and ran an amber light on Myrtle. Horns blared behind him. He glanced in the rearview and saw a dusty green Volvo had run the red light, skewing the crossing traffic.

He continued on north with an eye to the mirror. The Volvo kept pace. At the north end of town he speeded up on Highway 95. The Volvo paced him, staying four car lengths behind.

Okay. So who was following him? In his general experience, threatening people did not drive Volvos. Soccer moms drive Volvos. People who shop at the food co-op drive Volvos. Volvo owners listen to Minnesota Public Radio. They love wolves; they hug trees.

He squinted into the rearview. And this person didn't believe in car washes, because the dust on the windshield was as good as a tint; he could not make out the driver.

Broker scratched his chin and went with his gut: Volvo owners do not usually tail cops unless they are psychos.

Or reporters.

North of town the highway dipped and rose through a turn in a raw cut in the limestone river bluff. Heading into the incline, Broker floored the gas. When he lost the Volvo in the shoulder of the turn, he gained the top of the hill going almost eighty, braked sharply, and turned into a blind intersection on the left. Spitting gravel, he swung around and punched the accelerator as the Volvo raced to catch up. He pulled back on the highway and flashed his lights on and off, pulled alongside, and looked over at Sally Erbeck, the *Pioneer Press* reporter.

Emphatically, he held up his badge and pointed to the side of the road. She rolled her eyes and pulled over.

Broker parked behind her and approached down the shoulder trying to keep a straight face. He hadn't gone through the motions of a traffic stop in over twenty years.

"You should wash this car, lady," Broker said. "I can't see your brake lights."

"Oh c'mon," Sally said.

Broker put on a stern expression and said, "You ran a red light back there in town."

She sat up straighter and hung her head, mostly getting her defiant voice under control. "I'm sorry, officer; I thought I had the amber," she said, and Broker could almost hear her dad instructing her as a teenager. *Even if the cop is a total asshole, always show respect; always call him sir or officer.*

Struggling to maintain his stern expression, Broker continued. "Plus you're driving erratically. I could write you up for operating a motor vehicle while under the influence of journalism. That's a pretty serious offense in Washington County."

Sally stared at him.

Finally, Broker couldn't hold back the grin. "So what's up?" he asked.

Exasperated, she shot him a sidelong glance. "Not much. Just that the whole Catholic Church is under siege, and you got a dead priest, as in shot-in-the-head dead, in his confessional to boot."

Broker squinted at her. "Has somebody been tipping you, like anonymously?"

Sally batted her eyes. "You mean, like calling me up at odd hours?"

"Yeah."

"C'mon, that only happens in bad novels and B movies."

Just then a dark blue Stillwater squad and two white county cruisers zoomed past and headed north with their flashers turning but no sirens.

Sally didn't even say good-bye. She dropped the Volvo in gear and left Broker in a shower of gravel as she pulled back on the road and headed out after the cops.

Broker turned into the driveway right after Sally. He saw at least five other police cruisers, a couple unmarked Crown Vics, and a green ambulance from Lakeview Hospital.

Several cops were fanning out in the densely wooded area around the house, which was a basic St. Croix River place: basement built into a slope, one upper story, wraparound deck. Broker watched Sally get out of her car and approach the house. Several cops saw her but didn't stop her, so she continued around to the back. Broker saw Mouse standing in the shade of a basswood tree. He got out and walked over.

"Hey Mouse, what's up?"

"Go look."

"Is this a crime scene or a county fair?" Broker said.

"I'm, ah, relaxing the rules a little," Mouse said. Sweat soaked his face.

"I guess . . . you just let Sally Erbeck go traipsing through. I thought the general idea was you don't want civilians messing it up."

"We may have caught a lucky break here in a ghoulish sort of way. Appears this guy had a heart condition and caught the Big One in his yard. The neighborhood dogs were roving in a pack and found the body, probably twenty-four hours ago. There's no way to mess this one up any more than it already is. Go look. But, ah, watch your step."

Broker walked around the house and down the lawn to where a knot of Stillwater and county patrol coppers had gathered to direct traffic around points of interest strewn in the grass. Sally backed away from the group, walked over to a lawn chair, and sat down. Her face was pale and queasy.

Then Broker got a whiff of the rotten-meat stench plumped up on a platter of heat. A few more steps, and he glimpsed literally flesh and blood on the grass and what could be a gut pile. His first impression was: the cadaver of a road-killed deer.

But they were a long way from the road.

He took a few more steps and saw that the remains were human. One of the cops walked stiffly away, ducked into the bushes, and lost his breakfast.

The corpse lay on its back and was distorted by the mutilation of genitals, belly, and face. Entrails had been chewed and jerked out in red, white, and purple ribbons across the grass. Eyes gone, no mouth. The face had been gnawed down to the bone. All the exposed meat was coated with a glistening swarm of green flies that hummed like a small hardworking motor.

"Dogs," said one of the cops. "Regular old Rover and Spot."

He pointed through the trees at a house over two hundred yards away. "The neighbors had been up north on vacation. They came home last night and heard dogs scuffling in the woods, didn't think much of it. Then this morning they heard them again and the man came to investigate. He thought maybe the dogs had run down a deer."

"Wild dogs?" said Sally Erbeck. Like a good soldier, she had returned.

"Nah, just your everyday faithful Fido. They're probably at home nuzzling the kids." The cop, a husky sergeant, smiled at

Broker. He was enjoying his moment with the white-faced reporter.

"And all those flies?" Sally said.

"Bluebottles, they show up fast in the heat, when a body starts to release gas and fluids. Now if this guy hadn't been chewed on by dogs, the flies would settle into the orifices; eyes, nose, mouth, and the genital anal region—but as you can see, there ain't no eyes, nose, mouth, or . . ."

"I get the picture," Sally said, walking away.

"What's going on?" Broker said to the sergeant.

"Mouse said to let the press take a good look, no restrictions, long as they don't actually step in it," the sergeant said quietly. Then his heavy features composed into a swoon of pure delight. "Oh my," he said.

Broker turned and saw a blond television reporter in a lime green pants suit striding toward them with her cameraman in tow. Her perfect features were clenched in an enamel Botox smile.

"Margo Shay, Channel . . ." She got a look, and her smile clotted into a gag reflex.

"It ain't exactly ashes to ashes, dust to dust, is it?" the sergeant said, striking a thoughtful pose.

Broker left the sergeant to his forensic epiphany and went back toward the house, where he found Mouse facing another camera crew and several print reporters. Mouse shifted from foot to foot like an old lion gathering himself to jump through yet another ring of fire.

"We're still waiting on the medical examiner, so anything I say is strictly off the record and for background. But we found a whole cabinet full of medication, so we speculate this person might have suffered a heart attack in his yard at least twenty-four hours ago," Mouse said.

"What kind of medication?" a reporter said.

"Lessee." Mouse consulted a small spiral notebook. "Lasix, Bumix. Some digitalis and, ah, I think it's Coumadin—that's a blood thinner, basically rat poison is what it is."

"Rat poison?"

"Yeah, really thins out the little fuckers' blood so when they squeeze through itty-bitty cracks they start really gushing inside," Mouse said.

"So the dogs didn't kill him?" another reporter said.

"Highly doubtful. Almost certainly not. Usually, domestic dogs will feed on a corpse only if there's fresh blood. So maybe he had a nosebleed or something; that might explain the pattern of mutilation from the face down the front of the torso," Mouse said.

"Are we talking regular dogs, house pets?" a reporter asked.

"The neighbor who found the body this morning chased off five or six dogs, two of which he recognized," Mouse said. Then seeing Broker, he waved off the reporters. "I think it's better to wait on the Ramsey County medical examiner."

Mouse took Broker by the arm and walked him into the shadows under the deck. "Lookit this. We put the dog stuff over the radio, and there's sheriff deputies here from St. Croix County, Wisconsin, Forest Lake, Cottage Grove. And, ah, it must be a slow day in St. Paul because the 'A Team' from BCA just arrived." Mouse pointed at two guys in suits who were striding down the driveway.

A Stillwater cop and county patrol sergeant Patti Palen were standing a few feet away. The Stillwater cop said, "The tall guy in the blue suit with the dark hair, is that . . . ?"

Patti said, "You mean the guy in the *thousand-dollar* blue suit."

The Stillwater cop said, "Yeah. So that's him, Davenport?"

Patti said, "That's him. He bailed from Minneapolis, now he's with the state."

The Stillwater cop said, "I hear he cuts notches in his gun."

Patti's face was deadpan, her timing perfect. "The way I heard it, he cuts notches in his dick."

The Stillwater cop said, "BCA ain't gonna be the same."

Patti said, "No shit, looks like the Sears catalog is out and *GQ* is in."

Broker rolled his eyes and turned to Mouse. "This is a circus. You know what you're doing?"

"Orders. I been on the horn to John E. He said throw it wide-open. I got guys keeping an eye out so the press doesn't disturb anything. But how can you contaminate a scene like this? There's pieces of this poor pilgrim spread out for a hundred yards in every direction," Mouse said. "The point is, it takes the heat off our dead priest for a news cycle."

"Gotcha. Who was this guy anyway?" Broker said.

Mouse scratched his flattop. "His name was Scott. Some kind of photographer."

"Our boy called again last night. It sounded like he was in a casino," Broker said.

"Don't worry, they'll spot him," Mouse said. "In the meantime, prepare yourself to hear, see, and read a lot about the dogs of Washington County this weekend."

Then Broker spotted Lymon Greene walking uncertainly up from taking a look at the body.

"Lymon," he called out, "you got a minute?"

"I've never seen anything like that before," Lymon said.

"About time you got wet," Broker said.

"Is that some kind of joke?" Lymon said. He was clearly upset; sweat dotted his skin like BBs of mercury.

Broker shook his head. "No joke. Part of the job is protecting the public from seeing stuff like that. The civilians live up on top the water. We get to see what swims under it." Broker paused a beat. "Like the Saint."

Lymon nodded and motioned Broker to follow him up the driveway. They counted three TV vans. Cops from other jurisdictions were coming down the drive three abreast.

"It's like a circus sideshow," Lymon said.

"You got the sideshow part right," Broker said.

When they reached Lymon's car, he reached in the open window, took out a manila folder, and handed it to Broker. "Benish said you were out here, so I thought I'd bring these," Lymon said.

The folder contained several glossy black-and-white photographs of Victor Moros lying in a small pool of blood on the carpet of his confessional. He was a stocky, strong-featured man, more Indian than Spanish, with longish black hair. His eyes were closed in death, but his mouth was open in a grimace of even, white teeth.

Lymon tapped a sheaf of faxes that were in the folder along with the photos.

"Cause of death, a .22 long fired point-blank into his temple. The two other wounds, one in the neck and in the cheek, would not have killed him if he'd received medical attention promptly. So they speculate the killer lured Moros close to the screen, shot twice, then came around and put one in his head. They found plastic residue in the wounds, like from a commercial container. A pop bottle. They think the killer might have used a homemade silencer.

"No cartridges found on the scene. No latent prints, no blood or body fluids. They're still running tests on fibers and residue on the carpet.

"I talked to Albuquerque, and they say Moros was a solid, old-fashioned plodder. Nothing remotely in his past that suggests he's anything other than what he was. They put the whole incident down to media-induced hysteria.

"The father and mother who accused Moros out there have been in town all summer. No vacations to Minnesota."

Broker reached in and put the folder back on the front seat of Lymon's car. "This is your kind of stuff, not my kind of stuff," he said.

Lymon's face was unusually candid. "Your kind of thing is Harry, right? Fast and loose, high risk, and no rules. Benish just told me about what happened between you two back in St. Paul. About Harry's wife."

"Let's get out of here, walk a little," Broker said. He pointed toward the highway. They walked the rest of the way up the drive, crossed Highway 95, and followed an asphalt bike trail that meandered under the shade of the trees.

"So how do you handle what happened with Harry's wife?" Lymon said.

"You don't handle it. It's always there, walking beside you, like we are now," Broker said.

"I hope I never get put in that situation."

"Chances are you won't. A big part of living is believing that bad stuff happens to other people. Usually it works that way."

"Up on top of the water."

"There it is. But you're right. Harry is my kind of thing."

Lymon studied Broker carefully. "Explain your kind of thing."

"Sure. Start with fundamentals. What was the world's first recorded murder?"

"You're patronizing me," Lymon said, guarded.

"Uh-uh. C'mon. Answer the question."

"Cain kills Abel. God asks Cain where his brother is, and Cain says, 'I know not. Am I my brother's keeper?'" Lymon quoted.

"God interrogates his suspect." Broker nodded. "The suspect denies the crime. But Cain gets busted. That's a fairy tale. What's missing that would make it real?"

Lymon stared at him.

Broker continued. "What's missing is the tip that put God onto Cain. Once you add the snitch, you have the world's first solved crime."

"And you think Harry's the snitch on the Saint."

"There it is. My job is getting Harry to talk."

They walked in silence for thirty seconds. Then Broker said, "The gossip says you're sleeping with Gloria. Are you?"

Lymon avoided Broker's eyes and looked into the trees. "I might have strayed a little . . ." He held up his left hand, palm inward, and stared at the gold band.

"Bad question. Nobody tells the truth about sex. Or the Saint," Broker said.

Lymon made a face.

"So what'd she do, take you like an antidote to Harry? She's still in love with him, isn't she? Must be hard on her, being stuck on a guy who shouldn't have his ticket punched into the twenty-first century," Broker said.

"The human heart is . . ." Lymon said.

"Dog food, remember?" Broker nodded back toward the house. "Was Harry protecting her?"

"What do you mean?"

"Let me put it a different way. Where was Gloria the night Moros got killed?"

"Down in the gym, working out."

"Anybody see her who can vouch for the time?"

"Me."

"Anybody see the two of you?"

"No, we were alone."

"So you could have been somewhere else."

"Prove it."

Broker squinted at the younger man. "That's what Harry used

to say when people suggested he killed Dolman." Broker turned and walked back toward all the cop cars lining the driveway. He was about ten feet from his car when his cell phone rang.

It was Janey Hensen, and she was crying.

"Broker, I need some help. Drew and I had this fight, and he totally lost it, says he's moving out, and the thing is, Laurie is—she took it kind of hard and she hurt herself. . . ."

Hurt herself? "Did you call nine-one-one?" Broker said.

"It's not like that exactly. I need some help talking to her," Janey said.

"Okay. I'll be right over."

Chapter Thirty-one

You will regret this.

Broker did not play games with women. And one of his basic rules was not to meddle in other people's marriages, especially when an old girlfriend was involved.

Janey and Drew lived in a Victorian on the South Hill that looked like a three-layer wedding cake. From their front porch you could look over the town and see north down the river valley. Drew had kept Restoration Hardware in the black when he rehabbed this tusker.

Then all the trivia dropped away when Janey met him at the door and he saw the bloody towel in her hands.

"She cut her hands up. I don't think it's bad enough for the emergency room, but it's just horrible," Janey said.

"Calm down, breathe through your nose," Broker said as he moved swiftly into the house toward the sound of the crying child.

Laurie sat on the kitchen floor blubbering. She held her hands out in front of her with bloody gauze stuck to her fingers. More blood was smeared on her T-shirt and shorts.

Immediately, Broker looked for signs of serious injury.

Blood smears, no great quantity. Nothing arterial. He removed the gauze pads and evaluated the wounds on Laurie's hands.

One fingernail was split to the quick, and tiny bits of abraded skin hung from several fingers. Her knuckles were a mess.

Quickly, he felt over the rest of her body; he asked her to move her feet, asked if her back or neck hurt. As Broker worked through his checks, Janey said, "Laurie, honey, this is Phil Broker; he's a friend, a good friend." She turned to Broker and said, "I'll show you."

She swept Laurie up in her arms, settled her on a hip, and carried her out the back door.

Janey was talking too fast; her eyes and hair were spiky with tension. "About an hour after Drew made his scene and left, I found Laurie out here, in the corner of the yard."

She put her hand on the back of Laurie's head and pressed her to her chest, instinctively murmuring, "It's okay, it's okay . . ." as she led Broker to a corner of the yard where tall hostas and ferns grew in the shade. "There," she said, inclining her head.

Broker saw the freshly dug hole in the flower bed. Several gauze pads and some ripped pieces of dirty cardboard were scattered around.

"She . . . she was digging with her bare hands," Janey said, rocking Laurie back and forth. "Samantha was Laurie's cat and slept at the foot of her bed for years. We had her put to sleep last May, and we buried her out here in the flower bed. Then today, after Drew left, Laurie disappeared, and I found her crying out here. And I went out there and . . ."

Janey balled her free hand into a fist. "She's just six years old, for Christ sake. It's not fair she has to go through this. It's just not fair. How could he do this to a kid, his own daughter? Fucking men. Goddamn fucking men and their fucking."

"Shhh, easy, let's get her back in and look at those hands." Broker put his arm around her and started her back toward the house. But Janey was clasping and unclasping her hand, blinking rapidly. So Broker said, "Focus, Janey. We gotta do something about Laurie; forget the other for now."

"Laurie, right," Janey said.

They went back in the kitchen, and Broker sat Laurie down on a chair, then squatted to get at her level. Laurie was tall, with blond hair plaited in two braids. She had blue eyes like her father. She had tears in her eyes like her mother. He looked to Janey.

"I'm on it. Hot water. A clean sponge. Some disinfectant . . ." Janey said, starting to move.

"And hydrogen peroxide if you have it, clean towels, and all the first-aid dressings you have, adhesive tape, and a sharp scissors," Broker called after her.

As Janey set about assembling the items, Broker spoke to Laurie. "First we have to clean up your hands and see how bad they are."

"Leave me alone," Laurie sniffled.

"I will, but first we have to wash your hands."

"I don't want to wash my hands," Laurie cried and waved her hands feebly in the air.

"They must hurt a lot," Broker said, his voice conveying just a touch of admiration.

"They do hurt," Laurie admitted.

"Well, we don't want to get stitches, do we?" Broker said.

"Stitches?" Laurie said. Apparently that jogged a precrisis memory. "I don't want any stitches."

"Well, then you better let me look. If you don't, we might have to go to the hospital."

As Broker was examining Laurie's hands, Janey put a pan full of hot water down. Then she put down a sponge, more gauze pads, adhesive tape, and a brown plastic bottle of hydrogen peroxide.

"Hold her," he told Janey. Janey kneeled down on the floor and put her arms around her daughter. "It's all right; Mommy's here," she said. She held her tight as Broker cleaned away the coagulated blood and dirt and tried to ignore the girl's screams. These intensified as he trimmed away the abraded skin with the scissors, then peaked when he poured the peroxide. Her hands foamed up white with tiny red bubbles.

"Hold her, good; Laurie; you're doing fine."

After blotting the hands dry, he took the tape and gauze and started bandaging. Soon she looked like a taped prizefighter just about to put on the gloves.

There was more holding and soothing with Janey, and in a few minutes Laurie was over the worst of her tears. Then she stopped crying altogether and said, "Am I a broken home, now?"

"What?" Broker said.

"There's a boy in my first-grade class named David Knoll, and he's a broken home. Are you going to live here now?" Laurie said.

Broker cocked his head. "No, no I live someplace else."

"Mom yelled at Dad and said he had a girlfriend. I wondered if you were her boyfriend?"

"No, actually, honey . . ." Broker reached in his pocket and pulled out the five-pointed county deputy star.

Laurie's eyes widened, and she asked in a whisper, "Are you a wizard?"

"No, no; he's a police officer," Janey said.

"Are we in trouble?" Laurie asked, hunching her shoulders. "Is that why Dad left?"

"I'm here because I have a problem," Broker said quickly. "You see, one of the things police officers do is rescue cats that get in trees. Well, I took this cat out of a tree today, and now I have it at home. But it's not a grown-up's cat. It's a kid's cat because it doesn't want anything to do with me."

"What color is it?' Laurie asked.

"Ah, it's gray I think."

Janey moved closer to Broker, their shoulders grazed. The anger in her face transformed into something warmer. Broker turned his attention to Laurie, took one of the clean towels and wiped her nose.

"Let's take a ride. Go out to the river, collect a cat, and maybe order a pizza," Broker said.

"You sure?" Janey said, and the expression on her face was far more probing than her words.

"You two need a breather. So we take a drive, clear the air, and I bring you back," Broker said. He looked around the kitchen at the too-bright Italian patterns in the wall tile. The copper pots and pans hung on hooks like brass shouts.

"Okay. He could come back, and I want her more prepared for"—Janey closed her face around a harsh thought—"whatever."

Janey went upstairs, leaving Broker in the middle of the light, airy downstairs that had lots of houseplants in planters and throw rugs on the gleaming hardwood floors. The Mission Oak furniture and the floor lamps had been selected with an Art Deco flair. The color coordination of the sofa, chairs, and carpet was impeccable. And the kid who lived in all this perfection had been driven to dig up a dead cat.

Janey returned with a stuffed bunny that had blue vertical stripes, and which Broker recognized as Goodnight Bunny from the book of that name. Then he went out and backed the Crown Vic right up to the back door so they didn't show the whole neighborhood Laurie's bandaged hands.

As they were pulling out of the drive, a stout woman in her fifties stood at the right side of the driveway.

"Who's that?" Broker asked as they drove by.

"Mrs. Siple standing with her big ears right on the property line as usual," Laurie said, obviously imitating something her parents had said.

"What's her story?" Broker asked.

"She hates Dad," Laurie said from her mom's lap. "She called the cops on him." Then Laurie dropped down low in the seat and chanted under her breath, "Hag. Witch. Prune. Daddy's going to put her in a book."

Janey shook her head. "She made all these ridiculous charges, but it was really about the property line."

"It's a small town," Broker said. The biggest single complaint to police in the city of Stillwater concerned property line violations.

Broker made small talk with Laurie. They discussed his favorite movie when he was a kid, which was *Peter Pan.* And his favorite food, sloppy joes. What about pizza? Laurie asked. Broker said he'd never had pizza, maybe they could try some now? Laurie liked that idea.

They drove north on 95, past the cop car rally in A. J. Scott's driveway, to Milt's place. They put Ambush the cat in a plastic carry basket, drove back past all the cop cars again, picked up the pizza Janey had ordered on her cell, and returned to the house on the South Hill.

While Laurie got acquainted with Ambush, Broker took directions from Janey and went to call on Drew.

Drew Hensen kept a studio at the north end of town over a rambling antique warehouse. Broker parked and studied the layout. Access to the studio was up a flight of wooden stairs; there was a long porch overlooking Main Street.

Broker crossed the street, went up the steps, and peeked in through the screen door; there was a small kitchen, a futon in an alcove, and one big room full of shelves, books, a taboret, a computer, and a drawing table at which Drew sat, hunched over.

Broker knocked on the door. "Drew. It's Phil Broker."

Drew came to the door and cocked his head. "Hello, this is twice in two days. Come in."

"It's about your daughter," Broker said.

Drew, who'd worked around a lot of cops, was immediately alert. "What about my daughter? Is this *official*?"

"No, no; Janey called me up . . ."

Drew stared. Refocusing. "Janey called *you* up," he repeated.

Pipes rattled in the wall, and then a slender blonde came out of the bathroom. She was dressed for the weather in tennis-type skirt, a sleeveless top, and sandals. Her blue eyes were magnified behind granny glasses.

"This is Lisa Mertin; she writes children's books," Drew said.

Broker and Lisa said hello. Drew turned back to Broker and said, "Now what about Laurie?"

"She cut up her hands. She was upset and tried to dig up Samantha," Broker said.

Drew winced at Broker's language. "Christ. Janey and I had a fight, and there you go—the kid soaks it right up." He turned to Lisa and gestured at the drawing board. "Look, this isn't going to work out today."

"No problem. Take care of home," Lisa said. She picked up her purse, came over, and pecked Drew lightly on the cheek. "I hope everything's all right. I'll leave you two." Then she walked from the studio.

Lisa impressed Broker as being sharp and businesslike, with none of the bovine qualities that Janey had attributed to the other woman.

"Lisa is one of my authors; she was in town for a book signing today, so she dropped by to discuss this new project we're working on," Drew said.

"Whatever. Drew, look, I think you better go see Laurie," Broker said.

Drew blinked several times and then stared at the empty doorway where Lisa had just disappeared. "We're trying something new. You see, Rowling's success with *Harry Potter* tells us that kids don't want all this PC coddling. We should prepare them for the real world: villains, danger, and even death. I was thinking of calling it *Bullies, Bad Guys, and Things That Bite.*"

Drew's eyelids fluttered after he finished speaking. Broker's gut read on the man hadn't changed since they'd met years ago; Drew still kept a one-second delay between himself and reality.

Finally, Drew shook his head. "The dead fucking cat?"

"Her hands are torn up a little; she doesn't require stitches, but . . ."

"Torn up." Drew paused a beat and then said, "I suppose you've been talking to Janey."

"A little. I ran into her at the grocery store last week."

"Uh-huh. Well, you should know, she's been pretty twitchy lately. Since the terror attack in New York, she's obsessed with being vulnerable. She worries about poison in the food and water; smallpox being released at the State Fair . . . she watches C-SPAN coverage of the congressional hearings on terrorism.

"And then there's the personal side. I tell her Lisa is dropping by the studio, and she accuses me of having an affair. Christ—I work with six female kids writers in Minnesota. Two of them are fat, and two of them are lesbians," Drew said.

"What about the other two?" Broker said a little too fast.

Drew made an attempt to stare Broker down, decided against it, and looked away. "Okay, so I blew up in the kitchen. And Laurie saw it. Now this has happened. What's next?"

Broker looked around the studio, and his eyes settled on the big duffel bag full of clothes sitting on the futon in the alcove.

Obviously, Drew was leaving some stuff out. Like walking out of his house with a packed bag. Broker said in a level voice, "I think you should go see to your daughter."

"And I want to see her," Drew said. "I just don't want to see . . . who's with her right now."

Broker said nothing, but his arms were crossed tight over his chest in a body language knot. Drew pulled the studio door shut. Side by side, he and Broker went down the stairs two at a time. On the street Drew shook Broker's hand, mumbled a fast thanks, turned, and jogged toward the line of parked cars.

Broker got in his car and drove back to the house north of town where the dogs had found the body. The voyeur rush had subsided, and now only a few county cars remained. Mouse was talking to Joe Timmer, the chief investigator for the Ramsey County medical examiner. As Broker walked up, they were indulging in copper gallows humor about how the news media would handle the incident.

"Ten ways to tell if Rover has been eating corpses," Timmer quipped.

Mouse's cell phone rang. He raised the phone and said in a tired voice, "Whatta ya say?" He listened a moment, gripped the toothpick in his mouth between his clenched teeth, and snapped his eyes on Broker.

"Got him," he said after he'd hung up. "He's at Mystic Lake."

Chapter Thirty-two

Angel watched Carol Lennon write a check for a bottle of Clos du Bois merlot at the MGM liquor store across from the Cub-Target strip mall in Stillwater.

Carol taught art at Timberry Consolidated High School. She was forty-two years old, had divorced in her twenties and never remarried. She had large oval brown eyes and smooth unblemished skin. Her plain angular face was absolutely clean of wrinkles or crow's-feet. Her luxuriant black hair had not a trace of gray, and she wore it straight back in a long ponytail. If she'd been shorted some in the chest department, she made up for it with magnificent dancer's legs, which she usually concealed under long dresses. But this sultry early evening she wore flaring tan shorts, a green sports top, and leather sandals.

The earth colors went nicely with her slightly olive skin.

Carol had a particularly fluid way of walking, and, as she left the crowded store, several men turned to look. One of them smiled and cocked his head as if he had just relived a special memory of a small-breasted woman with a great ass and knockout legs.

I don't trust Miss Lennon around the young boys, the anonymous caller complained. She reminds me of that teacher who was in the news, who had the baby with the high school sophomore.

Angel had been observing Carol for two weeks.

She now knew that the anonymous caller had been absolutely right-on.

Carol had a penchant for a muscular young boy who—she reflected back on what A. J. Scott had said—could have modeled for Michelangelo. Angel suspected that Carol offered him marijuana, got him high, and then engaged in sex acts with him. He had showed up at her house last Friday evening, and, from what Angel had glimpsed peeking over the fence, the playing around was carried on under the guise of posing for life drawing.

This Friday night, Angel suspected the boy would appear again, and she was determined to get a closer look.

Angel watched Carol get in her car and drive across the street to the Cub parking lot. Just like last Friday night. She was doing her weekend grocery shopping.

Which gave Angel time to get in place. She went to her car and slipped into the hot traffic snaking back into the old residential district of Stillwater. Carol Lennon lived on a quiet street on the North Hill.

Angel parked downtown. This wasn't like Moros or A. J. Scott. Angel felt no need to talk. So no wig. Just her sunglasses, running duds, and the backpack with the pistol, silencer, medallion, and the latex gloves. The only new item she carried was a short crowbar to pry open one of Carol's rotting basement windows that she had scouted. She jogged down Main, then puffed her way up Myrtle Hill, turned right on Owens at Len's Grocery, and took Owens north out of town.

Waiting for the twilight to crochet in and thicken.

Then, as the shadows lengthened and blended, she angled back toward Carol's house.

Carol Lennon lived in a tidy rambler with a landscaped, and very fenced in, secluded yard. Angel glanced left and right. Lights were coming on all along the quiet leafy streets, the alleys filling with night. The garage was built under the front of the house. The backyard gate was unlatched.

Angel slipped down the alley, through the gate, into the backyard. Carol's house was more accessible than George Talbot's wide-open homestead full of family and pets. Carol didn't have a dog. She had two cats. And no security system. So Angel had no trouble getting in close.

Quickly, she ducked under a trellis thick with grapevines that ran along the side of the house. She knelt, forced the punky basement window with the crowbar, and went inside.

The cats were indifferent, especially the black shorthair who even rubbed up against Angel's shin as she came up the stairs. Carol's house smelled of sandalwood incense and the Alpine air-freshener machine that buzzed on top of the armoire in the living room.

For a few moments Angel thrilled at moving secretively through this strange house. *House invasion. Lying in wait.* The excitement tweaked her senses as she padded into the solarium addition that extended into the backyard, and stepped from the humdrum living quarters of a schoolteacher into a lush riot of plants, light, and color. Carol's own private Babylon.

Obviously, the girl had a green thumb.

Carol's jungle of houseplants thrived on the summer heat; the chlorophyll air was loamy with damp potting soil, peat moss, and vermiculite. Elephant-eared philodendrons were crowded in with palms, dwarf pines, a ming aralia, and scheffleras.

There was even an orchid under a grow light. Carol was especially fond of snake plants, several of which grew to seven feet tall. And she liked prickly pear cactus . . .

And fifteen-year-old boys.

So this was where Carol wiggled out of her old-maid skin. A low futon couch sprawled amid the plants. A big sand-filled urn held stumps of incense sticks. The broad coffee table was made from the varnished hatch of an old sailing ship. Under it Angel found an ornate wooden chest banded with inscribed metalwork and dense with colorful designs.

From India or Pakistan maybe. Teachers had the summer off; they were big on vacations.

Angel opened the chest and found where Carol kept her stash of weed.

And her porn flicks. And her paraphernalia. Her slippery stuff, her vibrator.

With one ear cocked for the sound of a car in the driveway, Angel couldn't resist taking a look. So she put a tape in the VCR. It wasn't just stuff with guys. There were pictures of farm animals.

Amazing.

A bechained dominatrix strapped on a plastic dildo and made this guy in a black leather mask bend over . . .

Angel carefully put it all back the way it was.

She'd studied the solarium and the dimensions of the backyard and made her plans. A small prefabricated toolshed sat in a corner of the yard; just big enough for a lawn mower, fertilizer spreader, a wheelbarrow, sacks of peat, composted manure, and a rack for garden tools. If you left the shed's door ajar, you could see everything that went on in the solarium.

And that's just what Angel did. There was just enough room for her to squeeze in and, leaving the door open a crack, she had a decent field of view. She'd walked off the distance. Twelve paces, about thirty-six feet across the thick grass to the solarium screen door.

She had not eaten or consumed liquids for the last three hours. If Angel was one thing, it was regular. No call of nature would interrupt her vigil.

So. Hide in the shed. Wait to see if the boy showed. Then, wait for him to leave.

If Carol deserved the full visit, Angel would give it to her.

Chapter Thirty-three

Broker observed that, for an old fart, Mouse still really enjoyed goosing the flasher and speeding in his Crown Vic. Drving over one hundred miles per hour, he zigzagged through the Friday afternoon traffic going west on Interstate 494 and then veering south on I-35W until he had to rein it in slightly—but only slightly—as he plowed right through red lights on County Road 42.

The Mystic Lake Casino complex was twenty minutes of freeway driving from the Twin Cities metro, which put it about an hour from Stillwater. Mouse made the drive in thirty-five minutes flat. The casino dominated the center of a mile-square parking lot like a twin-domed hit-me factory where people punched machines on three shifts, twenty-four hours a day.

"He's bound to get tricky," Broker said.

"We been over this. Not with both of us he won't," Mouse said.

Broker and Mouse showed their badges to two security cops in black blazers who were waiting under the front-door portico in valet parking. One stayed with the car; the other escorted them into the main circular gambling hall.

Broker wondered if maybe this was what the inside of Harry's mind looked like: a smoky cavern filled with the low roar of slot machines and the shuffling shadows of the players.

They were walking fast around the periphery of the sunken gaming parlor. "He's in the High-Stakes Slots alcove. And believe me, we got him so he isn't going anywhere," the security guard said.

"How? Are you restraining him?" Broker said.

"Nothing so crude. You'll see." The guard smiled.

"How'd you get onto him?" Broker said.

"You'll see," the guard said.

They stopped and were met by two more black blazers and two casino floor workers: a man and a woman in red shirts and black vests.

"We all set?" their escort said.

"All set," said the woman.

"Let's go," said the escort.

High-Stakes Slots was a sparsely attended alcove done up in Art Deco, with a marble floor, tall snake plants, and a stone sculpture. Harry Cantrell slouched on a stool at the end of an arcade of machines in front of a huge slot machine that looked, to Broker, like a twelve-foot-high Wurlitzer jukebox.

A blue light flashed atop the tall machine.

Three red 7s were pasted across the video drum. They were a close match to the three 7s tattooed on Harry's right arm.

With bloodshot eyes he watched them come down the aisle. "So what took you so long? I can barely keep my eyes open," he said. His Cherokee cheekbones were puffy with bloat, and his tan was turning yellow.

"Just take it easy," Broker said.

Harry's face hung on in his cigarette smoke by a bare shred of willpower.

The escort pointed to the three sevens. "He hit a jackpot on our one-hundred-dollar machine. When our people came to verify the win, they noticed the tattoo—and they mentioned it to Security. We held up his check until you got here."

"We appreciate it," Mouse said.

"No problem; funny thing is, your be-on-the-lookout mentioned he'd probably be drinking. We're a booze-free facility," the escort said.

Harry said, "I confess, I got a bottle of rum in my room. I been spiking my Pepsi. Main reason I came is this machine. I always wanted to nail this sucker."

"And you did," the floor worker said. She handed Harry his driver's license and a receipt, which he signed.

"How do you do it?" Mouse asked.

Harry handed back the receipt, got his carbon copy, accepted the check, and tapped his forehead with a shaky finger. "It's a mind-set. You gotta study Ulysses S. Grant. Main thing about Ulysses was he never let losing bum him out. He'd lose ten thousand men. Go to bed, get up the next morning, and attack. You gotta believe that, in the end, you're going to win."

"Okay, Ulysses" Broker said, "it's time to go."

"Led you on a merry chase, though," Harry said, getting slowly to his feet.

Mouse took Harry's left elbow, Broker took his right; the security men went two in front, one behind and led them through the crowd to the door.

Harry pulled up short. "Gotta stop at my room."

"No stops," Broker said.

"Yeah, we do," Harry said. "Papa Echo—I spell phonetically: *PE,* man. *Physical Evidence.* I've got physical evidence on the Saint."

Broker and Mouse looked at each other.

"Bullshit," Broker said.

"Exactly what have you got?" Mouse said.

"Hey, it's in my room. I ain't gonna talk in front of the whole fucking world." Harry pulled a key card envelope from his back pocket and handed it to the security escort.

"Okay," Mouse said. "But you try anything this time, I'll put my cuffs on you."

"Yeah, yeah." Harry raised a Lucky Strike toward his exhausted grin. He missed his mouth, hit his chin, and the cigarette fell to the floor.

"Worth a look," Mouse said.

"I'd cuff him, just to be safe," Broker said.

"What?" Harry said. "I ain't even drinking, I'm not resisting nothing. I'm ready to go take my medicine. Hell. I just heard that Viagra works better if you're booze-free."

"Okay," Broker said.

Harry remained quiet but stumbled occasionally as they negotiated the corridors and malls to the adjoining hotel lobby; then they got into the elevator and went up to his room."We'll just be a second," Mouse said to the security escort, who used Harry's card to open the door. The escort nodded. He and his colleagues took up positions in the hall.

Harry's room was totally undisturbed, just a leather travel bag on one of the beds.

"Open it," Harry said.

Broker unzipped the bag. He saw several new pair of socks and underwear still in their plastic wraps. A shaving kit. "What am I looking for?"

"Green plastic box on the bottom," Harry said.

Broker moved items aside and found the box sitting on a sheaf of paper. He took it out. An old piece of adhesive tape was stripped across the top with faded ballpoint notation: *Brass/.38/ GR/158 Speer Wadcutter/4.8 grain.*

"GR," Broker said.

"Gloria," Mouse said with no surprise in his tired voice.

Harry squinted at Broker. "'Fraid so. Remember, I told you how she made a grab for Lymon's pistol after Dolman was acquitted; how she was screaming, 'I'm gonna do the so and so'?"

"I didn't know that," Mouse said.

"Yeah, well, if your friendly local detective won't hand over his pistol, what's your next move?" Harry said.

"Go buy one of your own," Mouse said.

Harry shook his head. "She already did that; just before the trial we went down to the big Cabela's in Owatonna. The background checks should be on file. She picked the Colt .38-caliber Detective Special, said it fit her hand. Two-inch barrel, six shots; goes in the bedroom night table or the glove compartment; she didn't want to fuss with a safety. She just wanted to point and shoot if somebody came back on her from one of her cases."

"You were with her when she bought it?" Broker said.

"Uh-huh. And taught her to shoot the thing out at my place." Harry pointed at the green plastic box. "Reloaded ammo for her to practice with. So after I see the scene with her and Lymon in the courthouse, I go over to her place that night and, you know, tell her to give me her gun to hold for a while . . ."

Broker and Mouse watched Harry's next thought try to scale a spasm of shaking and collapse short of speech.

"Take your time," Broker said.

"Fuck you," Harry said as he started to move toward Broker.

"Easy," Mouse said.

Harry waved his hand to indicate the bottle of Don Q rum on the writing table in back of Broker. "You wanna hear this, I get to do it my way, and my way is with that bottle."

Broker wasn't about to hand Harry a glass bottle. He picked up the bottle, poured several inches of rum into a plastic cup, and handed it to Harry.

Harry slowly drank the contents of the cup, grinned, and quoted, "Man takes a drink. Drink takes a drink . . ." He laughed, a bad-sounding laugh that was shaking things loose inside and ended in a fit of coughing. When he recovered, he said, "I think this is where the drink takes the man." He opened his fingers and let the plastic cup fall soundlessly to the carpet. "Okay. So I go over there and ask for the gun, and she bats her eyes and says somebody stole it. Dolman was shot two days later."

"The medallion," Mouse said.

Broker heard the resigned, lockstep undertone in Mouse's voice. "What about the medallion?" he said.

Mouse spoke slowly, like plodding underwater. "Nobody ever said a word about this, and everybody knew. You been in Gloria's office. She had this picture of Tommy Horrigan on her bookcase. When they were preparing for trial, her receptionist brought in this St. Nicholas medallion and hung it on the picture frame. You know, St. Nicholas, protector of children, like that . . ."

Broker's forehead creased in a question. He looked at Harry.

Harry lowered his eyes to the carpet, toed the plastic cup he'd dropped, and said, "Yeah."

Broker turned back to Mouse, who said, "The next day after Dolman got whacked, the medallion was gone."

"What? Everybody knew?" Broker said.

"It's not like we really *knew*," Mouse said.

"Yeah, we did; I did," Harry said. Then his wavering eyes settled on Broker. "Some people get dealt a shitty hand, they learn to live with it, huh? I guess Gloria couldn't stand seeing Dolman walk out of that courtroom a free man."

Broker told himself he was alert, ready for any tricks Harry might pull. But the black glare of alcohol hate in Harry's eyes came lightning fast.

"I wouldn't rat her out for Dolman; *some people* might, but not me!" Harry shouted, making his move.

"Mouse," Broker warned. But Harry sidestepped and body-slammed into Mouse, yanking Mouse's baggy shirt aside with his left hand as his right hand swept in the opposite direction, cleanly lifting the .40-caliber pistol from Mouse's holster. This time, Broker didn't spin his wheels. Instantly, he had the .45 out from under his shirt, thumbing off the safety.

Like two dancers obedient to an inevitable choreography, Broker and Harry faced each other, the pistols coming up.

Harry snapped off the safety. Teeth clenched, he said, "Your little girl is going to be a fuckin' orphan."

Nothing happened.

"C'mon, let's go," Harry said.

Their beating hearts were six feet apart. Maybe three feet separated the pistol muzzles.

The veins on Harry's hands and wrist and forearm bulged as he squeezed the pistol grip. "You gonna learn—"

"Go on, tough guy, pull the trigger," Mouse taunted.

Harry sneered, "—there's worse things than dying, mother-fucker..."

"Yeah, like in-patient treatment at St. Joe's for alcoholism," Mouse said, reaching in his pocket and pulling out a fistful of bullets. "All those weepy fucking losers telling their lame life stories in those groups, and you're gonna have to sit there and listen, and they don't even let you smoke anymore."

Broker lowered his gun. "You're gonna love the Detox program. They wake you up with cattle prods, put you to sleep with showers of animal blood." He smiled as he said this, but—even empty—the sight of Mouse's gun in Harry's hand wasn't something to smile about.

Harry relaxed his grip on the pistol, looking from Broker

to Mouse and back again. "You two . . . ?" he said.

"What were you doing, Harry, provoking me into ending your misery?" Broker said.

"That sure puts a new spin on the term *suicide by cop.*" Mouse chuckled. "Think we'd go into a room with you with loaded guns, you fuckin' moron?"

Harry tipped his wrist back, aiming the pistol at the window, and pulled the trigger. The hammer fell on an empty chamber. He dropped out the empty magazine and let it fall to the carpet. Suddenly weak, he handed the .40-caliber to Mouse and settled to the floor and sat cross-legged. Broker also pulled the trigger to show that his weapon was empty. Then he shoved it back in the hideout holster and sat down across from Harry.

Mouse snatched the rum bottle off the desk, picked up the green plastic box from the bed, and lowered himself to the floor with some difficulty. "Fuckin' knees," he said.

They sat in a circle. Mouse passed the bottle to Broker, who took a ritual swig, grimaced, and offered it to Harry.

Harry slowly shook his head. "I'll pass. I been thinking of quitting."

Mouse put the green box on the carpet between them. Moving in slow motion, Harry removed one of the bright brass casings from the grid of cubbyholes filled with empty cartridges. He held the primer end up and said, "Every firing pin leaves a distinct impression on the primer, like a fingerprint. The one Gloria's Colt left was dramatic, obvious to the naked eye. See?"

They squinted at a fishhook impression dented into the primer.

Broker and Mouse had the same thought at the same time. Their eyes clicked together.

"Right," Harry said. "The six casings left next to Dolman's body. They were wiped clean of fingerprints, but they have the exact same firing pin signature. I could recognize it blindfolded.

Get them from BCA evidence and look for yourself." Harry paused a beat. "There's something else. Remember I told you somebody had been snooping in my computer files?"

"Yeah, but I thought . . ." Broker said.

"I was just drunk, huh," Harry said. "Well, I did some snooping of my own and I found a stack of printouts in Gloria's desk. She went into my trash bin and retrieved these anonymous tip reports I checked out and tossed. You should look at them. Victor Moros was right on top of the pile."

"We'll check them out." Grimacing, Mouse pushed himself to his feet and said, "We got work to do."

"Yeah, like get a judge off a golf course to write a warrant," Harry said.

Broker took Harry's arm to help him up. Harry shook off the hand and said, "Watch it. I still might punch your ticket."

"Yeah, well, maybe next time you'll be sober and more in touch with it," Broker said.

Chapter Thirty-four

Angel was in position for twenty minutes when she heard Carol's Mazda pull in the front drive. The garage door rail rattled up; the engine noise muffled as the car entered the garage. Then the door came down.

Carol was home.

Angel squirmed around to get more comfortable, sitting on a damp sack of peat moss. Lights came on in the house; the moving pattern of light and shadow marked Carol's movement through her rooms. A door opened. Carol, barefoot, padded out onto the terra-cotta tiles.

Carol's hand dropped to her waist, and she shed her shorts with a flick of her wrist and a shimmy. She raised one leg, and let her underpants slide down the other leg and caught them expertly on her toe, kicked them up, and caught them in one hand in a gesture that was almost endearing. She crossed her arms in front of her chest, and elbows up, she peeled off the sports top.

Angel squirmed deeper on her peat moss. *Steady. Be steady.*

Carol paused for a moment to tap the CD player, then tugged

the binder from her ponytail. As the leaden sounds of Chris Rea's "Road to Hell" jumped from the speakers, she let her hair swing free. Then she walked a circuit of her space, trailing her hands on the leaves of her plants.

Coming down from the day. TGIF.

Carol slipped back into the house and returned wearing a brief orange silk kimono that hung loose, untied, sleeves to midforearm, hem at mid-thigh. A green dragon coiled on the back. She carried a bottle of wine and two long-stemmed glasses.

Expecting company.

So Angel watched Carol sit on her futon sofa and work the cork from the bottle, set the corkscrew aside, pour a glass of wine, and recork the merlot. Then Carol went into her banded chest and removed the baggie of grass and cigarette papers and rolled a joint. A match flared, and Carol inclined back on her couch.

This was the worst part. The waiting. During the waiting the doubts crowded around her in the dark. The scent of the dope reminded her of A. J. Scott. She made a mental note to watch the news tonight, to see if he'd turned up yet.

Then she tried to concentrate on the here and now, which only prompted her to speculate that probably there were spiders in here along with the mosquitoes. She pictured a fat gray leopard spider as big as a mouse.

She shivered.

Get thee behind me. Concentrate on Carol.

She's on the list.

But then the wait ended abruptly when Angel heard the gate open. Carol's student entered by the same route as had Angel, coming down the dark alley. Sneaking in.

Carol slithered up from the couch and made a halfhearted gesture at tying the robe. She met the boy at the door to the solarium, and they conversed in low tones that Angel couldn't hear clearly.

But their body language was easy to decipher, awkward and needy as two dumb animals edging toward the trough.

Snatches of conversation drifted on the soupy air.

"Can I get you some wine?" Carol.

"How about a hit on that joint?" Him.

Carol wagged a finger. "The wine's bad enough."

The boy looked around, and his eyes stopped on a direct line with the ajar door to the shed. "Yeah, right," he said.

And Angel held her breath. *He's staring right at me.* But then she thought, *He can't see me*—not because she was invisible but because she was out in the dark yard and he was standing inside, in the light. All he probably saw was his own reflection on the curved transparent panels of the solarium.

He had a jock's blond buzz cut, wore baggy over-the-knee shorts and a T-shirt artfully torn to emphasize his lifter's delts, lats, and triceps. A barbed-wire tattoo circled the biceps on his left arm. He wore an ear stud in his left ear.

Maybe he swaggered at the gym. Inside Carol's house he moved uncertainly and had to be reassured. So she guided him from the solarium into the house proper.

When they reemerged, he'd been outfitted with a robe identical to Carol's, which he wore with the shuffling self-consciousness of a seven-year-old playing a wise man in a church Christmas pageant.

Carol poured a glass of wine, which he held awkwardly: clearly, he'd prefer a beer or a can of Mountain Dew.

He sipped the wine as Carol assembled her gear. Drawing pad, a short stepladder. A tackle box. She placed the stepladder among the philodendrons and dwarf pines. Teacherlike, she took the wineglass from his hand and led him to the ladder.

Carol had him sit and arranged him, positioning a knee here, a shoulder there. The boy quivered at her every touch. A loop of

Carol's hair fell over his throat; the silk robe grazed his skin. She eased the robe from his shoulders and let it fall around his belly so the tight curls of blond pubic hair peeked in the hard wedge of his lap.

When Carol returned to her couch and picked up her charcoal, her own robe had worked open, revealing a glimpse of inner thigh, a shadow of stomach muscles. Carol obviously stayed in shape. But not a gym type.

Yoga maybe.

Then, for half an hour, Carol sketched, occasionally asking if the boy needed a break to stretch. Angel was the one who needed the break, for crying out loud—her hamstrings were starting to cramp from squatting in the shed.

By the time Carol finished up her sketch, her robe concealed little, and slowly the boy's robe was sliding deeper down around his hips. His chest now glistened with sweat. More and more, he appeared to be holding his breath.

Waiting for it.

Carol moved forward with a towel and gently wiped the sweat from his chest and shoulders and upper arms. When she leaned over him, Angel imagined her tidy breasts grazing, touching.

In a minimal gesture of intimacy, the boy reached out awkwardly, to caress her hair, but she stiffly steered the hand away. Insisting on having all the control here. In a deliberate movement, she straightened the sweat towel and folded it and made a pad for her knees. Then she kneeled before him, her back to Angel, who saw the robe start to slip down her shoulders, down her back. Her skin was pale, startlingly so; she must avoid the sun. SPF 40.

Carol was now naked from the waist up. As her head dipped forward, Angel wasn't immune to the lust of the eye. She opened the door wider and squinted, straining to see the boy's expression.

Too far for fine detail. She should have binoculars. Opera

glasses maybe. His eyes must be arias as he grabbed Carol's head in both hands for balance.

Abruptly, Carol raised up and removed his hands.

"Don't touch," she said distinctly. The words clinked in the night like two dropped coins.

Obediently, the boy's hands groped at his side, treading air, as Carol resumed the ritual.

And it went on forever, and Angel's thighs were burning, and she had to stretch out her left leg and flex her foot, which was full of sawdust and stinging needles. C'mon, c'mon, she exhorted her foot.

And you, she exhorted the boy, you c'mon.

When he finally did, it was shocking. Foreshadowing, because as Carol lurched her whole body forward to accept it, she flung out her arms straight to either side. Angel couldn't resist opening the door wider to get a better look. She had seen this move before, in a movie about Anne Boleyn, who, kneeling before the headsman, adopted this absurd posture when she bent forward to lay her throat upon the block.

Angel's eyes strained, involved in the mindless animal glee smeared all over the boy's face.

When it was over, the boy dressed quickly, clumsily, uncertain if he should express some affection, a hug, a good-bye kiss. Expertly, Carol fended him off. She turned away as if a kiss would be distasteful. Flushed and vaguely smiling, with his eyes still pinwheeling, the boy was steered past Angel's hiding place, back toward the gate, and ushered out.

Carol returned to the solarium, trailing her fingers on the leaves, until she settled back on the couch, poked around in the incense urn until she found the roach.

Angel. Up and moving now. Soundless. Invisible. Crossing the grass, coming out of the inky night.

Carol stretched out, puffed, and raised her eyes toward her

glassy ceiling. Angel was close enough to hear the pleasurable hiss of Carol's inhalation, drawing sharply on the dope: *Owwwshhhhh.*

Angel coming in closer. *Look at the bitch, lying there, eyes rolled back dreamy like a boa constrictor, digesting.*

Angel thrust open the screen door and stalked into the solarium, a little awkward, the sleep needles not all the way out of her left foot. Her right hand hung close to her side, the green plastic silencer held back, out of sight behind her thigh.

When Carol opened her eyes, she saw Angel coming straight toward her, knocking aside the leaves of the ming aralia, kicking over the stepladder. Still frozen in shock, she did not comprehend; Angel's wraithlike expression, the extended left hand, the accusing finger.

"What the . . . ?" Carol started to rise. She looked reflexively across the coffee table, toward the cordless phone.

"I saw you with that underage boy," Angel said. "And you a teacher. What do you suppose his mother will say?" Angel picked the words carefully for effect. They worked; Carol was momentarily stayed, subdued.

"Who are you?" she said, her voice looking for traction between fight and flight. Carol swallowed, tried her voice. It cracked. She tried again, found it this time, and said, "What's that in your hand?"

"Take it," Angel said. She tossed the silver chain and the medallion into Carol's lap.

"What the fuck?" Carol groped at the medallion.

"Wipe your chin," Angel said, disgusted.

Carol winced, ran the sleeve of her robe across her jaw. Down deep on a preconscious level, her brain just now sensed how total and black Angel's shadow was, that it was a pit into which she was meant to disappear. The first hard tremble hit her. "Why are you . . . wearing . . . gloves?"

"Shut up and listen. I won't tell anybody what you've done if you pray with me. Now first, kiss the medal."

"You're nuts." Carol. Stronger now.

"Do it." Angel. Stronger.

"And then what? You'll leave me alone?" Carol slowly raised the trinket to her shuddering lips.

Angel's right hand came up and pointed the silenced pistol. "Now put it in your mouth."

Carol's voice cracked again. "Please, can we work this out a little?"

"IN YOUR MOUTH!"

Angel moved forward and shoved the silencer against Carol's forehead. With the gloved fingers of her left hand, she roughly jammed the medal into Carol's mouth. Carol gagged, and through the latex Angel felt the warm interior: the gums, the corrugated pinkness on top against her knuckle, the—

Quickly, Angel withdrew her hand. Just as quickly Carol spit the medal out onto the floor.

"I should make you wash out your mouth with soap, that's what I should do," Angel said.

Instead she aimed right between Carol Lennon's eyes.

Seeing the pistol bore in, Carol went limp as if overcome by shock and resignation. In that instant, Angel relaxed, took a breath . . .

But Carol uncoiled like a spring, kicking wildly at the gun hand, and screamed, "HELP, SOMEBODY, HELP!"

No one had fought back before.

Angel froze for an instant. In that pause, Carol windmilled both fists, knocking the gun hand askew.

Angel pulled the gun back in line with Carol's face—feral now, teeth bared, a grimace wrinkling her brow and cheeks like war paint—and jerked the trigger.

CRACK-CRACK-CRACK!

The angry face spun away as a loud pain punctured Angel's ears. The three shots sounded like bombs going off. Then Angel got it. *Silencer gone, ripped off in the struggle.*

Carol was down, pitched forward on all fours. She struggled for one wobbly beat to push up, then collapsed. Angel knelt, picked up the medallion, and stuffed it in the wreckage of Carol face. Then Angel froze.

Very close, just on the other side of the fence, a man shouted, "What the hell . . . ?" Then, "Carol, *Carol; you all right?*" He had an adrenaline foghorn for a voice.

Not supposed to happen. Not.

Scrambling now, freeing the dangling silencer from the gun barrel. *Hold on. Don't drop it. Christ, the spent cartridges?* But there was no time. She dashed for the gate.

Footsteps. Rapid, scuffing in the alley, also headed for the gate.

Angel shrank back against the fence as a short thick man thrust open the gate and stepped into the illumination of the yard light. He wore shorts and a green tank top that rode up over his flab. At his waist, next to the tiny cell phone, Angel saw red dots on a ring of flab. Heat rash. And she realized that if she could see his rash, he could see her face.

She raised her left elbow in front of her head to hide her face and came around the gate swinging the clubbed pistol. Her left hand held the green plastic bottle. The half-blind swing landed with panic strength on the man's forehead. He pitched to his knees, waving his arms.

Angel felt his heat and sweat against her bare legs as she shoved past him. But she was out, in the alley, running fast. By the time she turned onto the street, she could hear him screaming, "Nine-one-one? Yes, goddammit, this is life and death."

Oh, shit. The cell phone.

For the first time, it occurred to her that she could be caught.

Chapter Thirty-five

Now Mouse drove at a slow, almost solemn tempo. After dropping Harry off at St. Joseph's Hospital in St. Paul, he and Broker settled into their own thoughts. Broker had contracted a case of the Harry-Gloria blues, the main symptom being a heavy reluctance to follow through on the suspicions that Gloria Russell had convicted Ronald Dolman with a pistol when she couldn't get him in court; and that Harry had erred hugely on the side of omission. He stared at the green box of shell casings sitting on the pile of printouts in the foot well of Mouse's car. He had no interest in confronting Gloria Russell. Other people would have to do that.

He was done with this.

As if clairvoyant, Mouse picked up the theme. "I ain't going to pick her up for questioning. Uh-uh. Not me. John's back tonight. He can make that call. I mean, what have we really got? Some shell casings. Gloria's going to say, sure, they're from my gun—but my gun was stolen just before Dolman was whacked."

"And you still have two different things going on—Moros

wasn't killed with a thirty-eight; he was a twenty-two," Broker said.

"I hate this thing," Mouse said.

"Yeah, but you gotta get a warrant. You gotta at least look," Broker said.

"Yeah, I know." Mouse finally roused himself, pulled out his cell, and punched numbers.

"Where are you?" he asked when Benish answered the phone. "You're at home firing up the grill. Listen, Harry gave us some pretty compelling stuff on Gloria being the Saint. Yeah, I shit you not. Meet me at the shop. We're gonna need a warrant for her home, her car, her office, and anyplace else she might hide a thirty-eight-caliber Colt Detective Special. Get Lymon in gear and have him run a background check on Gloria purchasing the gun last summer. And put somebody on her place, try to get a line on her movements. We're going to want to talk to her." He paused. "Harry? He went . . . quietly. Yeah, give him a couple of days to come down; then we'll go out and take a statement."

They were coming through Lake Elmo, going northeast on Highway 5. Mouse's car radio grumbled occasionally, the volume turned down.

Broker reached down and pulled up the sheaf of printouts he'd taken from Harry's bag. He started to flip through them, then sat up straight and said, "Holy shit, Mouse."

"What?"

"This. Holy fuckin' shit! Lookit the top sheet—it's the complaint against Moros."

"Yeah?"

"And we got a real problem here because the second sheet is about someone taking pictures of a little girl putting on a bathing suit," Broker said.

"So?"

"A. J. Scott."

It took Mouse a second. "*Our* A. J. Scott from this morning?"

"Address checks," Broker said, tapping the sheet of paper.

"Jesus Fucking Christ!" Mouse pulled onto the shoulder and put the car in neutral. "We made some assumptions . . ."

Broker nodded. "Heart medication in his bathroom cabinet doesn't have to equal heart attack in his yard."

"There was no medallion," Mouse said.

"There was no mouth to find it in."

"Jesus, you're right. The dogs could have taken it," Mouse said. "And even if somebody shot Scott, how the fuck could you tell—"

"You better call Joe Timmer over at the ME and tell him to start looking for bullet holes in all that hamburger," Broker said.

"Two shootings in Stillwater in one week?" Mouse said, steering back on the road. "Give me a fucking break."

Five minutes later, they were swinging around the LEC, heading for the underground ramp, when the dispatcher's voice surged up out of the routine static: "*Anyone in the vicinity of Beech Street, North Hill Stillwater. We have a possible fatal shooting and an armed suspect fleeing on foot. Address is six thirty-eight Beech.*"

Mouse hit the brakes and locked eyes with Broker.

"Get a name," Broker said.

Immediately, Mouse snatched his radio handset and keyed it: "*One hundred, this is one oh six. Do you have a name on the victim?*"

"*Wait. Two cars talking. One oh six, go ahead.*"

"*This is one oh six. Do you have a name on the victim?*"

"*Ah, wait. Everybody else shut up on the net. Two oh seven, come in.*"

"*Two oh seven.*"

"*Do you have an ID on the victim?*"

"*Ah, roger that. Carol Lennon. Schoolteacher, Timberry High.*"

"Let's get to that shooting," Broker said, holding up the print-outs. "She's the fourth sheet."

When all hell breaks loose, women make the best dispatchers.

"Ten thirty-three, emergency traffic only. All units, shots fired in Stillwater, victim down . . ."

It had something to do with multitasking.

"Suspect fled west down Maple on foot from six thirty-eight Beech Street . . . suspect described as white female in dark running shorts and dark tank top." The dispatcher's voice strove for calm. *"Use caution; suspect's got a gun."*

It was ninety-nine dead-still degrees out, the humidity 82 percent. The surge of radio ten codes hot-wired the moisture in the air. A dozen cops leaned forward, stepped on the gas, and fired up their adrenaline jets. A computer program immediately set in motion the units nearest to the address. At the Washington County Comm Center, Dispatch—call sign one hundred—and the first cop on the scene worked on basic emergency first aid.

"Clear the airway, see if she's breathing. EMS en route."

"She ain't breathing, and there's something stuck in her mouth . . ."

Broker's fist slammed down on the dashboard. "Aw, shit!"

"Some kind of locket on a chain."

Mouse loosened the safety strap on his holster and stepped on the gas. Lights and sirens. Broker put out his hand to steady himself on the dashboard as Mouse plunged into the summer traffic.

Broker's heart kept pace with the runaway cop radio rap.

"One hundred, two twelve is twenty-five on scene. Confirm ten seventy-two: Victim is DOA. Stop EMS. We want to keep the scene as clean as possible."

"Ten-four, all units copy—victim is dead. Use caution. Two twelve, one hundred. What about the neighbor?"

"He's got a lump on the head, but he's ambulatory; after ques-
tioning we'll run him to Lakeview emergency.

"Ten-four."

Mouse pushed the Crown Vic through a grid of residential
blocks, toward the sound of sirens. He held his radio handset in
his left hand. His right hand tapped on the computer keyboard.

"One hundred, one oh six, en route."

"Ten-four."

"Two twelve. One hundred. What's your status?"

"We got another one like the priest."

"Calm down out there."

Now they could hear the wolf pack sirens starting to gather in
on the neighborhood. Mouse shook his head, tapped on his computer keys. "The only thing missing is a full moon," he said.

Broker noticed the display on Mouse's MDT screen flicker,
bringing up a screen full of different color type. White lines of
type blipped to blue lines. "What's going on?"

"This is the duty roster. White is off duty; blue is on duty. Guys
are piling on." Mouse tapped one of the blue lines. "See, seven
niner just logged in blue. That's Lymon. He's in ahead of us."

Cross streets named after trees: Linden, Laurel, Maple. Broker
turned onto Beech. An ambulance from Lakeview. Six squads:
two from Stillwater, two county, Oak Park Heights, and Bayport.
Cops with flashlights working the lawn, the fence line. Light and
movement and sound coming in from the adjoining streets, where
more cops were cordoning the neighborhood. Stopping cars.
Asking questions.

A Stillwater cop was standing on the front lawn of the address.
He waved at Broker and Mouse. "In the back. In the back." They
parked and ran to the back of the house.

Badge number two twelve, the Stillwater sergeant who was
commanding the scene, leaned over a street map unfolded on

the hood of a squad. A county deputy held a flashlight on the map.

The sergeant nodded to Mouse and Broker as they walked up. "You hear? We got another one," he said. "And this time it's out in plain view. Still in her mouth." Then he opened the gate and pointed toward a well-lit solarium porch.

Carol Lennon lay sprawled on her back in front of a futon couch, starkly naked in the askew orange kimono.

The sergeant went on, "The neighbor found her facedown, he was talking to nine-one-one, he turned her over to try CPR."

Her eyes were stuck open, exaggerated by blood from the wound in her face that had pooled in the eye sockets. The elbow and the wrist of one arm were twisted at an unnatural angle of stress. Shards of shattered wineglass sparkled on the floor.

Broker could see a long swirl of dark hair soaking in a wide pool of blood on the terra-cotta tiles. A tall snake plant was tipped over, the hairy roots exposed, the long green blades bordered with blood.

The sergeant pointed to the stocky man in shorts and a lime tank top who was holding a gauze pad to his forehead. "He's the next-door neighbor. Charlie Ash. He was out watering his lawn and heard shots and breaking glass. So he came to investigate and the shooter whacked him in the head when he came through the gate."

The guy nodded. "I went to check Carol, like the nine-one-one operator told me, and I turned her over to, you know, clear the airway, and she had this thing in her mouth."

"We heard," Mouse said.

"Where do you want us?" Broker asked.

The sergeant drew a semicircle on the map with his finger encompassing the area west of their present location. "We're clamping off everything to the west and stopping anyone moving on the streets or driving out of the cordon." He turned to the neighbor. "You're sure this was a female?"

The guy nodded wearily. "Even with blood in my eye, I noticed she was pretty built from behind. Definitely a female."

"So we're looking for a female, dark shorts, dark sports top," the sergeant said.

A county deputy approached with a big black-and-tan shepherd on a leash.

"Good, we can get a track started," the sergeant said. The he stuck his head in the squad and keyed his radio. "*One hundred, two twelve. Status on the state police helicopter?*"

"*Trooper nine is airborne. ETA fifteen minutes.*"

"*Ten-four.*"

A squall of voices competed in the static.

"*All units not directly involved in perimeter go to alternate channel . . .*"

Then out of a jitter of static: "*One hundred, seven niner. Woman running north on McKusick, along the lake.*" The voice sounded agitated, as if it was spinning in a washing machine.

The radio channel went dead silent.

Mouse said, "Lymon."

Broker nodded, recognizing the shaken voice.

"*Leaving the car. Won't stop. Told her to halt. Just turned off the path and ducked into trees north end of the lake. Will pursue on foot.*"

"Take the mobile, take the mobile," Mouse said, gritting his teeth.

"What?" Broker asked.

Mouse hunched over the map, tapped his finger, and said, "I know exactly where he's at. The lake ends here, and then there's this swamp. He's chasing her down this wooded finger that runs in between." Mouse bit his lip. "It gets real fucked in there, broken ground, this woods on the other side of the lake before you get to this single windy street."

Broker saw the problem. Lymon was chasing someone into a

marshy woods in the dark. And it sounded like he didn't take his mobile radio. Broker also sensed that most of the squads converging on the area, which had started to set up a perimeter, now were bolting toward the lake.

The radio squawked a confirmation: *"Gimme a cross street on McKusick . . ."*

"Which end of the Lake . . . ?"

The cops were talking at once, stepping on their transmissions. A cluster was taking shape in the night.

The sergeant reached in his car and grabbed his handset. *"Units on perimeter, it's tricky in there, no through streets; you have to swing around east end of lake. Copy?*

"Ten-four."

"I gotta stay here, wait for John," Mouse said.

The sergeant nodded, barked to the Stillwater cop blocking the gate. "Terry, go in around the other side of the lake and see if you can get ahead of this goddamn footrace."

The cop nodded and started toward his car.

"You going or staying?" Mouse said to Broker.

Broker pointed to the Stillwater cop, followed him, and piled in his car. Lights, no siren, they raced around the lake. Broker saw in detail the difficult terrain Mouse had warned about. The solitary curving road they drove down had few streetlights. And the houses dissolved into darkness. The street ended in a cul-de-sac.

"I don't like this," said Terry, the Stillwater cop. "Only a couple of streets on this side, and they wind all over."

"Lymon's in there, no radio," Broker said, squinting into the darkness. "Person he's chasing could be armed and maybe just killed somebody."

They got out of the car and walked between the houses. Immediately the ground slanted downhill in a jumble of treacherous footing.

"I don't know," Terry said, slapping his long-handled flashlight against his palm. To turn it on was to give away their position. So he strained to see in the dark. Then he cupped his hands to his ears, listening.

Broker figured there were twenty cops on the scene now, and like him, they were bracing for a melee of shooting in the dark. He and Terry edged to the extreme limit of the yard.

"Now what?" Terry said.

"We wait and listen, maybe—" Broker was cut off by a yell about one hundred yards ahead of them.

"Halt. Police. Halt. Police."

A flashlight stabbed the darkness. Immediately, Broker and Terry started into the broken ground, feeling their way toward the commotion.

"No, no." A gasping hysterical female voice.

"They got her," Terry said; then he switched on his flashlight and crashed forward into the dark. Broker followed at a much more cautious pace.

The ground was hilly, eroded, and thick with impassable brush. Bits of tense conversation drifted in the night.

"On the ground, facedown."

"No!" Gasping. "He's chasing me. Him back there."

Then Broker heard Lymon yell, "You got her?"

"We got her, but we ain't got a gun. Must have ditched it."

A blond-haired woman dressed in running gear thrashed in the flashlight beams as she was being handcuffed. "Ow, shit, what are you doing?" she screamed. "If I have *scars* . . ."

"Calm down."

"Not me, you moron. This *black guy* just chased me through *the fucking woods*. Call the fucking cops!"

The cops exchanged looks by flashlight.

Someone said, "Uh-oh."

Chapter Thirty-six

She heard the sirens, the neighborhood dogs barking in their yards, and realized the cops could have dogs too. Angel ran in a blind panic for half a block, then ducked, panting, behind a parked car to think.

Get yourself straightened out. Get a plan . . .

First she'd have to get off the streets and get under cover. The cops would own the streets.

A swarm of sirens was building in the night. Most of them up ahead, in the direction she'd been running. Instinctively she got up and moved in the opposite direction, away from the sirens. Off the street now, she picked her way through the dark yards . . . weaving around hedges and fences.

She reached the end of the block and burst into the open to cross the intersection. And nearly collided with some damn kid on a skateboard doing solo routines. The boy immediately grabbed his board and stepped back.

But he'd glimpsed her. The light was not good enough to see her face, but Angel realized she was running with a pistol in one hand and her makeshift silencer in the other.

She ducked back into the yards, praying she didn't encounter dogs. Twice she had to backtrack when she ran into six-foot fences.

Angel darted across a street and ran toward a trio of houses with dark windows. Three blocks to the west, a circular wind of red flashers lashed at the motionless trees and rooftops. But here it was still dark.

They were concentrating on the direction in which she'd initially run.

But that damn skateboard kid . . .

Okay, right now, hide; catch your breath. She scrambled up a limestone retaining wall into a yard and crouched behind a dwarf lilac hedge. She wiggled the backpack from her shoulders and stuffed the silencer and her latex gloves into it. Put it back on. Her bare knees tickled in the night dew collecting in the grass. She was dizzy. More than fear. The scent of foliage and humid earth made her head swim.

She could hear snatches of staccato disembodied traffic from the cop radios. And still the sirens were coming. They were cordoning the streets, but still to the west.

Then a cop car roared past her in a scream of sirens and whooping red lights and pulled a screeching U-turn almost right in front of her.

Angel's heart started to count down to implosion in her chest. The cop car stopped. A man jumped out and ran into the shadows about a hundred yards from her. The cop in the car turned on a searchlight. The long beam swung across the facades of the dark houses; it played across the porch behind her.

Her hand closed over the pistol. *I won't be taken alive.*

The idea of putting the filthy barrel in her mouth repelled her. Better to put it to the temple.

Won't be taken.

Won't.

Chapter Thirty-seven

Angel may not have been invisible anymore, but she was the next best thing: absolutely motionless. Several minutes passed, and the cop car, with its probing light, moved away. She was instantly up, running in a low crouch through the shadows. Then another light barred her path.

She ducked down and made herself small under a wide juniper as the police car searchlight swung back and forth like a white lantern down the street.

She watched the curve of her ankle pulse red as flashers atop police squad cars passed down the next block. Everywhere, she heard the static squawk of the radios.

Time to move.

"Lady, the guy chasing you *is a cop.*"

Broker and Terry could see them now: two officers, one in Stillwater blue, the other in county tans. They were pulling the handcuffed woman to her feet. She was lean, sun browned, and pissed off in the weaving flashlight beams. She wore black shorts and a green halter that passed for gray in the dark. Her blond hair was pulled back in a ponytail. Her trophy legs were cut and bleeding from thrashing through the brush.

Lymon Greene walked in circles, hands on hips, chest heaving, trying to catch his breath. His left knee was banged up, and a string of blood twisted down his shin.

"Bag . . . her . . . hands," Lymon said, gulping for air.

"Right," one of the arresting cops said. Then he jogged toward the street.

"So where'd you throw the gun?" the other cop asked her.

"The gun?" Her eyes widened, flashing white. "Oh you poor, dim fucking moron," she snarled. "My husband is a *lawyer*."

Broker approached Lymon and put a hand on his shoulder. Lymon's T-shirt was drenched with sweat. But he was grinning. "Man, jogging around the neighborhood doesn't even start to get you ready for this kind of steeplechase."

Broker studied him, glad that this chase had ended without bullets finding flesh. "Did Benish get ahold of you?" Broker said.

Lymon shook his head. "No. I was on my way to the grocery store and heard the radio call and came running."

"You don't know about Harry?" Broker said.

Lymon shook his head, blinking; distracted, still into the drama of the chase, he watched the two cops who'd cuffed the protesting woman walk her toward the street. Then his grin froze when an urgent voice came over the mobile radio mike clipped to a Stillwater cop's epaulet.

"All units, we have a problem. She's going east, toward the river . . ."

"Say again."

"We got a boy on a skateboard who saw a woman with a gun her hand running east through Everett and Maple."

"One hundred. All units copy?"

Aw, shit. They piled into cars and converged on the North Hill. Immediately, it all felt wrong to Broker: the cops were road-bound; the suspect was working through the yards in the dark.

"Lemme out," he yelled. "We gotta comb through the back-yards." He jumped from the rolling cruiser and jogged into the shadows.

Angel held her breath as the cop car shone its light into the yards on either side. The officer stopped two blocks away, got out of his car, took a handheld flashlight, and shone it into the overgrown ravine that abutted the street. Then his radio squawked. He turned off the light, got back in the car, and drove away.

Shaking, she took a fast inventory. Okay. They'd talked to the skateboard kid, figured out she'd doubled back, and now they would start cordoning these streets.

But the cop had given Angel an idea.

She was a Stillwater girl. It was a hill town, and in between the hills lay wooded ravines. She struggled to get her bearings and realized she was two blocks from a ravine that had a storm sewer running down its length. If she could slip into the intake grate at the bottom of the ravine, she could scurry underground and wiggle out on the bluff overlooking Battle Hollow. She'd come out close to her car, parked downtown.

She rose to a crouch and started maneuvering slow and low from shadow to shadow, feeling her way through the dark yards. But she could see people coming out on the street into patches of light, looking toward the red lights, the activity.

She hunkered along a hedge. There was a driveway partially screened by more lilacs. Then the open space. She looked behind her. A garage was attached to the house. No car in the drive.

Maybe no one was home.

A fence with grapevines ran from the garage to the edge of the ravine. If she could get into the backyard, she could move on the other side of the fence, behind the grapes. No yard lights back there, pitch-black.

She'd have to chance it. She duck-walked up the drive and crouched next to the doorway. Out of sight, hidden. A nice feeling but for how long? Too long. Too long. *You have to move.*

But it was comforting here in the dark.

She placed her hand against the garage side door. *Please be open.*

She twisted the knob and the door opened. The garage was empty, no car. She pushed the door open and rushed through, tripping on empty cardboard boxes, squinting in the dark. Found the back door, came out on a deck. The rolling backyard was hemmed in with lilacs, grapevines, and tall arborvitae. The obligatory pile of kid's plastic junk.

Even better, the flower bed on the other side of the fence was thick with grapevines and eight-foot sunflowers that screened her from the street.

And the light was almost gone. Really getting dark now. She eased in along the lilac hedge and began to cross the yard. That's when the dog in the wire pen in the next yard started going crazy.

On reflex, Broker moved in a crouch and pulled out the .45 as he tried to adjust his night vision. His shoes slid on the damp grass under his feet; mosquitoes buzzed in close, blowing little pincushion kisses.

Through breaks in the foliage and bushes he caught glimpses of police cars in the distance, people starting to congregate under streetlights.

This was bad. No radio. No coordination. Going mobile in the dark with guns was always bad. He'd operated at night in wartime, before night-vision goggles. Murphy's Law. Accident waiting to happen. He kept jogging, weaving around shrubs, avoiding fences; she'd be avoiding them too, not hiding, moving fast to get out of the area. He was sure of that.

She?

Was Gloria out there ahead of him running on those strong legs, with a gun in her hand?

He vaulted a low rail fence and heard a dog start to bark in a yard up ahead. Then he heard the animal go frantic, banging its body against kennel mesh. Broker sprinted through some thick shrubs toward the sound. He came out in a broad yard and . . .

The shadow darted, low from behind a tall lilac hedge.

"Halt, halt, halt." Broker yelled as he ran, bringing up the .45. He let go of the reins and let his senses drive, all kinetics now, all reflex . . .

The shadow ducked low, twisted, and was illuminated by the twinkle-crack of a muzzle flash. Broker felt a tiny bee buzz past his head.

Shit. She was firing at him. Still moving, he bent forward from the waist to make a smaller target, gripped the pistol in both hands, extended his arms, aimed low at her legs and pulled the trigger.

It was like squeezing a steel rock.

He'd forgotten to reload when they left the casino. Now he was running straight at a shooter who was taking her time to squeeze, not jerk, the trigger.

Like Harry had probably taught her.

Crack-buzz-crack-buzz-crack-buzz. More bees. A window shattered in the house behind him.

Broker dived, rolled sideways, and scrambled on all fours through a kid's plastic play set and crawled into the nearest cover, a patch of staked tomato plants. He lay absolutely still for a whole minute, during which he distinctly remembered leaving his eight .45 rounds in Mouse's car when they agreed to unload their guns before confronting Harry. Slowly, he caught his breath facedown in the rich black dirt, the mulch, and the thick chlorophyll fragrance of the tomato plants. He listened. But now all he heard was the onrushing cars, coming to the sound of the shots.

She was long gone.

Broker had other things to worry about. All the car doors slamming, the radios crackling—all the young coppers out there who'd never heard a shot fired in anger, their sweaty, overeager hands gripping their guns.

"Don't shoot," he yelled. "Over here, a friendly."

"Who's there? Come out with your fuckin' hands up," a hypertense young voice yelled back.

"Broker."

"Broke who?"

"Broker, you know," a different voice yelled. "Cool it. He's buddies with the fuckin' sheriff."

"Oh," the first voice said.

"All right everybody, stand down, holster the pieces. We clear? Okay? Come out, come out wherever you are, Sheriff Friend Broker." It was Mouse, breathing hard, but his voice unmistakable, coming in through the garage, then out onto the deck.

Slowly, Broker rose to his feet, knocking dirt from his chest as Mouse approached, flanked by two Stillwater cops.

"Were those shots you?" Mouse said.

"*At* me. I ran into her when she came through here. She took four shots—they went high—then she changed direction and headed for the ravine," Broker said.

Mouse told the two cops to fan out in an area search centered

on the ravine. He turned back to Broker and said, "Did you get a
look at her? Was it Gloria?"

"Too dark. Just a shape," Broker said. He shook his head,
looked into the darkness, and thought, *Goddamn Harry. If he
didn't get you one way, he'd get you another.*

She had bolted when she heard someone crash through the hedge
behind her; then the loud voice had ordered her to stop. She half
turned and picked out his moving broken shadow against the
shrubs, saw the shadow's arms come up, extended. Trying to get
off the first shot, she planted her feet, swung the Ruger up in the
classic Weaver stance, and pulled the trigger.

He went down. Out of sight. She turned and ran.

Sprinting now, across the lawn, she hurdled over the edge of the
ravine and slid through the bushes, past the chain-sawed trunk of
a large cottonwood that had fallen.

The cottonwood's upper branches were still intact, the foliage
wilted and dead. But it tangled up the bottom of the ravine with
irregular lines that broke up her shape. Under the tree's cover, she
hunted for the sewer grate.

Her hands found the slanted steel bars among the branches. She
slipped off the pack, pushed it through the grate, and squeezed
through herself.

Inside, underground, dank, with sand and debris left by the last
bad storm weeks ago, before the hot spell. All black where she
was. No flashlight. Basically, it was a big concrete pipe that ended
in a catch pond at Second Street. Every one hundred yards there
was a steel ladder leading up to a manhole opening.

She could hear them ganging up out there. Think. They'd block
the other end, seal her in.

She wiggled back out of the grate, took off the pack, and used one of the latex gloves to remove the makeshift silencer. She tossed it in through the grate.

Then, very carefully, stepping on rocks where possible, she backed away from the sewer entrance and slowly crawled up the far slope through the thick brush. Behind her she heard the cops moving down into the ravine from the street.

Very slowly, she emerged from the ravine and slipped across a dark dead-end street and went through another yard. The controlled panic of being hunted gave way to a warm sweat of elation. As she started down the bluff toward Main Street, she took in deep breaths of the sweet hot air.

It was time to call it quits. Maybe after she was gone, someone else would take up the cause.

Not her. She was done.

But if she was finished, she intended to have some control over the way her life ended. She wasn't going to be snared like a rat in a . . . sewer.

She had thought about this in great detail. And now she knew exactly what she had to do.

Chapter Thirty-eight

Men and women in uniforms, barefoot civilians in shorts, men without shirts, kids—they all came out from the dark houses to see the cops cordon off the entire North Hill around the ravine.

They got somebody trapped in the sewer.

They hoped. Broker leaned forward, forearms planted on a steel rail running along the limestone wall that overlooked the ravine. Not far away, Lymon sagged against a car. There was never a good time for a situation to totally unravel, but the heat definitely made it worse. The adrenaline jag of the chase had blown back on them, and now a knot of cops sulked around the woman Lymon had pursued through the woods. Freed from her handcuffs, she stood with her arms crossed, listening to an officer who took great pains to explain the murder, the description of the suspect . . .

"We're really sorry about the mix-up," the patient cop said.

"I know my rights. I want everybody's badge numbers," she said.

Another group of cops was talking to a teenage boy with a

skateboard under his arm. Benish was with that group, scribbling notes in a pad in the bad light.

Down the wall from Broker, flashlights played over an old limestone sewer spillway. The newer underground storm sewer intake was located about thirty feet farther down into the ravine. Cops had strung crime scene tape and were searching the area around the sandy apron in front of the intake grille. The branches of a fallen cottonwood obscured the grille and made it hard to see.

The shouts went back and forth.

"There's this clay-type dirt. We got a fresh cleat pattern from a running shoe. She crawled in here."

Another cop gingerly fished a green pop bottle out from inside the sewer intake and held it with a pen stuck through the neck. "What do you make of this? It's got punctures and duct tape . . ."

And: "She definitely slipped into this sewer intake. We got people blocking the other end."

Mouse—arm up, neck scrunched to the side in cell-phone silhouette—walked up to Broker. "Somebody has to go in there," Broker said.

"Yeah, somebody young. And that ain't you or me," Mouse said. He gestured with the phone. "We got it sealed. SWAT's on the way. We'll watch this end, and the manholes on top. They'll go in on Second and push through. If she's in there, we got her."

The cops fanned out along the length of the ravine and waited for the SWAT team. Broker sat down and adopted a wait-and-see attitude; he did not directly think of Gloria hunkered down under the ground gripping a pistol. And he didn't revisit the experience of being shot at point-blank in the dark less than half an hour ago.

He was past the adrenaline spike of the chase, coming down. He fingered the deputy's badge in his pocket. He tried to stay in the moment. And at the moment he smelled like tomato plants and fresh dirt.

Then the tension cranked up again when the SWAT members went into the sewer. The radios cracked, and everybody leaned forward, waiting . . . and . . .

"Get ready, something's coming. Ready, ready . . ."

Hisses and chittery growls came from the sewer, and then three raccoons scrambled between the bars of the grille and raced through the blocking force.

One of the SWAT guys popped his head out of the intake and said, "She ain't here."

The gathered cops dispersed in a wider search pattern. Broker accompanied Mouse, who went over to Benish and told him to locate Gloria Russell and find out where she was tonight.

"Where's she live?" Benish said.

"How the fuck do I know?" Mouse said. "You're a cop, find her. Take Lymon. Hey Lymon, c'mere."

Lymon walked over to them, then stopped, plucked his Palm Pilot from his pocket, and hunched over to read something off the tiny screen. His face tightened; then he reached out and grabbed Benish's arm so hard Benish said, "Ow."

Broker and Mouse joined closer with Lymon and Benish. Lymon thrust the small screen up for them to read: LYMON, I'M SO SORRY. GLORIA.

"Go, go!" Mouse shouted, pounding Lymon on the shoulder. He grabbed Broker, held him back. "John just arrived at the victim's house on Beech. I ran it down about Harry and Gloria. He wants to talk to both of us."

One of Sheriff John Eisenhower's favorite maxims was that nothing good happens at the end of a car chase. He arrived at the address on Beech Street to find cops, paramedics, and some citizens already openly discussing the Saint.

Broker and Mouse parked down the block and walked toward the lights.

The medical examiner was there and the Stillwater mayor with his police chief. The state crime lab van from BCA had backed up to Carol Lennon's gated yard, an area that was now as brightly lit and tightly secured as a space shuttle launch.

The crowd of citizens swelled, some of then grinning the kind of rubbernecking smiles that reminded Broker of old photographs of gawkers at a lynching. At least one Saints baseball jacket was being worn in the impossible heat.

It was starting.

Sally Erbeck moved swiftly toward the sheriff. As she passed Broker she gave him a quick wink. It was truly amazing to see the way the lines of her face streamlined forward; it was a fresh kill, and she was on the scene. Broker wondered if she had a police scanner surgically implanted in her ear.

John Eisenhower held up a hand to halt Sally, signaling with his fingers that he'd talk to her in five minutes. He detached from a knot of coppers and walked over to Broker and Mouse.

"Mouse told me," John said. "What a mess. You had to go round and round with Harry. And she took a shot at you—could you ID her?"

Broker shook his head. "Too dark." He took the deputy's badge and ID card from his pocket and handed them to John.

"Not now, Broker," John said. He pushed the badge and card away and then warmly squeezed Broker's arm. He turned to Mouse. "This here"—he indicated the crime scene—"is BCA's now. But we have to find and question Gloria. She's ours."

"Benish and Lymon are looking for her right now. We're gonna need a warrant, the whole schmeer," Mouse said.

Art Katzer, the lean head of Investigations, had also returned. He pushed through the crowd with a cell phone glued to his ear.

He said, "Somebody from the governor's staff just called; he's thinking of coming out here if it's the Saint."

"Great," John said.

Broker felt deformed. He was the only nonuniformed person in a ten-yard radius who didn't have a cell phone growing from his ear. Now Mouse was on his again. Broker watched Mouse's lined face tighten. At the same time, he heard a spike of radio static ripple through the crowd. The uniforms started melting away toward their cars.

Mouse had this look on his face, as if thinking: *Why am I always the guy who has to tell the kids their parent is dead?*

"They found her," he said.

John and Katzer lowered their cell phones. "You mean they're questioning her," John said.

"No, they *found* her," Mouse repeated. Then he raised his right hand, extended his index finger, curled his other three fingers, made his thumb into a hammer, pointed the finger at his head, and let the thumb fall forward.

"She ate the gun."

The address was on the South Hill, an imposing two-story red-brick school building constructed during the New Deal. It had been remodeled into condominiums. Benish sat on the steps of the entryway with a baleful guard-dog look in his eyes. Elbow planted on his knees, he was methodically pulling on a rubber band he wore around his wrist.

Broker had ridden over with Mouse. They parked in front. As they walked up the sidewalk, Mouse paused and stared at the letters chiseled in stone over the door. The tiny glow of recognition flared in his eyes, then faded back to sorrow. "I went to elementary school here," he said in a quiet voice.

Benish snapped his rubber band, exhaled, got up, and said, "Second floor, top of the stairs on the right." He raised his chin at the cop cars converging on the street.

Broker watched some neighbors stand frozen in the red slap of the flashers. The sudden police presence transformed them into shell-shocked refugees in their own yards.

"There's a deputy in the lobby with the tenants. I'll try to keep the crowd down, but it's going to be a zoo in about three minutes," Benish said.

Broker and Mouse entered the building, nodded to the copper who was questioning a small crowd of people gathered in the lobby. Then they climbed the stairs, broad slate with heavy oak blond banisters and black wrought-iron filigree. At the top of the stairs, on the right, the door to number six was open. The doorway was very tall, splendid with old wood, with a wide glass transom window on a chain.

Mouse ran his hand down the varnished wood of the doorway and said simply, "I learned to read in this room."

Lymon met them. Broker noticed that his eyes were hard and steady, as if he'd aged ten years in the last two hours. "In here," Lymon said.

As they stepped through the door, Lymon said, "She's in the bathroom. But we gotta be careful; there's feathers all over the place." They edged past a small kitchen and down a hallway.

Lymon raised his hand. They stopped. He pointed at the clay-caked soles on a pair of running shoes that lay casually strewn, one on its side, on the hallway oak flooring.

The gunshot-ripped pillow lay on the bathroom tile floor. As if in a miniature snowstorm, the sink and tub were carpeted with the white lint.

"I guess she used the pillow to muffle the shot," Lymon said, then stepped aside so they could see. Moving cautiously, they eased in the bathroom door.

A pair of dirty gray running shorts, a sports top, and a pair of grimy socks lay on the floor. A wafer of dark plastic lay next to them. The Palm Pilot.

Like someone who didn't want to make a mess, Gloria Russell lay toppled into the bathtub. And, like Carol Lennon, she was naked. Unlike Carol's face, hers was turned away. A scum of dirt and tiny bits of leaves formed a swirl of sediment in the bottom of the tub. As if she'd showered first. The tiny feathers had drifted down and settled on the bare soles of her feet. There were abrasions on the left knee consistent with scraping through thick brush.

There was very little blood, just the single entry wound above her right eyebrow. Her right index finger was still tangled in the trigger guard of the gun she'd used, a Ruger .22 automatic that lay under her twisted arm.

Lymon pointed to the gun. "Look at the barrel housing, on the end."

They looked and saw a gummy residue and tiny pieces of frayed duct tape.

"The exhaust fan was on, and the door was closed when I got here. I turned off the fan with a pen; it was blowing the feathers around. Maybe the fan helped suppress the sound of the shot, like the pillow. The neighbors didn't hear," Lymon said. They carefully backed out of the room. "The closet," he said.

He led Broker and Mouse back to the entryway hall and pointed to the askew folding closet door. A canvas gym bag sat inside. Using a pen, Lymon lifted the flap on the bag. Inside there were several crumpled pieces of paper, one of them with blood on it. Broker knelt and tried to make it out; a computer printout of a kid, dancing maybe. Beneath the paper Broker saw a wig, a portion of a Saints logo peeking from the folded material of a jacket.

"What's that other stuff?" Mouse said.

"Some kind of padding, I don't know. I didn't want to dig around," Lymon said. "And there's this." He poked a pencil flashlight into the pack.

Broker craned his neck and saw a plastic baggie in the bottom of the bag, a glint of tiny chain links and silver.

"But no thirty-eight," Mouse said. "We'll have to tear this place apart looking for it."

Broker had had enough; he stood up. "I don't see any reason for me to stick around here," he said, moving toward the door.

Lymon followed him into the outside hall and said, "Remember when you asked me about the night Moros was killed, where she was?"

"Yeah," Broker said.

"I saw her in the gym. But I split, and she stayed. So she was alone. There would have been plenty of time," Lymon said.

Mouse joined them, and they looked down the stairs at the lobby filling up with the sheriff, the mayor, the police chief, the state guys, and a dozen blue and tan uniforms.

"That whole game Harry ran on folks, drawing the Saint rumors to himself—he was trying to protect her," Lymon said.

"Yeah. Ah, Christ, now somebody has to tell him in the hospital," Mouse said.

"Me," Lymon said.

"You sure?" Mouse said.

"Me," Lymon said firmly.

"Okay. That's it. I'm leaving," Broker said. He turned to Lymon. "Welcome to the job, huh." He extended his hand, and they naturally hooked thumbs, clasped wrists, did a finger snatch on the release.

"Where'd you come by this shit?" Lymon said.

"What, this?" Broker said, opening his hand.

"Yeah, the old Soul Brother dap shit," Lymon said with some spark in his new tough eyes.

Broker flashed on Harry driving dead drunk from casino to casino past midnight. The wind rushing in his hair had sounded like helicopters on the phone. "It was something long ago," he said.

They left Lymon on the job at the head of the stairs and went down and pushed through the crowd. Outside, Broker raised his head, as if to sniff the wind. But there wasn't any wind; just the heavy air and too many cop cars. A few houses down, a surreptitious lawn sprinkler hissed, defying the watering ban.

Cody, the young narc, walked up, handed Broker a slip of paper, and said, "From Dispatch. Sorry to lay this nickel-dime shit on you, but you've been requested by name at a domestic downtown. Some woman named Jane Hensen. Says it's personal."

"Aw, shit." Broker grimaced. He looked at the address on the slip of paper. Drew's studio.

Mouse handed his car keys to Broker and said, "Go on, take my cruiser. I'll be busy here all night. Bring it back tomorrow."

Chapter Thirty-nine

Broker got in Mouse's cruiser and left the crowd of people, vehicles, and equipment that had descended on Gloria Russell's suicide.

A dark blue Stillwater squad was parked in front of the warehouse. Broker pulled in back of it, got out, went up the stairs, and walked into the studio.

The town cop was a young guy Broker had never seen before. He had removed his hat and wore his hair high and tight and was buckled and harnessed with gear. His mobile radio squawked in the center of the studio, calling attention to the place Broker had just left. The cop stood between Janey and Drew, whom he had positioned in separate corners—Drew at his drawing table, Janey on the couch. A tipped bookcase and about twenty books lay on the floor between them.

"You Broker?" the cop said.

Broker just nodded.

"You were in on the chase up the hill?" the cop said.

"Yeah, what a mess," Broker said.

"I heard, on the radio. I would have been there, but I got this call first." He narrowed his eyes and leaned forward. "Is it true it's the Saint? They found a medallion in her mouth? And about the prosecutor?"

Broker nodded again. "So what have you got here?"

Janey and Drew began to speak at the same time. The young copper held up his hand. "People, we've been through this; you will speak in turn, you will not raise your voices, and you will listen to Mr. Broker. If I have to come back, we will continue this discussion at the county jail."

Drew and Janey shut up. The cop said to Broker, "You know the Hensens. Right?"

"Yes, I do," Broker said.

"Okay. The husband called for assistance. Said the wife was wrecking his studio. Reason I called you—their little girl, Laurie, is in the bathroom. She's the only one with any common sense; she says she won't come out until everybody stops yelling. The thing is, her hands are all cut up and bandaged, which looks like rough stuff I have to report—so naturally I have questions. They both said you could explain."

Broker nodded a second time. "They had a fight; he walked out. Laurie's way of dealing with it was to go in the backyard and dig up her dead cat. That how she tore up her hands."

The copper growled at them, "If it was up to me, you'd have to pass a competency test before you'd be allowed to have children."

"I can take it from here," Broker said.

"Good luck," the cop said, heading for the door. "I'll be up the hill at the scene if you need anything."

"Thanks, I think we're good," Broker said. He stood with his hands folded in front of him as the officer left. Then he went to the bathroom and knocked on the door.

"This is Phil Broker, remember? I let you take the cat home; gray, shorthaired?"

"I'm not coming out till they stop yelling at each other," Laurie said.

"Okay. We'll do something about that. You wait right here. I'll be back in a minute," Broker said.

"Okay," Laurie said.

Broker turned back to Janey and Drew, who sat facing each other with their arms folded tightly across their chests.

"Okay, why are you yelling at each other?" Broker said.

"We have agreed to separate," Janey said. "He wants to move out and live here. Fine. I just don't want him to run his parade of bimbos past Laurie. Just keep it away from my kid, okay?"

"What? Lisa—a bimbo? C'mon Janey," Drew said, "she has a master's in child psychology for Chrissake."

"Ohhh, a *master's* . . ." Janey wiggled her fingers.

"So this is a custody dispute," Broker said.

"Yes. I want Laurie to spend tonight here with me. Janey says she has to go home," Drew said.

Broker jerked his thumb toward the bathroom. "What about her? She's involved in this too."

They were silent for a moment, then Drew sat back, refolded his arms, and said, "I promised to take Laurie to Camp Snoopy tomorrow."

Broker looked at Janey. "Is that okay with you?"

"Of course. It's tonight I'm worried about," Janey said.

"There you go again; just settle down," Drew said.

Drew was also staring at him. Broker looked down and noticed that his shoes were caked with drying mud from his night walk around Lake McKusick, his jeans and shirt were gritty from diving in the tomato patch.

Drew said, "It's no big deal. I have to work. She can watch movies on the TV with the headset."

"Where will she sleep?" Janey asked. "Certainly not back there where you . . ." She pointed at the alcove where Drew had his futon.

"No, no; I'll take the small futon off the chair and make a pallet in front of the VCR."

"I suppose that would be all right," Janey said. Grudgingly, they nodded to each other.

"Okay, I'm going to bring Laurie out," Broker said. He went to the bathroom and knocked on the door. "Fight's over. Time to come out."

Slowly, Laurie opened the door. "I heard," she said as she squinted past Broker at her father. "Can I watch three movies?" Laurie asked.

"Not *three* movies," Janey said.

So Broker watched them work out the details. Absently, as they talked, Janey began to pick up books and stack them back in the shelves. Immediately, Drew stooped to help. Broker thought the behavior bizarre, yet also comforting. Or saddening. He wasn't sure which.

Finally, Broker and Janey left the studio and stood on the sidewalk.

"Hop in, I'll give you a ride," Broker said.

They got into Mouse's car. As they drove away, Janey brightened with a forced eagerness. "Don't take me home yet. Let's take a drive. Now that we're both separated persons, we could go somewhere and have a drink. A lot of drinks. In fact, we could get drunk," she said.

Broker studied her across the front seat. Scraps of moonbeam caught on her teeth and the whites of her eyes. She was looking very warm and available. But the glimmers on her face reminded him of the tiny feathers stuck to Gloria Russell's cold skin. "I don't get drunk," he said.

"Not even during a moment of weakness?" Janey said.

He had the windows open, and the night pressed in feeling foreign; Galveston, New Orleans—someplace else. So hot you wanted to take off everything to cool down, and not just your clothing—your normal restraints. Broker thought about it. For the second day in a row, bullets had zipped past his head. He'd seen two dead women . . .

"Weak moment, huh?" he said.

"Yeah," Janey said.

"Separated," Broker said.

"Uh-huh. You know, Broker, you're, ah, all dirty," Janey said.

"We were chasing somebody tonight," Broker said.

"Did you catch them?" Janey said.

"Catch them . . ." He thought of his first wife, Caren; how after hunting season she would say, "Phil caught a deer," not "shot" it, not "killed" it. "Yeah, I guess we did," Broker said. "Okay, look; I'm going out to Milt's and jump in the river. You want to come along?"

Broker floated on his back and stared up at the stars. He considered a world in which Diane Cantrell and Gloria Russell had to die while he and Harry continued to live.

Janey surfaced beside him, a gleam in the moonlight.

"Just relax, just let it happen," she said.

An experiment at playing skinny dipping in the dark. Pale flashes of skin, like fish, curving out of sight. Laughter. Splashing.

Then the bodies grazing, just nibbles of touch at first.

So just let it happen. Forget the death. Embrace the life.

Chapter Forty

You think you lose it, *that it's gone forever, worn to nothing by the drip of familiarity that breeds contempt. You resign yourself that it's never going to happen again. Not happen like it used to, not heightened and intense, and then you discover it's been there all along and that all you needed was the right person to bring it back strong. Flint and steel. Sparks, flame, inferno . . .*

He was lost in his lovemaking.

God, it was like he was twenty-five again, and she made it all new. So good. Like secrets. All these cunning little physical secrets she revealed. Could she always do this? Or was it something kindled special between them?

Was it her? Was it them? It was like she was a mirror, and when he looked at her writhing in his arms, lips parted, eyes shut, slippery with sweat in this heat—all he could see was . . .

Himself.

But he wanted to please her; he wanted to slowly gather her in, then herd her, then push her into a run until they ended in a happy stampede.

Shhh, she said. We have to be quiet.

It's all right; it's all right, he said.

We're making too much noise, she said. But then she began to really like it and then she began to whisper loudly, Oh God, oh God; it's perfect, it's perfect, and now I'm afraid I can't stop. I'm afraid I can't stop.

I don't want you to stop, he whispered back.

Oh yes you do. Yes you do.

Drew Hensen was more than impressed. What a surprise Annie Mortenson turned out to be on a sultry Saturday morning. One minute he was waving to her from his studio porch, inviting her up for coffee. An hour later they were in bed.

Now he studied Annie as she began her transformation from wanton to quietly prim, drawing her knees together, sitting up, and pulling the damp sheet over her chest. She leaned back and fluffed her bangs.

While she was still wide-eyed and puffy-lipped, he reached over and ran his finger across her lower lip. "Is it true what they say about librarians giving the best head? I always wanted to know," he said.

She mock-arched her eyebrows and briefly took his finger in her mouth, then slowly slid it out, turned it around, and wagged it at him. "But if I give you some, that's all you'll want."

Drew actually had a little run of goose bumps with the temperature in the midnineties.

Annie laughed silently. "Is this how you give all the girls a tour of your studio?" she whispered.

"Why are you whispering?" Drew said. It was nuts, with the racket the TV was making.

Annie grimaced and stabbed her finger at the sound of the TV on the other side of the curtain that was drawn over the alcove where the futon on which they lay was located. "There's a little girl out there."

"Oh, c'mon, she can't hear anything. She's OD'ed on *Shrek* for the second time this morning," Drew said.

"It's not funny." Annie squirmed deeper in the sheet. "What if she would have pulled the curtain back?"

"We were under the sheet."

"Not all the time we weren't."

Drew stood up and slapped his stomach. "Well, I wouldn't worry about it." Abruptly he reached for the curtain.

"What are you doing?" Annie asked.

"I got to take a pee," Drew said.

"Aren't you going to put some clothes on?"

"Hey, Annie; she's six years old, she's my daughter."

"It's not right to walk around like that. At least dry yourself off." Annie flung a corner of the sheet at him.

Drew ran the cloth over his crotch and dropped it. "I'm not going to make my kid ashamed of her body."

"We're not talking about her body. We're talking about your body."

"Don't be so uptight," Drew said as he stepped past the curtain.

Annie hugged herself, stared at the space where he'd just been, and muttered, "That's what my dad used to say."

She'd thought he was going to be different. Heck, he drew pictures for children's books; he *should* be different. That's why she took a chance when she saw him standing on his porch this morning. He'd waved at her. He'd invited her a number of times before. But he was married then.

Now he had taken off his wedding band. He said he and his wife were separated, that he had moved in here. But he was smooth. A different smooth than Harry Cantrell. Harry was rough smooth, Drew was smooth smooth. But Harry had lied. After Harry got her good a couple of times, he still pined for that bodybuilding bitch. Already Annie was starting to worry that Drew would pull the same stunt. She'd seen the wife.

She pursed her lips and scowled. She didn't like the idea of him out there parading his pecker in front of a kid. Any kid.

Uh-uh. Not one bit.

The TV audio turned off, and she heard Drew talking with his daughter. "You're covered with grease and crumbs from last night; you need a bath."

"But I thought we were going to Camp Snoopy," Laurie said.

"We are," Drew said.

"Is she coming?" Laurie said.

"No, no, she's going home. But you have tomato sauce stuck in your hair. You know what that means."

"I know," Laurie said. "It means consequences."

"Consequences, right. You got to do what you wanted, and now you have to get cleaned up."

"You have to wash me because of my hands," Laurie said.

"Don't worry, I will," Drew said.

After a few beats of silence, Annie heard the bathwater running. Him peeing in the bowl.

Consequences, consequences, consequences.

The toilet flushed. He was in the bathroom with her, taking her clothes off. And him not wearing any.

She could feel the steam from the hot water billow like a sail in the heavy air. Snatches of their father-daughter conversation.

Like . . .

Slowly, Annie stood up and gathered her clothing, a pair of Levi's cutoffs, a loose T-shirt with the arms and neck scissored out—hot weather gear. She pulled them on and walked barefoot through the studio, paused in front of the full-length mirror on the wall, and checked the tiny cuts and slight bruising on her knees. Not bad. Ice packs had helped a lot last night. She put last night from her mind and went down the wooden stairs to the street.

The late-morning sky seemed to be in motion; flickers of light illuminated deep, convoluted canyons of black and gray clouds. The world struck her as such a beautiful place. Why did it always seem she was watching it from the outside? Why couldn't she step into it and lose herself? Be part of it.

Why did she have to go on cleaning up after other people, finishing what they started and left undone?

It wasn't fair.

She thumbed the remote on her key ring, and the door locks responded with a reassuring metal *shh-chunk*. She lifted the rear hatch, pulled up the floor cover, and removed the heavy saddlebag purse nestled in the concave bin in the middle of the spare tire.

When she returned to the studio, Drew was looking at himself in the mirror. He seemed to be trying to flex his not quite defined abdominal muscles. He had made a concession to modesty and slung a bright red towel low on his hips, sarong fashion. The towel had blue and green monkeys on it, and coconuts and palm trees.

"Where'd you go?" he asked.

Annie held up the purse. "Went to get my toothbrush." Among other things. Then she cocked her head toward the bathroom. She could hear Laurie talking in the tub. "Is someone else here? She's talking to somebody."

Drew shrugged and said, "She talks to her dolls."

Annie walked a circuit of the studio, making sure they were alone. When she returned, she said, "I have a minor confession to make. I read about you in something."

Drew acted interested, but his eyes wandered back to the mirror. "And what was that? A review of a book?"

"It was a complaint. You were accused of something; I thought of investigating you."

Drew turned and smiled. "You can *investigate* me anytime," he said, sashaying his towel around in a mock striptease.

"This is serious, Drew. I used to go out with this county cop, you know."

"Uh-huh. You told me."

Annie nodded. "Well, your name was on this list he brought over. Your neighbor complained about you walking around naked when her daughter had a play date with Laurie."

Drew's striptease ended abruptly. "Oh, Christ. Mrs. Siple. Are you for real? She tried to get us on a complaint about our fence encroaching on her yard. When that didn't pan out, she tried character assassination. I talked to a cop about it. He saw it for what it was; case closed."

"But you do walk around naked in front of kids," Annie said, setting her jaw slightly.

Drew shook his head. "Not other people's kids," he said firmly. "Jesus, talk about mood swings. How can somebody screw like a mink one minute and be such a prude the next?"

"Maybe you were a little too casual about nudity, but you seemed to be a good father."

"I guess I should say thank you very much."

Annie walked past Drew without a response. She went to the bathroom, shut the door behind her, and knelt at the side of the tub. Laurie was pink and shiny with several Band-Aids on her fingers and gauze wrapped around her knuckles. Because of the dressings, her hands were marooned on the sides of the tub. Otherwise she was perfectly formed. Three Barbies surrounded her, floating facedown, arms and legs extended, hair adrift like miniature drowning victims.

That's when Annie noticed the Nokia cell phone lying on the wet floor. She picked it up. "Is this your dad's?" she said.

Laurie clammed up and pursed her lips tight together. But she bobbed her head affirmatively. Annie slipped the phone into her purse. "This shouldn't be in here on the floor where it can get wet," she said.

"I really need my dad to wash me. My hands hurt if I get them wet," Laurie said.

"Okay, I'll tell him. But right now I have a present for you," Annie said.

"Oh—thank you," Laurie said apprehensively.

Annie took the medallion from her purse and carefully draped the chain around Laurie's neck. Then she gently patted Laurie on the cheek, stood up, and left the bathroom.

Chapter Forty-one

Drew puttered in his cramped kitchen area, getting an ice tray from the small refrigerator. He dropped some cubes into two glasses and added ginger ale. In the bathroom, Laurie began to sing a lackadaisical lyric of her own invention. Annie stood very still in the middle of the room with her purse slung over her shoulder. She had her right hand stuffed into its depths.

"You know what the really hard thing is?" she said.

Drew carried the two glasses of ginger ale to his round coffee table. "What's that?" He indicated one of the chairs, then sat in the other one.

"My father started making sexual advances toward me and my sister when we were not much older than Laurie in there," Annie said.

Drew's head came up abruptly. "That's horrible." He watched her for several beats. Annie had the feeling he was making some great male discovery about her and sex. "It must be difficult to talk about," he said, leaning forward, looking genuinely concerned.

Smooth.

"It is, but right now I need to," Annie said.

Drew nodded. "I'm a good listener."

"I guess what set me off was seeing you and your daughter and you being naked. That's like my dad; he'd wash us and then he'd show us how to—wash him."

Drew winced. "You mean . . ."

Annie nodded and studied his face. "Right, I *mean*." An edge hardened in her voice that Drew hadn't heard before. "By the time we were eleven, he had progressed to actual intercourse with Angela, my twin sister. Angela had always protected me. She convinced Dad to do it to her and leave me alone. I'd lie in bed and pray to God to help me. But the only person who helped me was my sister. I pretended I was invisible."

Drew studied her face. Annie thought the story fascinated him. Just as he'd seemed to be excited by making love behind a curtain while his daughter watched TV fifteen feet away.

But his voice was serious. "Makes sense, denial as a cloaking mechanism. It's one of the ways kids cope. Jeez, Annie, I'm really sorry . . . how long did this go on?" He removed an ice cube from his glass and slid it in little melting circles on his sweaty chest.

"Until we were fifteen; that's when Dad had a heart attack and died."

"What about your mom?"

"She denied it right up until her death. Angela tried to stuff it, too. She worked hard as an attorney, but she had to take meds for depression." Annie paused and set her jaw. "The meds didn't work for the cancer."

Drew winced. "Cancer? On top of . . . Jesus, Annie, what happened to you?"

Annie shrugged. "I went to college in Madison. I floated from library to library and wound up back here. But when Angela died, something just . . . snapped. That was just about the time Ronald Dolman was acquitted." Annie leaned forward. "You remember Dolman?"

"Sure," Drew said, "the child molester last summer. He was . . . wait a minute." Drew sat up, thinking out loud. "On the news last night, the prosecutor who committed suicide; they hinted she might have killed that guy last summer as well as a woman yesterday—that she was . . . ?"

"The Saint."

"Yeah, the Saint." The indulgent afterglow dropped from Drew's face. He narrowed his eyes. "What are we talking about here?"

Annie withdrew her hand from the purse and dropped the medallion and chain on the table.

He pushed the chain with his finger. "What's this?"

"St. Nicholas, he's the patron saint of children. That's why I gave one to Laurie just now."

Drew sat up and looked at the bathroom door. "Wait a minute, you *what?*"

"Hung it around her neck, to protect her."

Drew began to breathe more rapidly.

Here comes the first fear, Annie thought. "Do you know how Ronald Dolman died?"

Drew tensed forward in his chair. Instinctively, he measured distances: the distance between himself and Annie, the distance to the bathroom, the distance to the telephone on his drawing table.

"Someone shot him," Drew said slowly.

Annie nodded. "With a thirty-eight-caliber Colt Detective Special revolver with a two-inch barrel. Would you like to see it?"

Drew's chair banged on the floor as he startled and planted his feet, pushing away from the table when Annie smoothly pulled the revolver from her purse.

"Oh my God," Drew muttered. His eyes fixed on the bathroom door. "Laurie," he said.

"Laurie has nothing to fear. She's going to be safe. *Now* she is, I mean," Annie said. "You sit very still. I'm not through talking." She thumbed back the hammer and steadied the barrel at Drew's chest. "You don't know much about guns, do you?"

Drew shook his head. His eyes were riveted to the bullet tips he could see inside the pistol's cylinder.

"Well, I do. Harry taught me. This is a double-action revolver. Cocking the hammer makes the trigger pull smoother," Annie said.

It was silent in the room for a few beats. Just the faint sound of Laurie singing in her bath.

"Please, take it easy with that," Drew said.

"Settle down, drink your ginger ale," Annie said. "See, my sister had just died, and I was going through her things. She had this wig—well, that's a long story—but the thing was, I was going out with Harry, and he'd go off all weekend with that Gloria Russell. We used to do a lot of things together until . . . he bought her a gun and taught her to shoot." Annie brandished the pistol. "This gun."

Drew squirmed against the back of his chair, seeing the hate come to Annie's face.

"He'd have me over and get his kicks; then he'd stick me in front of the TV and go down in the basement and load bullets for her to practice with. So I started watching her, when she left her apartment, when she came back. It was last summer, so she left her windows open. There was a perfect tree under the window. I climbed up, slit the screen, went in her bedroom, and took the gun."

Annie drew herself up. "Then Gloria let Dolman get away. Harry came over drunk and said how she was raving about wanting to kill the guy. I even drove him over to her place so he could take the gun off her." Annie smiled. "But the gun wasn't there." She moved the pistol out of line long enough to give it an admiring look.

"Maybe Gloria failed, but her gun didn't. And the bullet casings left with the body could be traced back to her. All I had to do was return the gun to her apartment, hide it, and tip the cops." Annie's smile jerked on her lips. "But I kept . . . putting it off . . ."

The gun barrel wavered off his chest, and Drew started to rise in his chair. The gun snapped back. "Sit," Annie commanded. Drew sat.

"It was you, last night," Drew said. "The woman up the hill, the teacher. You—"

"Oh, she was easy. Now Gloria, that was hard," Annie said.

But as Harry always says, if you never take the long shots, you never win big.

So she bets it all that Gloria will be home. And it's just like she has Harry's lucky arm with the three 7s hugging her. Gloria opens the door and sees bedraggled Annie all beat up from ducking through the bushes.

"Help. This guy jumped me."

Barge past her, going into the apartment. Track dirt, shed bits of shrubs. Feigning shock, mumbling after the phone, compassionate Gloria tags along, does not notice the latex gloves. Wrong turn into the bedroom, return with the pillow. One hand stays in the pack on the Ruger, but the silencer is back at the storm sewer.

More shock, stumbling into the bathroom—then the one moment of cruelty. Face-to-face.

Harry sends his love, bitch!

One beat, two. Let it sink in. Then the gun comes out. Shove the pillow in her face to muffle the scream of protest, the sound of the shot. Make sure the angle of the barrel is credible for a suicide, jam it in, and . . . Gloria's dead, open eyes watch her enjoy a cool shower on a hot night.

Take the time now to be careful. Arrange the pistol just so in the lifeless hand. Scuff her up with the dirty clothes and shoes, leave them strewn on the bathroom floor. Even thought to bring a small branch to gouge her shin and knee. Then a moment of quiet cele-bration in the bedroom, slow tour of Gloria's closet to find a fresh change of clothes. Leave the pack in the closet; Angel's cheap wig, the bodysuit, medals, the Saints jacket.

One last touch. Send the world's first wireless suicide note. To her weightlifting buddy. The cop. His address is right in her queue. Message him on Gloria's Palm Pilot. A trained detective, and he comes running because he sees a dead woman's name printed on his gadget.

No one sees her go in or out. Perfect. Gloria Russell is the Saint. Harry's theory comes true. All she has to do is leave the .38 along with the Ruger.

But here it is, in her hand.

Annie stared at Drew, almost fondly. "Like I told you, I can't stop. Just like I couldn't resist coming over this morning because you were the last name on my list."

Drew balled his fists, desperate and angry, getting ready to fight. "You're crazy, really fucking crazy."

"DON'T SAY THAT!" Annie yelled. Her hand began to shake now, and Drew half rose, gathering himself.

"Crazy . . ." he said again, but he looked past Annie. She extended her arm, pointing the gun at his face, but she turned slightly and saw Laurie standing naked and dripping in the bath-room doorway.

"Daddy, I'm *scared*," Laurie sobbed.

Annie looked back and forth between them. She couldn't stop the shaking.

"Go back in the bathroom, honey," Drew said, finally finding his voice. He steadied, gathering himself. "Listen to Daddy."

"DON'T SAY THAT!" Annie shouted.

Laurie screamed and ran to the bathroom. When Laurie slammed the door, Annie jerked around at the sound. Drew made his move, coming over the table. Annie swung back and yanked the trigger. Drew's momentum carried him forward into her as the gun went off.

The loudness of the explosion shocked her. She was used to the silenced Ruger. She watched Drew's eyes go wide, then he toppled against her, and they both rolled to the floor. Annie was up quick. Drew lay facedown, leaking blood.

Annie staggered to get her balance. She blinked her eyes and swallowed to clear her hearing. Now what? She pushed through the door and entered the bathroom with the pistol hanging in her hand.

"I'm trying to help you," she explained. She reached out to grab Laurie by the shoulders, to reassure her. Laurie twisted away like a wet fifty-pound wildcat and screamed, "I WANT MY DADDY!"

"DON'T SAY THAT, GODDAMMIT!" Annie screamed back and grabbed at the girl to restrain her.

Chapter Forty-two

Broker and Janey sat on the deck sipping coffee and watching the clouds roll in. A grumble in the distance prompted Janey to turn her head. "Was that thunder?" she said.

"I think it was," Broker said. He could feel a cool shadow insinuate into the air, compressing the humidity like a spring.

Their eyes met, and they laughed, just as they'd laughed last night when they couldn't get past mild petting. Janey had slept in the guest room.

After a few beats, Janey said, "Well, look at us; so much for weak moments."

Broker shrugged and said, "Maybe weak moments are like straight-leg jeans; you gotta be young to be comfortable in them. We're pretty much padded with baggage, you and me." He briefly revisited his "weak moment" last year with Jolene Sommer, which had been pretty awful.

"I guess Drew doesn't let it bother him," Janey said.

"I don't know what to tell you," Broker said.

"Maybe it's his men's group . . . we go to this Unitarian church sometimes, and they have . . . don't laugh," Janey said, seeing the smile curl at the corner of his lips.

Broker held up his hands in a surrendering gesture. "Hey, I can dig it. I was in this big men's group once. Cut my hair short, wore green all the time, ate shitty food, and slept in the woods. No drumming, though, and no campfires."

"Very funny. What I mean is, Drew and these guys get very involved in discussing their evaporating testosterone or something . . . their vigor. I think getting older scares him."

A long muted crackle snaked across the sky. If his daughter were here, Broker would tell her that, far away, a thunder lizard was uncoiling his spiked ozone tail.

"I don't know. Sometimes a marriage comes down to basic triage. When things get ugly and bloody, you have to figure where you're headed—to emergency or the morgue," Broker said.

"Now there's a quaint—" Janey stopped in midsentence as two phones rang at the same time in the kitchen: the house phone and her cell phone on the table. "That's . . . weird," she said.

They got up and went to their respective phones.

Broker picked up and heard the familiar voice start in, "It's Jeff; first of all, everything's all right so don't worry, you hear me?"

The caller was Tom Jeffords, the Cook County sheriff. His neighbor on Lake Superior's north shore.

"What the hell? Is it the folks?" Broker said, bracing himself.

"No, it's Kit," Jeff said.

Instant Tilt-a-Whirl in his chest. "Kit?"

"She's all right. She's fine. It's just that she turned up in a motel room in Langdon, North Dakota, with a baby-sitter who had instructions to call me today."

Broker sat down as the edges of his vision came tunneling in. "Where the hell is her mother?" His voice shook between incredulity and real anger.

"Nina left her with this baby-sitter yesterday. Just the instructions to call. No other message," Jeff said. "I called the Cavalier County Sheriff's Department, and they've got deputies on it up the wazoo. Nothing to worry about. She's fine, so stay cool."

"Where the hell is Langdon?" Broker said, trying to stay cool.

"Up in the northeast corner in the middle of nowhere. Grand Forks is the nearest air link. Take these numbers."

Broker wrote down the numbers for the Cavalier County Sheriff's Department. And the Best Western where Kit was found. He listened while Jeff counseled him not to bother his parents until he had Kit in hand. Jeff said call anytime; he was there night or day. They said good-bye.

He immediately started to punch in the motel number when Janey appeared in front of him. She pressed her phone to her chest, and her face was cold with restrained fury. "That was Laurie, calling me on Drew's cell phone. He left her stranded in the bathroom, and he's got some woman there."

Broker held up his hand. "Wait a minute," he said. He had to think. Better to make his calls from the county office. He had to return Mouse's car, anyway. No sense troubling Janey with this new information. "Go down to the car. I'll be right there," he said.

Broker went fast through the bathroom and the bedroom; threw his toilet articles and a change of clothes in a duffel bag, locked the house, and jogged to the car.

Driving between eighty and ninety, he barely heard Janey's screed against Drew as he tried to stay focused. When they hit the north end of town, he was reassuring himself that Jeff was a strictly no-bullshit cop. *If he said Kit was all right, she was all right.*

Okay. So what . . . ?

Then he stopped and double-parked in front of Drew's building, where a small crowd of people stood on the street nervously pointing up the steps toward Drew's studio. Janey stepped out of the car, spoke briefly to someone in that crowd, and immediately sprinted up the steps.

Broker jumped from the car and raced after her.

" . . . gunshot up there . . . ," someone yelled as he rushed past.

Now what? Taking the steps three at a time. Going in cold, nothing in his hand. Nothing. Just going in.

Now screams.

The kid. Laurie in there screaming.

He was in and . . .

Drew, naked with a towel trailing off his butt, leaking bubbles of blood from his chest and his lips. He left a slick red smear on the hardwood floor as he crawled sidestroke toward the bathroom. Broker dropped to one knee, to check Drew, and Janey shot past him into the bathroom.

"LET HER GO!"

Broker leaped over Drew, threw his shoulder against the door, and shoved it against the recoil of struggling bodies on the other side. He set his stance and forced his way in. Inside the small room, Janey grappled with a woman who had just taken her hands off Laurie. Laurie was screaming and crouched waist-deep in a bathtub full of water as she swung her tiny bandaged fists.

Broker had seen this woman before.

Lunging, he thought with his hands. The woman was reaching down to the wet floor . . .

GUN.

Really diving now, off the ground, stretching because the pistol was coming up in line with Janey's face. He batted Janey aside with his right hand while his left hand whipped out and grabbed the muzzle.

KABOOM—*OHSHITFUCK!*

He felt the bullet punch through his palm.

The noise, pain, and shock welded a frozen white circle, and he was suspended for a fraction of a second as he hurtled toward the floor and crashed chest and elbow into the rim of the claw-footed bathtub.

And that hurt more than the goddamn bullet.

Jarred, he flipped down and hit the floor hard.

In that tiny beat he saw Janey—a Janey he had never seen before—pounce over him and close with the shooter. Broker, dazed, coming up off the floor, Laurie screaming, Drew crawling, his chin coated with blood.

And Broker looked up and saw something else he had never seen before as Janey went in snarling and clawed her fingers into the other woman's eyes.

The woman staggered back, her eyes now a torn red mask. Janey went after the faltering pistol. Seized it in her hand. As Broker struggled up from the floor, he had one of his basic rules reaffirmed, the one about never having a loaded revolver in the house. No safety mechanism. The ultimate in point-and-shoot.

Without the slightest hesitation, she thrust the pistol into Annie Mortenson's face and pulled the trigger once, twice, and would have kept yanking it if Broker hadn't come up fast and torn the weapon from her grip.

Laurie screamed louder and clapped her hands to her ears.

Broker's own ears were ringing, plugged, stinging from the shots.

Laurie's screams brought Janey to her senses. She saw the gouts of flesh and splinters of scalp that spattered the wall, the floor, her daughter.

Instantly, she wrapped Laurie in her arms and then whisked a towel from a rack and began cleaning Laurie's face.

"Get her out of here," Broker said. Then seeing the slumped woman's face, knowing it was futile, he knelt, put down the pistol, and put his fingers to her throat. He waited several beats and felt no pulse.

Janey stepped over Annie's body, plucking red matter from Laurie's hair with her fingers and flicking it away. Immediately, she started to kneel to Drew. Broker grabbed her arm and shoved her toward the studio doorway and the porch beyond.

"Take her out there. Leave this to me," Broker said. Then he turned and saw air bubbles suck red suds in Drew's back. Bright red blood.

Sucking chest wound. Exit wound.

He squatted, turned Drew's shoulder, and saw a similar but smaller pumping action in his chest.

Through and through. Okay. Seal a sucking chest.

He walked, not real steady but fast, toward the kitchenette, tossing the contents of a cupboard until he found a roll of Saran wrap, a spool of duct tape. Ignoring Drew's groans he forced him to a sitting position, wound the Saran around his chest, flung his arms out of the way, and then reinforced the impermeable barrier with the tape.

Drew's breathing improved enough for him to try to talk.

"Shut up, save your strength," Broker said as he reached for the phone on the drawing table. It had just occurred to him that the people down on the street had probably not called the cops.

Broker called 911, identified himself, gave the address, told the call taker he had a man down with a sucking chest and a woman dead on the scene. Broker described the first aid he'd given and said the wounded man was breathing and able to talk.

Then Drew started to topple over, so Broker put down the phone and hunkered with Drew and straightened him up again.

Drew wheezed, "Say . . ."

"What?"

"Sane . . ."

"Drew, be quiet."

"Saint. Her. Crazy. Said she killed . . . some woman. Take the blame. She had one of those medals." Drew rallied and forced out a whole sentence, "Broker, she said she killed that guy . . ."

Broker was too focused on the immediate demands of the situation to process what Drew was saying. He told Drew to be quiet.

"No, listen; she . . ." Then he pitched back against the bookcase and gasped, completely exhausted.

"You rest. Help's on the way," Broker said. He propped him upright with a chair so the internal bleeding wouldn't collapse the lung, wedged him so he wouldn't fall. Then he went to check on Janey and Laurie.

Janey had scrubbed the blood from Laurie's face and hair and had swaddled her in the towel. He bent to them, inspecting them for shock. That's when he saw the medallion around Laurie's neck. That meant something, but at the moment Broker wasn't entirely sure what. They were okay. Drew was okay too, if the medics stepped on it.

He put his hand on the porch railing to steady himself, beginning to feel real fuzzy around the edges. *Getting old, you pussy, letting a little paper cut kick your ass.* He studied the ragged hole through the meat of his left palm. Painfully, he moved his fingers. The machinery that operated the bones and tendons was still intact.

Another scar, he thought vaguely.

Equally vaguely, he now recognized the dead woman in the bathroom as Annie Mortenson. The librarian. Harry's exgirlfriend. He began to feel dizzy. He began to shake.

Funny, out in the winter snow, shock could be a sheet of fire. Now, in this heat, it wrapped him in cold shivers.

Down below he saw people come up the street and gather in a semicircle around the stairway. Several had bottles in their hands;

probably they'd just left bar stools. In the distance, bracketed by the first thunderclap of this July, he heard the wolf pack sirens.

Goddamn, he was tired of sirens.

Something soft and cool grazed his face, and at first he thought it was Janey. But then he realized he was feeling the first temperate breeze in weeks. And the sky was darkening, thickening up with real thunderheads.

Broker slouched against the rail and looked for the ambulance. As he waited, he watched one of the oldest scenes in the world: a woman rocking a terrified child in her arms and saying over and over, "It's all right. It's all right. Mommy's here."

Mommy.

He was looking at Janey and Laurie. He was seeing Nina and Kit. He turned and faced north and west, the direction bad weather came down from North Dakota—where Nina had ditched their kid.

Then he heard the darkness grumble, and down the river valley he saw white veins bulge in a bundle of black clouds. Ten seconds later, he heard the crash of the thunder overhead. When the ambulance screeched to a halt on the street, the big, fat, cool raindrops had already started to scatter down and sizzle on the baked concrete.

Okay. North Dakota. Gotta get organized.

Blood dripping from his wounded hand, Broker started down the stairs. A paramedic ran up, yelling, "Where's the sucking chest?"

"Inside, keep going," Broker said. He took two more steps and ran into a Stillwater cop whom he recognized but whose name he couldn't place just now.

"Whoa, hey Broker, you better sit down, man," the copper said.

"Outa the way, gotta go. Airport," Broker insisted. He shook his head to clear his vision because the raindrops splashing on his face were making his thoughts all runny . . .

"Sit him down; he's in shock."

Many hands were on him now, gentle but firm, pushing him down to a sitting position on the stairs. Someone mashed a compress into his palm. Raindrops and blood mingled in the white gauze.

"Airport, goddammit. Gotta get . . ."

"No problem," said a female paramedic in a soothing voice as she worked on his hand.

Broker gathered himself and surged up against the cops and medics.

They were too many. Too strong.

They didn't understand.

I gotta get to my kid.

Acknowledgments

Sheriff Jim Frank, Washington County.

Sergeant Neil Nelson, St. Paul Police Homicide Unit.

Deputy Sheriff Investigator Michael Lindholm, Washington County.

Supervisor Troy E. Ruby, Communications Center, Washington County.

Sue Giles, 911 Public Safety Dispatcher, Communications Center, Washington County.

(Rev.) John M. Malone, Pastor of the Church of the Assumption, St. Paul.

John X. Paquette, former Special Agent, Minnesota Bureau of Criminal Apprehension.

Judy Schiks, Family Court Services, Washington County.

Mark Ponsolle, Assistant County Attorney, Ramsey County.

Tracy Braun, Assistant County Attorney, Ramsey County.

Richard Buchman, Assistant County Attorney, Ramsey County.

Amy Becker, *St. Paul Pioneer Press.*

Keith Mortenson, Chief Investigator, Ramsey County Medical Examiner's Office.

Diane Olivieri, Fitness Director, River Valley Health Club, Stillwater, Minnesota.

Chris Lentz, Loome Theological Booksellers, Stillwater, Minnesota.

FarWorks Inc. and Creators Syndicate, for granting permission to describe and quote one of Gary Larson's Far Side greeting cards.

Kim Yeager, Bill Tilton, and Don Schoff.